Praise for Carla Neggers' *New York Times* bestselling Swift River Valley novels

"Appealing protagonists, good neighbors, small-town Christmas traditions, and Neggers's own recipes make for a fine romance."
—*Publishers Weekly* on *A Knights Bridge Christmas*

"A heady mix of romance, mystery and genuine Quabbin history packaged in an enchanting holiday tale."
—*RT Book Reviews* on *A Knights Bridge Christmas*

"Neggers does the near impossible: she brings a small-town, family-loving heroine and a footloose hero together in an engaging romance that has its fair share of surprises."
—*Library Journal* on *Echo Lake*

"Her people, places and things are colorfully and expertly rendered in this compelling work of fiction."
—*RT Book Reviews* on *Cider Brook*

"Neggers captures readers' attention with her usual flair and brilliance and gives us a romance, a mystery and a lesson in history."
—*RT Book Reviews*, Top Pick, on *Secrets of the Lost Summer*

"Only a writer as gifted as Carla Neggers could use so few words to convey so much action and emotional depth."
—Sandra Brown

"[Neggers] forces her characters to confront issues of humanity, integrity and the multifaceted aspects of love without slowing the ever-quickening pace."
—*Publishers Weekly*

Visit carlaneggers.com for more titles

Look for Carla Neggers' next novel
in the Sharpe & Donovan series

LIAR'S KEY

available soon from MIRA Books

CARLA NEGGERS

THE SPRING
at MOSS HILL

Recycling programs for this product may not exist in your area.

ISBN-13: 978-0-7783-1867-5

The Spring at Moss Hill

Copyright © 2016 by Carla Neggers

For questions and comments about the quality of this book, please contact us at CustomerService@Harlequin.com.

www.MIRABooks.com

Printed in U.S.A.

For my mother,
who taught me and so many others how to sew

THE SPRING
at MOSS HILL

One

"What do you think a private investigator would want me to stock in his fridge and pantry?"

The provocative question came from Ruby O'Dunn, up front by the cash register at the Swift River Country Store, a fixture in Knights Bridge, Massachusetts, for at least a century. Ruby was speaking to Christopher Sloan, a local firefighter. Kylie Shaw, out of sight in the wine section, had spotted them coming into the store. Now she wished she'd been paying closer attention to their conversation. Private investigator? What private investigator?

"He's from Beverly Hills," Chris said. "I'd start with that."

"He works for a Beverly Hills law firm. I don't know if he's actually from Beverly Hills."

"Close enough."

"It'd almost be easier if we were having him stay with my mother. She's got a fully stocked kitchen."

"She also has goats."

"Don't get me started. I cleaned out their stalls this

morning. It's bedlam at her place. Even staying there a few days would be a lot to ask. Moss Hill is a much better choice."

Kylie held tight to a bottle of expensive champagne. *Moss Hill?*

Moss Hill was a former nineteenth-century hat factory that had undergone extensive renovations and opened in March, with offices, meeting space and residences. She'd moved into one of its four loft-style apartments five weeks ago. So far, she was the only tenant. She accepted that the other three apartments wouldn't stay empty, but she hadn't ever—not once—imagined a private investigator moving in, even temporarily.

She missed what Chris said in response to Ruby. Ruby went on about wild mushrooms, artisan cheese and artichokes, but Chris finally told her to focus on basics. "Put a six-pack in the fridge," he said. "It'll be fine."

Ruby muttered something Kylie couldn't make out, and Chris left, apparently with a six-pack of his own.

Kylie placed the champagne in her basket. She'd promised herself she would take time to celebrate once the daffodils were in bloom, and they were definitely in bloom. The last time she'd come up for air and tried to celebrate had been in August. She'd ended up at a Red Sox game with a negative, burned-out carpenter who complained for seven innings. She'd been relieved when the game didn't go into extra innings and had told him she'd had a call from her sister, a veterinary student at Tufts, to get out of going back to Knights Bridge with him. Before that, she'd split a bottle of wine with a condescending sculptor in Paris, celebrating her first children's book as both author and illustrator. *These lit-tle children's drawings you do are sweet, Kylie, but...* He'd shrugged, leaving her to imagine the rest of what he was pretending to be too polite to say. She couldn't make a living as an illustrator, they weren't real art, they weren't any good, anyone could do it. It had been that kind of *but*.

She headed to the cash register with her basket. She could always have her champagne alone on her balcony and toast the stars and the moon, with gratitude.

Maybe invite the Beverly Hills PI.

That'd be the day. She didn't plan to do anything to invite his scrutiny.

Ruby was lifting a basket off a stack by the register. Kylie had met all four O'Dunn sisters around town—the country store, the library, the town offices where their mother worked—but didn't know any of them well. She'd moved to Knights Bridge last summer and kept telling herself she wanted to get to know people there, but so far, they remained acquaintances, not friends. Ruby and Ava, fraternal twins and the youngest O'Dunns, were theater graduate students, Ava in New York, Ruby in Boston. A natural redhead like her three sisters, Ruby had dyed her hair plum-black and tied it back with a bright pink scarf. She wore a long black skirt, a white T-shirt and a denim jacket, with black boots and no jewelry.

"Oh, Kylie, hi," Ruby said. "I didn't see you back there."

"I couldn't resist the wine sale."

"Ah. Champagne, I see. Excellent. Did you hear Chris Sloan and me talking just now? A private investigator will be here from California tomorrow. He'll be staying in the apartment across the hall from you."

"What's he investigating?"

"One of his clients is giving a master class at Moss Hill next Saturday," Ruby said. "Daphne Stewart—she has roots in town."

"She was here last September for the vintage fashion show at the library," Kylie said. "Hollywood costume designer. I remember."

"Did you go?"

"No, I didn't." She'd been fiddling with a project ahead of hitting the Send button. Work was always her excuse for not being more social. "I heard it was a great success."

"The fashion show raised a lot of money for the library and the historical society." Ruby hooked her basket on one arm. "Daphne's a character. Russ Colton—the private investigator arriving tomorrow—is making sure everything's set for her arrival. It'll be Moss Hill's first public event. You should come, Kylie. You'll be right there."

"Thanks. I'll give it some thought."

Ruby held up her basket. "I need to fill this up. I should get moving. Good to see you."

"You, too," Kylie said, but Ruby had spotted someone she knew and taken off down the canned-goods aisle.

Kylie set her basket on the counter.

A private investigator and a respected, longtime Hollywood costume designer on their way to town—to Moss Hill.

Just what I need.

She held back a groan. If she couldn't fake excitement, best to be neutral.

She unloaded her groceries. In addition to the champagne, she'd picked up plain yogurt, cheddar cheese, flax-seed bread, coffee and mixed spring greens, all local to her quiet part of New England, west of Boston.

After paying for her groceries, she stepped outside. The beautiful April afternoon greeted her like a warm smile from a friend. She took in the quaint, picturesque village center. She was standing on Main Street, opposite the common, an oval-shaped green surrounded by classic houses, the library, churches, the town hall and a handful of small businesses. The long winter had released its grip. The grass was green, the trees were leafing out, and daffodils were in bloom. She had been working nonstop for weeks—months—and getting out into the warm spring air felt remarkably good, almost as if she'd come to life herself.

She noticed dark-haired, broad-shouldered Christopher Sloan farther down Main Street. He was the fifth of the six Sloan siblings, with four older brothers. She couldn't imagine having five brothers. She didn't have any brothers. The O'Dunns and the Sloans and other families had lived in Knights Bridge for decades, even for generations. Ruby and Chris had grown up together. That created bonds and a familiarity that Kylie couldn't pretend to have in her adopted town.

Or want.

Not now at least.

She arranged her groceries in her bike bags, aware of a vague uneasiness about the arrival of a private investigator at Moss Hill. It wasn't just that she wasn't thrilled about it. She'd worked hard not to draw attention to herself during her months in Knights Bridge.

But it would all work out, she told herself as she climbed on to her bike. She had champagne, food and coffee. If she so much as sensed this Russ Colton was going to cause trouble for her, she could hide out in her apartment for days, content in her world of evil villains, handsome princes and daring princesses.

Moss Hill was quiet even for a Saturday afternoon. Kylie's mud-spattered Mini was the only vehicle in the parking lot, so new it didn't have a single pit or pothole. She could feel the ten-mile round-trip ride in her thighs as she jumped off her bike. She'd relished the slight breeze and the fresh scents of spring in the air on this warmest day of the year so far.

She grabbed her groceries out of her bike bags and gave them a quick check. Somehow she'd managed not to break or spill anything. She started to slip her phone into her jacket pocket but saw she had a voice mail.

Her sister, Lila, three years younger, still hard at work as a veterinary student in Boston. Also still a chronic worrier who was convinced her only sibling was turning into a recluse.

Kylie listened to the message, smiling at its predictability. "I hope you're not answering because you're off having a great time with friends. Call back whenever. Just saying hi."

Lila had known at four that she wanted to be a veterinarian like their father. She'd never wavered. Kylie had always been more interested in drawing pictures of the animals that came in and out of the Shaw clinic than in operating on them.

She hadn't been out with friends. She'd missed her sister's call because she'd turned off her phone while she was on her bike.

She'd call Lila back later.

Kylie left her bike on the rack by the front entrance and followed a breezeway to the residential building, the smaller of the two brick-faced structures that formed the mill, or at least what remained of its original complex. Built in 1860 to capitalize on the burgeoning market for palm-leaf straw hats, the renovated mill was situated on a small river on the outskirts of town. Its namesake rose up across the road.

Moss Hill was one of the many knobs and hills that formed the uplands that had helped make the region attractive as a source of drinking water for metropolitan Boston. The bowl-shaped Swift River Valley had caught the eye of engineers and politicians, and the massive Quabbin Reservoir was created in the decades prior to World War II. Four small towns were disincorporated, their populations relocated, their homes and businesses razed, their graves and monuments moved, and Windsor Dam and Goodnough Dike were built, blocking the flow of three branches of the Swift River and Beaver Brook and, through the 1940s, allowing the valley to flood.

Even before Quabbin, the mill had been in decline, little realistic hope for its future. Straw hats had been going out of fashion, and by 1930, the mill stopped producing them. Subsequent owners hadn't succeeded with alternative businesses. Eventually, the old buildings were boarded up and abandoned. A few years ago, a local architect and his business partners had bought the property and begun the painstaking process of demolition, renovation and refurbishment.

Kylie took the industrial-style stairs to the second floor. In addition to its four apartments, the building included a well-equipped exercise room, lounge and lower-level parking and storage. Although she'd grown up in the western exurbs of Boston, she'd never heard of Knights Bridge until a friend, an art professor recently hired by the University of Iowa, had told her about her country house. *You need a place to work for a few months, and I need a renter until I figure out what to do.*

Kylie had only meant to stay in Knights Bridge three months—long enough to catch up on work and clear her head. But three months had turned into six, then eight, and when her friend decided to sell the house because Iowa was just too far away, she had taken a look at Moss Hill.

She'd been captivated by the transformation of the old mill and had surprised herself when she fell in love with her second-floor loft-style apartment. She'd loved the house she'd been renting, too. Charming, quiet and romantic, it had cried out for kids, dogs, chickens—a family.

She unlocked her door and went inside, relaxing now that she was back in her space. She set her groceries on the counter in the kitchen area. She was only a little more than a month into living here, but the open layout suited her. Tall ceilings, arched floor-to-ceiling windows overlooking the river, brick and white-painted walls and gleaming wood floors combined old and new, the specialty, she'd come to learn, of the owner and architect, Mark Flanagan. He'd thought of everything to make the space comfortable, contemporary and efficient. His wife, who worked at a local sawmill owned by her family, had helped with the finishing touches.

Since her previous rental had come furnished, Kylie had been scrambling to get things pulled together for this place. A buttery-leather sectional had been delivered a week ago, and she'd finally given up a ratty futon she'd dragged out of her parents' basement and bought a decent bed, queen-size with washed-linen sheets. She hated scratchy sheets.

She'd brought her worktable with her. She'd made it herself in college out of a finished birch-wood door on trestles, and it had gone with her almost everywhere since then. Not Paris or London; she'd left it in storage then.

She put the champagne in the refrigerator. She needed something concrete to celebrate before she opened it. It didn't have to be big, but it had to be more than daffodils being in bloom. That felt forced.

Because it is forced, she thought.

She put away the rest of her groceries and flopped on the couch, tugging the clip out of her hair, which, despite being pulled back, was tangled from her bike ride. It was pale blond and past her shoulders, and she kept promising herself she would get to a hair salon. She was okay with a pair of scissors and could manage a quick trim, but she wasn't a pro.

Too restless to sit for long, she got to her feet, yanking off the lightweight jacket she'd worn into town. She kicked off her shoes and walked in her stocking feet to her worktable. She'd been working on *Little Red Riding Hood* for only a few days. It was the third in a series of fairy tales she was illustrating. She'd finished *Hansel and Gretel* and *Sleeping Beauty*.

She knew it would take some effort to get her into the world of a clever wolf, a dark forest and an adventurous girl with a picnic basket.

Kylie sank onto her chair, feeling unsettled, strangely out of her element. Had she made a mistake moving here?

But she knew she hadn't. As fantastic as it was, the house she'd rented had made her think about what she didn't have. This place worked fine, given her solitary ways and her bad luck with men.

She lasted twenty minutes at her worktable.

She was working on the perfect tree to go in front of the grandmother's house in *Little Red Riding Hood*. She was doing sketches by hand, on paper. She stared at the last one. Not good. It looked more appropriate for a story about zombies than a classic fairy tale.

She balled it up and tossed it into the recycling bin under her table, on top of the other discarded sketches. She debated switching to her computer and drawing on her art board, but she knew from experience that wouldn't work, either.

Her tree needed more time. It wasn't there, and working harder and longer wasn't going to make it be there.

Also, she was distracted.

She noticed Sherlock Badger tucked at the base of her task lamp and smiled. She'd put him together with bits of fabric, dryer lint, a few notions she raided from discarded clothes, a needle and thread and glue.

Now here was a guy, Kylie thought.

Never mind that he was only four inches tall.

He was a law enforcement officer in a series of picture books for young readers she'd created. He wasn't in all the books. He didn't live in Middle Branch, the fictional town where his Badger cousins had a house and a veterinary clinic on a river.

Kylie pointed her finger at him. "Not a word about my *Little Red Riding Hood* tree. Not. A. Word." She tossed her sketching pencils in their basket, one she'd picked up in Paris, before that ill-fated bottle of wine with the sculptor. "I'm not stuck. I'm just thinking."

She picked a piece of lint off Sherlock. He had a square jaw and a tough look about him, but he was solid, trustworthy and brave.

What would Sherlock do if a private investigator came to Middle Branch?

It would depend on what people had to hide, wouldn't it?

Kylie felt her throat tighten. She sprang to her feet, restless, uncertain. Three years ago, when she'd had the idea for *The Badgers of Middle Branch*, the first book she would write as well as illustrate, she'd decided to work under a pseudonym and keep Kylie Shaw separate.

She'd chosen Morwenna Mills as her alter ego.

A year later, when the Badgers had debuted, they had been an instant hit with young readers. More Badger books followed. Instead of telling everyone she was Morwenna, Kylie had kept it to herself. Even her family didn't know. *Lila* didn't know.

Would Russ Colton, PI, want to know?

He didn't have to want to know. All he had to do was start asking questions about the only resident at Moss Hill, and he could complicate her life.

Two

Russ Colton had considered all the ways he could get out of this trip to Knights Bridge, Massachusetts, but he was stuck. He had to go. Right now, he was on the deck of the hillside Hollywood Hills home owned by his friend Julius Hartley, also an investigator with Sawyer & Sawyer. Russ was trying to savor the last of his coffee, but he had Daphne Stewart eyeing him from across the hexagon-shaped table.

Finally she sniffed and sat up straight. "I know what you're thinking."

Russ looked at Julius for help. When Julius had heard Daphne coming up the stairs from the street, he'd suddenly developed a driving need to pick dead leaves off his multiple potted plants. He didn't meet Russ's eye now. *Thrown to the wolves*, Russ thought. More accurately, wolf, in the form of petite, copper-haired Daphne Stewart, a diva in her early sixties.

"What am I thinking, Daphne?" Russ asked her.

"This trip is a waste of time."

"It is a waste of time. You don't have to read my mind. I told you."

"You gave me your professional opinion. I get that, but I have a bad vibe about my return to Knights Bridge. I've learned to trust my vibes. They're not always right, I admit that, but they're not always wrong, either." She sniffed. "I'm willing to pay for my peace of mind."

She settled back in her chair, eyeing Russ as if daring him to argue with her. She wore a close-fitting top with a deep V-neck and slim pants, both in the same shade as her dark green eyes. Even early on a Saturday afternoon, she had on gold earrings, a bunch of rings and gobs of makeup. But she pulled it off. She looked good. She always did. As a costume designer, she'd told Russ, she felt she should make an effort with her attire whether she was running out for a quart of milk or attending the Academy Awards.

Julius piled more plant debris onto the deck rail. He was in his fifties—twenty years older than Russ—and newly married to a San Diego attorney. He had on expensive golf clothes, his usual attire these days. He had two grown daughters by his first marriage, both Los Angeles attorneys. The younger one was buying his house, now that he was moving into his wife's La Jolla home. Russ figured he could afford a Harry Potter cupboard in either La Jolla or Hollywood Hills.

"Why is this place called Moss Hill?" Julius asked Daphne.

She shuddered. "I hate that I know the answer. It's at the base of an actual hill of that name."

"Is there moss?"

"I don't know. Honestly, Julius."

He tackled a fernlike plant, grabbing a handful of brown matter. "Was it always called Moss Hill?"

"Yes. Sort of. It was called Moss Hill to distinguish it from the other Sanderson mills in the area. They're all gone now, most of them demolished when the reservoir was built."

Russ tried to control his impatience. He didn't care what the damn place was called. It was in this nowhere-town, and he had to get on a plane tonight, fly to Boston and drive there in the morning.

"My great-great-grandfather, George Sanderson, built the mill in the nineteenth century," Daphne said. "It produced straw hats until sometime after World War I."

"Like the straw hat Dick Van Dyke wears in *Mary Poppins*?" Russ asked.

Julius and Daphne both raised their eyebrows. Julius held his clippers in midair. "You've watched *Mary Poppins*? Seriously?"

"Marty and I watched it on a snow day back when our father was stationed in upstate New York," Russ said. "I was six. Marty was eight. I'd sing the chimney-sweep song to taunt him."

Julius snorted. "He didn't throw your ass in the snow?"

"No, he did. It had no effect."

Daphne shook her head. "I have a hard time envisioning you and Marty as little boys. You shouldn't run into snow in Knights Bridge this late in April."

"If it snows on me," Russ said, "I'm quitting."

"Oh, no, you're not," Julius said. "You can't quit this

week. I can't fill in for you. I'll be in La Jolla planning my new office in the poolside guest room."

"I can't believe you're moving down there." Daphne snorted with displeasure. "Do you have a clause in your sales contract with your daughter that you can get your house back if you hate La Jolla?"

"There is nothing to hate about La Jolla, Daphne," Julius said.

Russ admired Julius's patience. After ten years working with her, Julius was used to Daphne, and he considered her a friend. Russ did, too, although he'd only known her a few months, and today she was testing him.

"I'm not quitting Sawyer & Sawyer," Julius added. "I'm not going to abandon you."

"Will your daughter invite me to coffee on your deck?"

"When have I ever invited you? You just show up."

Daphnee pursed her lips, clearly fighting back a smile. "You're the devil himself, Julius Hartley. But now I have my young PI, Colt Russell. How do you like Los Angeles compared to San Diego, Colt?"

Julius gathered up his pile of debris and threw it over the deck into his backyard without a word. Russ picked up his coffee mug. He didn't correct Daphne. She knew his name. She was trying to get a reaction from him. He wasn't irritated, amused or concerned. This was just part of his new life.

"You're so serious," she said. "You remind me of Liam Neeson in *Taken*."

Julius joined them at the table. "You told me the other day he reminds you of Mark Harmon as Gibbs in *NCIS*."

"Gibbs was a marine," Russ said. "Neeson was CIA."

"And you were navy," Julius said.

Daphne waved a hand. "Whatever. Liam Neeson and Mark Harmon are both older than you, Russ, I mean Colt, but you have that same kick-ass look. I like it. I'll bet you can kill people with your left thumb."

"Easier with my right thumb."

Russ could tell Daphne didn't know if he was serious. She got to her feet. "Well, I like knowing you're in my corner as I prepare for this class. You know I've never taught a class, right? I don't even like to speak in public. Ava and Ruby O'Dunn were very persuasive in getting me to say yes. They appealed to my ego and my desire to help and encourage young designers. I fell for every bit of it."

"You'll be great," Julius said.

Daphne kept her green eyes on Russ. Finally, she sighed. "Well? Aren't you going to agree?"

"Agree with what?" Russ asked, mystified.

"That I'll be great."

He wasn't as good at client care and reading the cues as Julius was. "Sure," he said. "You'll be great."

"You're both awful men and total liars," she said with a cheeky smile. "I could stink up the room on Saturday, and you'd tell me I had the crowd in the palm of my hand."

"I never lie to you," Julius said. "Sometimes you choose not to hear what I'm saying, but that doesn't mean I've lied."

"Well, I give you permission to lie on Saturday, because it won't matter. Whether I stink or I'm terrific makes no difference. Either way, I am never, ever, ever doing this again."

"That's nerves talking. See how you feel after you get through this thing." Julius rubbed the back of his neck, looking awkward. "I've been meaning to tell you... I can't be in Knights Bridge on Saturday, Daphne. I'm sorry."

"Your wife again. La Jolla. This move. Next, you'll be telling me you're volunteering at the San Diego Zoo." Before Julius could respond, Daphne swung around to Russ. "I suggest packing bug spray. It might be black-fly season in Massachusetts."

With that, she bid them goodbye and trotted down the stairs, back to the peppy little car she drove. She lived in Hollywood Hills herself, but she operated in a different social circle from Julius—a different world altogether from Russ.

The slider into the kitchen opened, and Loretta Wrentham, Julius's bride of one month, stuck her head out. "Is the coast clear?"

Julius grinned. "You want me to go downstairs and make sure?"

"It's all right. I have nerves of steel." Loretta came out on to the deck. She was in her fifties, slim and fit, with short, graying dark hair. She wore tight-fitting jeans, a white shirt and sandals with three-inch heels that didn't seem to bother her. She set her ever-present glass of sparkling water with lime on the table and sat next to her husband. "That woman gives me hives."

"I thought you liked her," Julius said.

"I do, in small doses. She's fun, generous, interest-ing and a little nuts. She loves having you two at her beck and call."

"No one has Russ at their beck and call. Me, yes. Russ, no."

"You just play along better than I do," Russ told him.

"My point is," Loretta added, "Daphne will run you ragged if you let her."

Russ smiled. "It takes a lot to run me ragged."

"No doubt." Loretta grimaced as if the entire conversation about Daphne Stewart pained her. "She loves the idea of having a rugged, good-looking investigator show up in Knights Bridge as her advance team."

"Hey," Julius said, "Russ is going east, not me."

She rolled her eyes, but Russ thought she looked less tense. She and Julius had only met last summer, but now it seemed as if they'd known each other forever. "Daphne knows her stuff, I'll say that for her." Loretta swept up her water glass and took a big drink. "She warned me the first dress I picked out for our wedding wouldn't work. Although this was my first—and only—wedding, I didn't want to do the whole white-dress thing. I found a cute cocktail dress I liked. I thought it was cute, anyway. Daphne told me I would hate my wedding photos if I wore it. I'd look sallow and sad. Her words. Sallow and sad."

"And you were neither that day," Julius said.

"She's also responsible for the two of us meeting. Now I really do feel like a heel for avoiding her." Loretta nodded toward the plants Julius had trimmed. "They look great. This is such a nice spot. I'm glad it's staying in the family. We can come for brunch. Your daughter makes a great frittata."

Russ was out of there if they were going to talk frittatas.

But Loretta had narrowed her dark eyes on him.
"Julius has told you about my connection to Knights
Bridge, hasn't he?"

"Dylan McCaffrey and Noah Kendrick."

She gave the smallest of smiles. "That cuts to the
chase. Dylan and Noah are best friends. They grew up
together in LA and got rich together. Dylan in particular is involved in several new ventures based in Knights
Bridge. Adventure travel, an entrepreneurial boot camp
and an inn of sorts."

"Not to mention goat's milk soaps," Julius added.

Loretta kept her gaze on Russ. "The soaps and the
inn are Olivia McCaffrey's ventures, but, of course,
Dylan is involved. Olivia is the local woman he married
on Christmas Eve. Noah is engaged to Phoebe O'Dunn,
the former Knights Bridge librarian and the eldest sister
of Ava and Ruby, the twins who put together Daphne's
master class. NAK, the company Noah founded and
Dylan helped launch, is based in San Diego. They both
have homes there, but Knights Bridge—" she sighed
"—it's home for Phoebe and Olivia."

"Are they involved in Daphne's class?" Russ asked.

"She'll be staying at the Farm at Carriage Hill,
Olivia's inn. I don't know if either Olivia or Dylan will
be at the class. Olivia's a graphic designer, so she might
be interested. Noah and Phoebe are at his winery at
the moment."

Russ downed the last of his coffee. "Two friends
from California fall for two women from Knights
Bridge. Great, but I'm not seeing a role for me here."

"Loretta worries about Dylan and Noah," Julius said.
"They're like surrogate sons to her."

"Dylan's a longtime client," she said. "I started working with him when he was a defenseman in the National Hockey League. That he's now worth at least a hundred million and Noah over a billion…well, yes, I do worry about them. Knights Bridge is a small, idyllic New England town. It's easy to be lulled into thinking it won't attract people who might not wish Dylan and Noah and the people they care about well."

Russ got to his feet. "What are you asking me to do?"

"Have a look at their lives in Knights Bridge from your point of view," Loretta said. "Talk to Dylan. See what you think. You have more experience with security than either Julius or I."

"Is Dylan expecting me to talk to him?"

"He will be by the time your flight lands tomorrow. I'll call him myself. Noah, too. He won't be there, but Dylan won't make a move on anything that concerns Noah without talking to him first."

"All right. I'll let you know. I'm not sneaking around, just so we're clear."

"No problem," Loretta said.

"And my first priority on this trip is Daphne."

"Of course."

"Even if it's a waste of time," Russ added, half to himself.

Julius brushed a bit of plant matter off his polo shirt. "Be glad the O'Dunn twins are putting you up at Moss Hill instead of their mother's place. She has dogs, cats, chickens and over a dozen goats. That's where Olivia gets the milk for her goat's milk soap."

Russ stared at his friend and colleague. "Goats, Julius?"

"Nigerian Dwarf goats."

"I have to admit they're adorable," Loretta said.

"Have you ever seen a goat, Russ?" Julius asked.

"I have."

Loretta inhaled sharply. Her husband winced. "Afghanistan or Iraq?"

"Both. I doubt I've seen a Nigerian Dwarf goat, though. Nothing wrong with raising goats, but if I have to stay in this town for more than a few days, I'm going to want hazard pay."

Russ left Loretta and Julius smiling—and looking relieved—and took his coffee mug into the house. The sliders opened into the kitchen, which the daughter who'd bought the house was already planning on renovating. Russ put the mug in the dishwasher. He took spiral stairs in the adjoining hall to one of two upstairs bedrooms. The main living area was located on the middle level of the hillside house, and a master bedroom and bath were on the ground floor. Russ had moved into the smaller of the two upstairs bedrooms in March while he figured out what came next for him.

He'd never, not once in his thirty-three years on the planet, imagined working investigations for a Beverly Hills law firm.

Julius had refused to take rent money from him, saying he liked having someone there while he was in transition between Hollywood Hills and La Jolla.

Russ got out his worn duffel bag.

How the hell had he ended up here?

But he knew the answer. He didn't like it, but he knew.

Russ eased onto a cushioned stool at Marty's Bar off Hollywood Boulevard. Opened in 1972, it had survived the changes in the area because of its best and its worst qualities. Best, it served good drinks and good tacos, chili and burgers. Worst, it was a notch above seedy with its dark wood paneling, chipped tile floor and cracked vinyl cushions. Cheaply framed Hollywood photos hung crookedly here and there, featuring everything from black-and-whites of the Three Stooges to color shots of Elizabeth Taylor and Richard Burton. It wasn't a spot to see and be seen, but since neither interested Russ, he didn't mind.

His older brother greeted him with a big grin. Marty had chosen to put in an application there when he came to Hollywood eighteen months ago because they had the same name. To him, it was amusing, as good a place to tend bar as any before he got rich and famous. "What're you having, little brother?" he asked.

"Heineken, thanks."

It was one of a dozen beers the place offered on tap. Marty grabbed a pint glass—scratched but clean— and drew the beer. He was dressed head-to-toe in black. With his chiseled features, clear blue eyes and straight, medium-brown hair, Marty was classically good-looking. He had no visible scars, although plenty were hidden under his black attire. Russ had never been as good-looking. He was beefier, and more of his scars were visible, if from minor injuries. His eyes were a darker blue. A scary blue, a former girlfriend had told him. He didn't know what that meant, but she'd insisted it wasn't bad.

Marty slid the beer across the worn bar. "All set to head east?"

"As ready as I'm going to get. You still okay with driving me to the airport?"

"Yep. No worries."

Russ didn't see any sign of worry in his brother's face, but Marty had been taking acting lessons. He didn't like airports and anything that flew except birds and bugs, and not all of them. But it wasn't something the two of them talked about. Ever.

"Daphne offered to drive me," Russ said. "I declined."

"She told me. Smart move on your part. She'd throw her back out driving your Rover. We'd never hear the end of it. I suppose she could take her car and leave the Rover with me, but I don't see how that would get you to LAX alive. She tootles around here in that sporty little thing she drives, but I doubt she's driven on a big highway in years."

"It's hard to tell with her."

"I bet she'd have her own driver all the time if she could afford it. She must do all right, but no way does she have that kind of money." Marty paused to take an order from another customer, then grabbed a pint glass and poured another beer. "It's cool she likes this place."

And because she did, Russ thought, he was working with Sawyer & Sawyer as an investigator, living in Julius's guest room and on his way to Knights Bridge, Massachusetts. Russ had met Daphne when he'd come up from San Diego in February to check on Marty, make sure he wasn't living under a bridge. She'd been sitting two stools down from where he was now, drinking a French martini and bitching about some nonexistent problem. She'd found out Russ was just out of the navy, doing security and investigative work on his own in San Diego, and put him in touch with Julius.

"This place suits Daphne's contrary nature," Russ said.

"She likes to surprise people. Also I make a damn fine French martini, if I do say so myself."

Three young women came in and ordered margaritas, laughing and chatting about their plans for the evening as they sat on stools down from Russ. He left his brother to his work and took his beer to a small booth. He ordered fish tacos and settled in for the next hour, until Marty was free to take him to LAX. In exchange, he could use Russ's Rover while he was back East.

After Russ finished his tacos, Marty delivered a fresh beer and set a squishy, tissue-wrapped package on the table. "A present for you. Don't get taco grease on it."

Russ unwrapped the tissue to reveal a well-made Hawaiian shirt. "It has palm trees on it, Marty."

"Damn right. I figured now that you're a real PI, you need your own *Magnum, PI* shirt, just like Tom Selleck in the '80s—except you're not as tall as he is and you don't have his sense of humor."

"I don't live in Hawaii, either."

Marty grinned. "A little devil-may-care attitude wouldn't hurt you, Russ. Selleck was about your age when he was playing Magnum."

"Thanks, Marty. A Hawaiian shirt with palm trees on it won't stick out at all in Knights Bridge, Massachusetts."

"Go ahead, little brother. Put it on while I finish up."

Russ held up the shirt after Marty disappeared behind the bar. The palm trees were relatively muted. What the hell. It would make Marty happy for him to wear it, and it would be comfortable on the long over-night flight across the continent.

He changed in the men's room. When he got back to his booth, Marty was ready. "Looks great. You want to finish your beer or head out now?"

"Now's fine. Thanks for the shirt, Marty. I feel cool."

His brother laughed. "You are the definition of cool. Come on. Let's get you to the airport."

Marty drove. He hadn't had any alcohol, and he wasn't distracted by the prospect of spending the next few days in a little New England town to make sure Daphne Stewart could do her master class without in-cident. Not that anyone—Daphne included—was con-cerned or had any reason to believe there would be an incident.

Russ grimaced at the prospect of wasting the next few days of his life, but he said nothing.

"I'm buying a car," Marty said. "A friend is giving me a good deal on a clunker. All I need."

"You've managed to get where you need to go with-out a car."

"Friends, Uber and public transportation. It'll be good to have wheels for a few days. I won't take off up the Pacific Coast Highway, though. Promise."

"I recorded the mileage."

"Of course you did."

Russ hadn't, which Marty knew, but it was the game they played with each other. Marty, the irresponsible dreamer. Russ, the feet-flat-on-the-ground military type.

Wasn't that far off from the truth.

"Have you decided to take a permanent position with Sawyer & Sawyer?" Marty asked.

"I'm there now. That's all I know."

"You can't camp out at Julius Hartley's place forever. Unless the daughter who's buying it is available?"

Russ wasn't going there. He had no interest in either of Julius's daughters. "Right now I'm focused on this trip."

"I thought you'd worm your way out of this one. Daphne's got you by the short hairs, doesn't she?"

"She's a valued client and a good friend."

Marty sputtered into laughter. "You just did the civilian version of saluting smartly. Daphne's great, but she knows how to get what she wants. Think she'll go through with this class in this little town? We have a pool going at the bar. Most of us think she'll twist an ankle or get a sinus infection to find some way out of it."

"I resist any urge to predict her behavior. She's talking about helping to start a children's theater in Knights Bridge."

"With the theater-major twins? Seriously? Where's the start-up money coming from? Don't let Daphne fool you. I've seen her calculate a tip. She's careful with a buck."

"I'm not getting mixed up in what happens with this theater."

"You always were the smart brother."

When Marty pulled up to the appropriate terminal, he had a death grip on the wheel but otherwise seemed okay being this close to aircraft. He cleared his throat and turned to Russ. "I'm doing fine, Russ. I mean it. Don't insult me by worrying about me."

"What makes you think I'm worrying about you?"

"Because you're here, working in Beverly Hills. It's not what you want. You're here because of me."

"Tell you what, Marty. You don't worry about me and I won't worry about you."

"Never. You're my baby brother. I always worry. The reverse doesn't work." Marty pointed at him. "Shirt really does look great."

"I figure I can change when I get to Boston."

"Ha-ha."

"I'll see you soon." Russ climbed out and grabbed his bag from the back. "Thanks for the ride, Marty."

"No problem. Safe travels. I promise not to wreck your Rover while you're gone." Marty still held tight to the wheel as he leaned across the seat. "You have directions to this town?"

"Head west. Look for the goat signs."

Three

Daphne Stewart arrived at Marty's Bar as Marty Colton returned from dropping Russ off at the airport. "This is an awful little place," she said, hopping onto a bar stool. "But that's part of its charm."

"That's what we all think. French martini?"

"As only you can make one, my dear Marty. Did Russ bitch and moan about heading east?"

"You know us Coltons. We're stoic." Marty reached for a glass. "His flight hasn't taken off yet. You still have time to call him and cancel this trip to this little town."

"Then you'd lose your chance to drive his Rover."

"The sacrifices we make for our siblings."

"I don't have any siblings. I'm an only child. Thank heavens. I'd hate for anyone else to have had to endure my SOB of a father. What was your father like, Marty?"

"Solid."

She frowned at him. She'd heard something in his voice. A certain raggedness, or unease. Maybe it was just driving to and from LAX. Her idea of hell. She was relieved Russ hadn't taken her up on her offer to drive him, not that she'd ever doubted he would. "Is he still with us? Your father, I mean?"

"Nah. Died ten years ago. You didn't drive over here, did you?" Marty held up the martini glass. "I don't have to worry about you getting behind a wheel after having one or two of these babies?"

"I did not drive, no, and you never have to worry about me. I'm a responsible drinker."

"Does that mean you want me to go heavy on the pineapple juice?"

"It does not."

Daphne noted how he'd changed the subject from talk of his father, deliberately. Fathers could be a tricky topic. It had occurred to her, more than once, that the Colton brothers knew far more about her than she did them. Russ, because he worked with Sawyer & Sawyer and she was a client. Marty, because he made a hell of a French martini and she was a customer. She considered them friends, and she thought they considered her a friend, if along the lines of an eccentric aunt.

An aunt would know more about her nephews than Daphne did about Marty and Russ Colton.

She leaned forward. "Marty, darling, are you dawdling?"

"No, ma'am. I have your drink right here."

"You're such a brat. You know I hate being called ma'am."

He set her drink in front of her. "That will take the sting off the insult."

Chambord liqueur, vodka and pineapple juice, with a twist of lemon. It was Daphne's favorite drink these days. She took a sip. "Ah. Perfect, as always. Have you ever sampled one, Marty?"

"No. Never will, either."

"Russ tried mine a few weeks ago. I think you were busy and missed it. I could tell he wanted to spit it out, but he's a tough guy. He resisted. He said it tastes like spiked punch."

"To each his own."

"That's what I told him."

Marty grabbed a white cloth and mopped up where he'd prepared her drink. "Are you seriously worried you'll run into problems next week in this little town?"

"They're expecting fifty people at my master class."

"You can handle it. That's nothing in your world."

"What if one of them is fixated on me in an unhealthy way?"

"You'd have forty-nine people there to help you."

Daphne didn't want to explain her mix of emotions about returning to Knights Bridge. Paranoia, excitement, dread, dedication. Affection. She'd come to adore Ruby and Ava O'Dunn. She'd known their father when she'd lived in Knights Bridge, briefly, as a young woman. He'd died tragically ten years ago in a tree-trimming accident. Ruby, in particular, reminded Daphne of handsome, poetic Patrick O'Dunn.

"You okay?" Marty asked as he poured a beer for another customer.

She made herself smile and adopt her practiced air of not having a care in the world. "Did Russ tell you he caught a stalker targeting a young actor? He didn't tell me. The actor did. No charges were filed. Our stalker volunteered to return home to Portland and go back into therapy. All it took was seeing Russ on his doorstep. Russ didn't have to say a word." Daphne drank more of her martini. "He says it was his sunglasses."

"He does look like a badass in those sunglasses."

"But it wasn't just the sunglasses," Daphne said.

Marty shrugged. "Russ is very good at what he does. He's a natural at his job, but he's also worked hard at it. He had a lot of experience in the navy."

Marty delivered the beer down the bar. He had the ability to carry on multiple conversations. He was a dabbler, bartending, acting, screenwriting, grabbing whatever work he could to live his Hollywood dreams. Daphne understood and tried to help, to get him to focus on the work and not just the dream. But he was focused, Daphne thought. It was easy to underestimate Marty Colton.

She nursed her martini. She didn't want to have two drinks, but she also didn't want to gulp down this one and end up going home too early. She supposed she could switch to sparkling water, but she knew she wouldn't. When Marty returned, he tilted his head back, studying her. She wasn't fooled by his good looks and easygoing ways. He could be as incisive and critical as Russ. Worse, even, since he didn't have a client relationship with her. She was just a customer who liked the occasional French martini at the hole-in-the-wall bar where he worked.

"Do you wish you felt guilty for sending Russ to your hometown?" Marty asked.

"Knights Bridge isn't my hometown. I moved there when I was eighteen to get away from my father. I found solace and hope there, and I honed my sewing and design skills. I left at twenty to come out here."

"That took guts."

"I think we say that when things work out. When they don't, we say it was reckless, stupid, irresponsible."

"This class isn't a prison sentence, Daphne. You can bow out at the last minute."

"Imagine how that would look."

"Imagine how it would look to drive yourself crazy or drink yourself into oblivion because you keep trying to talk yourself into believing you want to do this thing."

"I do want to do it."

He raised his palms in front of him. "I rest my case."

Daphne finished her martini. She was being ridiculous, second-guessing herself. She'd made her decision. She'd made a commitment to Ruby and Ava. Of course she had to go to Knights Bridge next week. With the day drawing closer, jitters were normal.

She thanked Marty and let him put her drink on her tab. It was a late night for her. Usually she was in bed by ten o'clock.

When she arrived at her bungalow in Hollywood Hills, Daphne was glad she'd opted to take a cab. Her one martini had gone to her head. She was careful not to stagger, because who knew if the cab driver was taking a video, texting his friends—anything was possible these days. Once she was inside, with the door locked, she felt tears on her cheeks. Oh, good heavens, she thought, was she crying? It had to be the martini.

"You need food."

She went into her kitchen, hoping she could find

something to eat. Her house was only fifteen-hundred square feet, but she loved it. She'd bought it after her last divorce and had it painted a warm sunshine yellow in celebration of her new freedom. She'd decorated the interior in creamy neutrals, with the idea that a man would never live here again. So far, so good on that one.

Hard to believe it had been twenty years.

She discovered hummus and cut-up vegetables in the fridge. She arranged them on a plate, poured herself a glass of water and headed out to the patio, turning on the lights since it was darker than the pits of hell. She checked her chair cushion for spiders before she sat down. She hadn't become a fan of western spiders in the forty years she'd lived in Southern California.

As she ate her dinner, she watched the turquoise pool water ripple in the light and smelled the roses off to the side of the patio. They were pink and peach, and she could see them from her studio window while she worked. Everything was on one floor—she could grow old here.

Her house wasn't anything special by Hollywood standards, but it was what she'd imagined when she'd boarded her first bus west all those years ago. Her life wasn't perfect, and she'd made plenty of mistakes, but she'd done all right. She had nothing to prove to anyone, including herself. That wasn't what this master class next Saturday was all about.

"Yes, my dear," she said as she dipped a carrot stick into the hummus. "If only you believed it."

Did she want Russ to come upon something that would force him to recommend she cancel her Knights Bridge appearance?

She remembered the first time she met him at Marty's Bar. Rugged, focused, task-oriented and so obviously very worried about his big brother. She had no one to worry about her. Some of that was by her own design. Even now, she could hear her father telling her he was smacking her because he was worried about her.

Damn. She wished she had another French martini instead of carrots, celery, broccoli and hummus.

Her great-great-grandfather's old mill as a theater…a place for children to come and learn about acting, costume design, lighting…ultimately about themselves.

Can I do this, tie myself to Knights Bridge?

Do I want to?

She inhaled deeply. The ghosts of the past were grabbing her from behind. She tried to shake them off, but they clawed at her, refusing to let go, forcing her back to those early days when she'd first arrived in Knights Bridge as a teenager. She hadn't lived there long, but her life there—working in the library, living in a cottage on Thistle Lane—had transformed her.

She remembered walking to the mill at Moss Hill one fine spring morning with the full intention of flinging herself off the dam. It was early on after her arrival in Knights Bridge. She figured people would think she'd slipped amid the tall grass, broken glass and debris.

An unfortunate accident befalling the last descendant of the mill's original owner.

A fitting end to the Sandersons.

She hadn't jumped. She'd decided the dam wasn't high enough, and it was too damn risky. What if she just got banged up and lay there alone, no one to find her?

She really hadn't wanted to die a slow death.

She'd walked back to town. She vividly remembered her annoyance at getting blisters.

It wasn't long after that little brush with oblivion that she'd started sewing, copying dresses she saw in movies and magazines and dreaming of a different life.

She didn't want to go back to who she'd been forty years ago. She was Daphne Stewart now, not Debbie Sanderson, the abused, insecure teenager with no money and no prospects.

Four

Russ collected his rental car in Boston. He'd reserved an all-wheel-drive car because he didn't know the terrain in Knights Bridge, and potholes and rutted dirt roads were a distinct possibility. And because Loretta had warned him. *Get a good car. I'm always in fear of wrapping myself around a tree when I'm out there.*

He had a text waiting for him when he got behind the wheel; it was from Marty. You there?

He typed an answer. Yep. Why are you up?

Working on a screenplay. On a roll. Stay in touch.

Will do. Get some sleep for me.

Russ tossed his phone on the seat next to him and started the car. Marty might be working on a screenplay, but he'd be up anyway, waiting for his brother to land safely in Boston. Russ felt like a heel for not texting him sooner, but Marty would never say anything. His fears, he'd told Russ more than once, without getting specific, were his burden. He would deal with them in his own way.

Gritting his teeth, Russ drove out of the airport and made his way through a tunnel and onto Storrow Drive. With Boston's notoriously poor signage and the unfamiliar roads, he regretted not using GPS to get him to Knights Bridge. He'd slept little on his flight. Nothing new there. At wheels up, he inevitably saw Marty in his hospital bed ten years ago, with morphine keeping the pain at bay.

Your brother sustained severe injuries but we think he'll survive.

Think? You're not sure?

Russ had turned then, seeing his mother in the doorway. She'd had no color except for her own bruises and lacerations. But she was on her feet, not on morphine, not fighting for her life—not her physical life, anyway.

Russ... I can't do this. I can't.

He'd thought she was talking about her older son. *He'll make it, Mom. Marty's strong.*

Your dad was strong and he's dead.

I know. I'm sorry.

Marty's an adult. We're not obligated in any way. It'll be months...months and months...

Mom?

Her dark blue eyes had fastened on Russ, and he'd realized she was talking about Marty and his recovery, and how she couldn't do it. She couldn't be there for him. She had sustained relatively minor injuries in the helicopter crash that had killed her husband, the father of her two sons, and at that moment, realizing the loss she'd suffered, the months of rehab ahead of Marty, she wished the crash had killed him, too.

Maybe not all of her had wished it. Maybe only a part of her, traumatized and grief-stricken, had wished it. Maybe she'd believed she couldn't get through it—couldn't cope with seeing her son in pain, the ups and downs of a long, uncertain recovery, and her shortcomings would hurt his chances of getting back to a hundred percent.

Not that a hundred percent had ever been an option.

She'd rallied, if only because of the expectations of the people around her. Russ tried to tell himself what he'd seen that day at the hospital was the fight-or-flight reflex at work. His mother had wanted to flee from her suffering son, and who was Russ to blame her? He'd taken as much emergency leave from his naval duties as he was allowed to bury his father and see to his mother and brother.

In the end, he'd abandoned his brother, too.

An insane roundabout brought Russ back to the present. He was on the road to Knights Bridge, Massachusetts. Marty was hanging out in Hollywood. Their mother had three miniature poodles at her home in Scottsdale and liked to joke she had full charge of the television remote now that she lived alone. Russ called her once a week. She never called him. He didn't know when he'd visit again now that Marty had moved away from Phoenix.

Traffic thinned as he drove west into the countryside, and he rolled down the windows, letting in the cool morning air as the sun climbed into a blue sky and chased away the memories. He could be in Knights

Bridge in time for breakfast, but he'd grabbed coffee and a protein bar at the airport. They'd suffice. He planned to keep things simple in this little town. In, out, head down, do his job, then he'd be back on his way west.

Kylie poked a stick at the wet, browned leaves that clogged a spring, tucked amid moss-covered rocks in the woods above the mill, about a third of the way up Moss Hill. She liked to think of the spring as her secret discovery, but a nearby stone wall indicated the land had once been cleared. Others had been here long before she had ventured off a trail last summer and come upon the spring, a precious spot where fresh groundwater had broken through to the surface.

She didn't want to take the time to push the leaves aside and wait for the water to clear in the small pool created by the spring's trickle. Normally she would. She loved this spot. She would come up here on breaks from her work. She would sit on a rock by the spring and allow the landscape to envelop her, cradle her, as all her distractions and intrusive thoughts fell away.

Not this morning.

She breathed in the smells of a gnarled hemlock, the early spring greenery, the mud and the cold water of the spring. She shut her eyes, listening to the narrow stream below the spring flow downhill over rocks. She could hear birds twittering in the trees. She breathed deeply, feeling her heart rate calming after her trip to town yesterday and her bad night last night. She'd awakened at dawn and gone out to her balcony to watch the sunrise.

After a hearty breakfast of Scottish pinhead oatmeal, yogurt and coffee, she'd tried to work, but her head hadn't been into *Little Red Riding Hood*.

She gave up after ten minutes, got dressed, put on trail shoes and headed up Moss Hill.

She'd brought her phone and a bottle of water, but she hadn't left a note on her kitchen counter, as she usually did, describing her route and the time and date of her departure.

Sometimes the spring wasn't easy to find. Everything looked so similar up here. She'd go too far and end up in a field or atop Moss Hill, or just miss it when it was right under her nose. This morning she'd had no trouble, following a narrow, seldom-used trail partway up the hill, then veering off through a gap in a stone wall to the stream and up to the spring.

She set her stick in the sodden leaves and mud next to the spring and stood straight. She could feel the air warming, the pinks and lavenders of the sunrise long melted into a blue sky. Rain was in the forecast for tomorrow, but it was pleasant now.

Russ Colton would be arriving sometime today. Once she got that out of the way—knew he was on the premises, doing his thing—she could concentrate.

At least she could picture him, had a good idea of what he looked like. Last night, tossing and turning, she'd remembered that an investigator had come to town ahead of Daphne Stewart's visit in September—in his fifties, supposedly a decent guy. Kylie hadn't met him, but she'd seen him in town. Gray-haired, casual, not the least bit intimidating. There'd been some confusion between him and Phoebe O'Dunn over Daphne Stewart and Noah Kendrick, now Phoebe's fiancé, but everything had worked out, apparently a case of multiple misunderstandings.

That California investigator had to be the one on his way now. This Russ Colton.

Kylie started back through the woods to the stone wall and the trail. Her left side was wet and muddy, but she didn't care. She might be restless, but the spring was one of her favorite spots. She wished she'd thought to ask what time this California PI was getting here, but she wasn't sure that would have helped with her distractibility. But she felt better, and if she couldn't get a lot done today, she could at least draw a few trees for Little Red Riding Hood's grandmother's house.

When she got back to her apartment, she lasted ten minutes at her worktable.

She sighed at Sherlock Badger. "I know. It's crazy."

He stared back at her. He looked unsympathetic. *Just start*, he would say.

Most days it would be good advice. Not right now.

Kylie grabbed her phone and keys and headed back out. She'd seen ducks on the river from her balcony.

Yes.

She'd check on the ducks.

Kylie took the stairs to the lower-level garage. Each apartment had its own parking spaces and storage compartment. She'd left her Mini in the parking lot, so her two spaces were empty. She didn't have anything to store yet. She'd put her bike in the compartment once winter returned. In the meantime, she wanted to buy a kayak or a canoe and the requisite gear. They could go in storage. Maybe a tent? No. She hated camping.

She could easily lose an hour wondering about what could go in her storage compartment.

Refocusing on her mission to see the ducks, she went out through the back and crossed the driveway that wound into the garage from the parking lot. She stepped onto a strip of soft, newly planted grass level with the river. The landscapers had added a few shade trees, now just saplings supported with ropes and stakes. The river was down from its early-spring runoff peaks, but still running high. Two ducks swam peacefully in the quiet millpond, with no apparent concern for the nearby dam and rushing waterfall. Above the dam and pond, the river widened and turned shallow, flowing over rocks and boulders toward the mill its waters had once powered.

The sounds of the water didn't soothe Kylie's agitated mind.

She had the keys to the heavy back door to the main building and unlocked it, heading inside. The ground level held a kitchen, storage rooms, the mechanical room and a large health club she was welcome to use in addition to the exercise room in her building.

She switched on a light and went upstairs to the main entry. She didn't have keys to any of the interior rooms except the health club. No one would be around on a Sunday morning, but she wanted to have a look at where Ava and Ruby O'Dunn were hosting the master class with Daphne Stewart. Moss Hill's sole meeting room was located on the other side of glass doors and a glass partition. More glass doors opened onto a balcony that jutted out over the river, a perfect spot for a romantic photo. The space was ideal for weddings and parties of

all kinds. It was empty now, its gleaming wood floor
obviously original to the building given the unevenness
and glossed-over nicks and discolorations.

Kylie peered into a glass case in the entry. It had been
empty on her last visit here but was now filled with a
display of antique straw hats that had been made at the
mill in the nineteenth century, a nod to the building's or-
igins. Moss Hill had character, one of its chief draws for
her. She noticed the display also held museum-mounted,
blown-up photos that depicted the mill's history, from
when it had been a thriving business employing scores
of workers to a century later, when it had been abandoned, left to decay and a wrecking ball, and, finally, to
the present, with its comfortable blend of old and new
setting it up for another century of use.

She heard footsteps echoing behind her and turned
just as a man she didn't recognize appeared behind the
glass doors in the meeting room. He was tall, broad-
shouldered and frowning right at her.

She decided not to take any chances.

Pretending she hadn't seen him, she retraced her
steps, running down the stairs to the lower level and out
the back door. She didn't breathe until she was outside.
She shivered in the cool morning air. She'd encoun-
tered all sorts as construction on Moss Hill had wound
down—engineers, carpenters, electricians, plumbers,
landscapers—as well as Mark Flanagan's employees
and clients now that he had moved his offices here. She
hadn't gotten a good look at the man who'd interrupted
her snooping, but he wasn't anyone she'd met before.
She'd remember. He hadn't been wearing a coat and
tie. A denim jacket, khakis. That didn't tell her much.

If he decided to come after her, she needed to get moving, because he'd be fast.

She pulled off her running jacket and crossed the grassy strip to the driveway that led to the garage under her building. When she reached the pedestrian entrance, she stopped, keys in hand, and groaned.

She had the wrong man. Russ Colton wasn't the investigator she'd seen last summer. He was the man up in the meeting room.

Had to be.

"How to draw attention to yourself when you don't want attention," Kylie muttered to herself. "Run like a lunatic."

What now? Go up to her apartment, lock herself in and hope for the best? Buck up and introduce herself to her new neighbor, act as if she hadn't seen him and bolted?

Take a long bike ride?

Fly to Paris?

The bike ride won.

She went inside and took the stairs up to the main level and headed out to the breezeway and the bike rack. She wore a thigh-length dark purple sweater, black leggings and sneakers with highly visible bright orange laces.

The man from the meeting room was standing by a blue sedan in the parking lot.

No avoiding him now.

"You must be Russ Colton," Kylie said, leaning against her bike. "Ruby O'Dunn mentioned you'd be arriving today from California. Kylie Shaw. I live here."

"You're my new neighbor, then. Sorry if I startled you."

He walked toward her. He'd put on sunglasses, which had a way of making him look even more humorless.

She decided not to deny he'd startled her. He probably wouldn't believe her, anyway. "No problem." She grabbed her bike helmet off the handlebars where she'd left it yesterday. "Did you just get here?"

"Here to Moss Hill. I arrived in Boston a few hours ago."

"Ah. You took the red-eye. It has an appropriate name, doesn't it"

He smiled. "It does, but it's not the reason I'm wearing sunglasses." He pointed a thick finger at the blue sky. "The sun is."

A sense of humor. Kylie was encouraged. "I work at home. Feel free to knock on my door if you need anything."

"I will, thank you. What kind of work do you do?"

"I'm a freelance illustrator."

"You're not registered for Daphne Stewart's class next Saturday."

"I only just learned about it. I've been busy with work the past few months and haven't paid attention."

"Do you know Ava and Ruby O'Dunn well?"

Kylie shook her head. "Not well. Do you?"

"I haven't had the pleasure of meeting them yet. I'm here on behalf of Daphne Stewart."

"So Ruby said. Fantastic she's taking the time to give a lecture in little Knights Bridge. It's very generous of her." Kylie tried to look nonchalant. She wanted to keep the focus away from herself. "When I saw you—"

"Deer in the headlights." He gave her an easy smile. "You froze for a split second, and then you bolted. I sometimes have that effect on people. Again, sorry."

She returned his smile. "I didn't freeze. I just bolted. Do people tend to run when they see you?"

"Not always. Sometimes I wish they'd run, and they don't."

"Comes with the job, I imagine. I had a different Russ Colton in mind. I thought you'd be the man who accompanied Miss Stewart last time she was in town. I didn't meet either of them, but I saw him."

"You were expecting Julius Hartley?" Russ grinned. "That's awesome. I can't wait to tell him."

"Sounds as if that one will keep you two laughing over your beers for a while." Kylie couldn't wait to get out of there. "Well, it's a beautiful day. I love springtime in New England. I'll be off on my bike ride now. Good to meet you, Mr. Colton. Enjoy your stay."

"Thanks. Enjoy your bike ride."

He returned to his car as she climbed onto her bike. As she rode across the parking lot to the exit, she was positive he was watching her, but she didn't look back to make sure.

She turned up the road, away from the village, welcoming the cool air and the sounds of the river tumbling toward the dam.

Russ Colton wasn't what she expected on a Sunday morning at Moss Hill.

Any morning at Moss Hill.

As she rounded a curve, she felt her phone vibrate in her pocket and remembered she hadn't called her sister back. She stopped next to the guardrail and checked her messages. A text, but not from Lila.

It's Ruby. Join us for lunch at Smith's at 12:30.

Kylie blinked at the text. Lunch? In the ten months she'd lived in Knights Bridge, no one in town had ever invited her to lunch, nor had she invited anyone to lunch. She hadn't even realized Ruby had her phone number.

Something was up.

Thanks but...

Kylie hesitated, then deleted the but.

Thanks I'd love to join you.

Great.
And that was that. She was joining Ruby O'Dunn for lunch.

Five

Russ got his bag out of the back of his rented car. He'd watched Kylie Shaw until she disappeared around a bend on the winding country road in cute little Nowhere, Massachusetts. She was blonde, pretty and quick. He hadn't expected her to get the jump on him outside the meeting room.

And she was cagey.

"Now, why is that, I wonder?"

An interesting development, his Moss Hill neighbor.

He took the covered breezeway to the residential entrance. Ruby O'Dunn had left keys to the two buildings in a flowerpot. First place Russ would look without instructions. Basic security at the renovated hat factory—his home for the next few days—was rudimentary but could easily be improved should the need or desire arise.

He'd had no trouble finding Knights Bridge or Moss Hill, even without GPS. When he'd pulled into the mill's parking lot, he'd noticed the mud-encrusted bike, unlocked, leaning crookedly on a stand. Now it was occupied by his neighbor.

She obviously wasn't thrilled to have him bunking across the hall, but she'd been expecting Julius Hartley. Probably would take a while to sort that one out in her mind. Russ had that effect sometimes. Maybe it was his scary eyes.

He could always unzip his jacket and show more of the palm-tree shirt Marty had given him.

Russ located his apartment and went inside, dropping his bag on the floor by the front door. He liked the industrial loft feel and modern furnishings of the place. Late morning sunlight streamed through the huge arched windows overlooking the dam and river. The design allowed residents privacy and solitude while also not being too isolated, at least by Knights Bridge standards.

Nice.

It'd do for his short stay. He'd done worse in his day. Much worse.

Did Kylie Shaw like being isolated? Was that what he was sensing with her caginess—it had more to do with his intrusion into her space? Moss Hill had only been open a matter of weeks. Where had she lived before here?

Lots of questions, likely none of which had anything to do with Daphne's upcoming visit.

He checked the kitchen. As promised, Ruby O'Dunn had stocked the pantry and refrigerator with essentials. The place was mopped, vacuumed and dusted, and there were clean sheets on the bed and fresh towels in the bathroom.

"All good," Russ said, fetching his duffel bag. He set it on the queen-size bed. He hadn't expected to feel at home the first second he walked into the place, but he did.

He returned to the main room and stood at the windows. It was a good drop to the river. He could see two ducks cruising in the reeds on the riverbank. He wondered if there'd be ducklings soon. Across the river, fields, turning green with the arrival of spring, rose up to a white farmhouse with a dark-wood barn.

Russ fought a yawn. This was a beautiful spot— better than he'd expected—but he was here to do a job, not to admire the view. Julius and Daphne—and to a degree, Loretta—had supplied him with the basics about Knights Bridge, but he didn't need to know anything that didn't involve his reasons for being here. He did *not* need to know town gossip. Who was sleeping with whom, who was looking for work, who was in rehab. Not his concern.

Was finding out more about his neighbor across the hall part of his job or a diversion?

Could be both. Kylie Shaw was on the premises where Daphne would be speaking in a few days, and she had pretty blue eyes. Not scary at all.

A quick shower, a change of clothes and more coffee, and he was back out the door. He decided to check out the riverside—where Kylie had run when she'd spotted him—and descended the stairs to the ground-level garage, then headed outside. He followed a walk to an overlook a few feet above the dam.

He leaned over the black-metal rail and watched the water rush over the solid, old dam, creating a misting spray as it tumbled onto the giant boulders. He got a bit wet but didn't mind. The temperature probably felt warm to the locals after the long New England winter, but to him it was refreshingly cool, not cold but not warm, either.

He was in no hurry as he returned to his apartment. He had nothing planned for the day. He'd figured he'd see what was what when he got here and go from there. He could have taken a later flight or spent the day in Boston, but this was fine.

As he started to unpack his duffel bag, Ruby O'Dunn texted him. He'd emailed her his number before he'd boarded his flight but hadn't followed up when he'd landed in Boston, given the early hour. He glanced at her text. Welcome! Settled at Moss Hill?

He typed his answer. All set.

A bunch of us are getting together for lunch. Join us?

Where?

Smith's off the common in 30 minutes.

Will do.

I've invited Kylie Shaw across the hall from you. She'll know the way.

Ruby typed faster than he did. Ok.

See you soon.

Russ slid his phone back in his jacket pocket. Were Ruby and Kylie friends? Had to be. Otherwise why invite her to lunch?

Maybe his instincts were off, and Kylie Shaw wasn't trying to keep to herself.

Might as well check with her. He walked across the hall and knocked on her door.

She looked thunderstruck when she opened up. She only cracked the door, as if she didn't want him to see the place was a mess. "I'm…um… You're here about lunch." She gave a vague wave with a slender hand. "Ruby texted me."

"I didn't realize you two were friends."

"We're not. I mean…" Kylie bit her lower lip. "I don't know anyone in town that well."

"But you're going to lunch?" Russ tried to make it sound like a genuine question and not an order. But he wanted her to go to lunch. Her behavior was borderline unusual. "I was on a plane all night. It'd be great to have someone else drive."

"You don't look jet-lagged."

"Trust me. I am." True, maybe, but he'd be fine to drive. "Yours is the Mini, I gather. Clever private eye that I am, I figure it has to be since it's the only other car in the parking lot."

Kylie nodded without enthusiasm. No smile at his humor. "I'll meet you downstairs. Give me five minutes."

To what? Gulp? Do yoga breaths? Russ shrugged. "Okay."

"Five minutes."

She shut the door.

Russ went back to his apartment and got his car key in case Kylie changed her mind, and he had to drive into town. But he would bet she wouldn't change her mind. Something about lunch both intrigued and rattled her.

It was early but not too early in California. He texted Julius: I'm about to have lunch at Smith's.

Order the turkey club. Don't go near the salads.

No update?

Quiet here. Why?

Later.

Russ headed downstairs and out to the Mini, a cream color underneath the dried mud and dust. Of course it was unlocked. He opened the door to let in some spring air while he waited.

Kylie joined him. She was in the same outfit she'd had on earlier, but she'd changed out of her orange-laced shoes into black ankle boots. It wasn't the sort of thing he normally noticed, but the laces had been tough to miss. She gave him a tight smile. "All set."

She might have been going on a secret mission behind enemy lines.

"I noticed your car is as muddy as your bike."

"There's a thing here called mud season. It just ended. I haven't had a chance to clean my bike and car since then." She pushed a palm through her pale hair, then gave him a forced smile.

Russ slid into the passenger seat while she went around the hood to the driver's side. It was a little car. His left thigh almost touched her right thigh. He thought she noticed. It wasn't an obvious giveaway, just a slight shift toward her door as she started the engine. "I'm not used to having anyone in the car with me," she said. "Last one in the passenger seat was a dog."

"A big dog?"

"Not as big as you."

"That would be a hell of a big dog."

"It was a chocolate Lab that had run off from the Sloan farmhouse about a mile away. I found him rolling in the mud on the riverbank."

"Mud seems to be a theme in your life. I'm glad I don't scare you anymore."

"You wouldn't have scared me to begin with if I'd seen the palm trees on your shirt."

"You noticed them? The observant artist. My palm trees aren't intimidating?"

She smiled. "Not by themselves."

"Need the rest of me, huh?" He thought he saw color in her face, but the light shifted as they continued down the road. "The shirt's new. A gift from my brother."

"To remind you that you're an outsider here?"

"Trust me, I don't need reminding." He pointed out his window. "Was that Moss Hill back there, across from the mill? Are there hiking trails?"

"Yes, and yes. I was on one of the trails this morning."

"Alone?"

"Yes."

"No dog?"

"No dog."

"If I lived way the hell out here all by myself, I'd have a dog. In fact, I'd have two dogs. Maybe a couple of goldfish, too, although they aren't much good in a fight."

"Do you have a dog in Beverly Hills?"

He shook his head. "No dog, and I don't live in Beverly Hills," he said, leaving it at that. "How long have you lived at Moss Hill?"

"Since mid-March."

"Before that?"

"I rented a house up the road."

"But you're not from Knights Bridge."

"I moved to town last summer." There was a slight testiness to her voice, as if she'd told him only because she knew he'd ask. "Are you from Beverly Hills?"

"Nope. Army brat. I joined the navy. I've been out two years."

"Thank you for your service," Kylie said quietly.

Russ hadn't expected that from her. He didn't know why. "It's a privilege to serve," he said. "Where did you live before Knights Bridge?"

"All over."

Vague answer. He watched her drive, one hand on the wheel, the other on the shifter. She wasn't tentative so much as tense. Not used to men? Not used to lunch? Didn't like Ruby O'Dunn? He wanted answers, but he didn't want to pepper her with too many questions. He was at her mercy. Imagine if she dumped him on the side of the road.

"Are there bears here?" he asked.

"Black bears."

He settled back in his seat. "I'm not big on bears."

She glanced at him as if she were trying to figure

out if he was serious. But she turned, eyes on the road. "Do you know who all will be at lunch?"

"You, me, Ruby. I don't know who else, if anyone. Why? Do you have enemies in town?"

"Just curious," she said, and pointed to more ducks in the river.

Russ figured he had ten minutes, tops, to pull himself together before he got sucked into some small-town nonsense that had nothing to do with Daphne—or Noah Kendrick and Dylan McCaffrey. It was jet lag. Boredom. Curiosity.

His neighbor's pretty blue eyes, her slender hands, the curve of her breasts under her purple sweater.

He hadn't had a woman in his life in far too long.

The jet lag, boredom and curiosity made him vulnerable to doing something really stupid.

And he wasn't paid to be stupid.

"Did I lose you?" he asked.

"Sorry. My mind wandered off."

"You know you're driving, right?"

"It didn't wander off like that. I'm paying attention to the road." She smiled at him. "No worries."

He begged to differ, but he said nothing. If Kylie and Ruby weren't friends, why lunch? Could be a simple question of politeness. He fought back a yawn, debating whether to watch the picturesque scenery or the attractive, intriguing driver. Finally he decided he could do both.

Six

Smith's was located in a 1920s house that had been converted into a restaurant, around the corner from the country store. Kylie had dined there a number of times, alone, tucked in a booth with her sketch pad. At first, she hadn't thought much about socializing with the people of her adopted town. She was here temporarily, as an artistic retreat—to work, not to hang out with the locals. She liked people. She liked being around people. But that wasn't why she was in Knights Bridge. When she'd moved into Moss Hill and started to consider making the town home, she'd figured friends and socializing would come in due time—when she had more head space for them and allowed herself out of the retreat mind-set.

And there was Morwenna.

Would Russ Colton want to know about Morwenna Mills? Why would he care?

Because he's the type who cares about every detail.

Morwenna was a big detail, if not one that had any bearing on Daphne Stewart's master class on Saturday.

Russ followed Kylie into the restaurant. Ruby O'Dunn jumped up from a long table in the back of the eatery, greeting Russ as if they were old friends. She introduced him to Mark Flanagan and his wife, Jessica, who were also at the table, joining them for lunch.

Mark smiled at Kylie. He was a tall, lean man in his thirties, an architect who specialized in older buildings. He wore a black windbreaker, a dark gray flannel shirt and jeans, his usual outfit. "Glad you could make it," he said.

She had the distinct impression he hadn't expected her to accept Ruby's invitation. There'd been something imperious about the text, and Kylie had suspected declining would cause her more problems than accepting. The faint feeling she'd done something wrong lingered, even with the warm greetings. Had Russ told Ruby about their meeting at Moss Hill—how Kylie had run from him? She gave herself a mental shake. She was overthinking.

She was hungry—maybe she just needed food. Regardless, she had to settle down.

Mark returned to his seat next to his wife. Dark-haired and green-eyed, Jessica was a Frost, one of the longtime families in town. She wore jeans and a flannel shirt but also a silver Celtic-knot necklace that Kylie suspected Mark had given her. Mark and Jess had known each other forever, but they were newlyweds, married last fall at her sister's inn in town.

"Moss Hill is great," Russ said, sitting next to Kylie and across from Ruby. "Thanks for putting me up there."

"I keep thinking we need to come up with a name for

the meeting space," Jess said. "'Meeting space' is too bland. I'm looking forward to Daphne's class. I know zip about costume design, so I won't be one of the students and experts in attendance."

"We want to make sure we have at least fifty people," Ruby said. "Ava thinks we'll get closer to seventy."

Mark shook his head. "It won't be that many."

He was a cut-to-the-chase type, Kylie knew from previous encounters with him. From what she'd seen of Russ Colton so far, she suspected the two of them would get along well. She'd always had the feeling that Mark and Jess looked out for her, alone up the road in her rented house and now at Moss Hill.

The waitress arrived at their table, and they put in their orders—turkey clubs for Mark and Russ, the tuna melt for Ruby and the house-made broccoli-cheddar soup for both Jess and Kylie. Kylie didn't trust herself to dive into a club sandwich, given how self-conscious and keyed up she was. It wasn't just having a private investigator at Moss Hill or the unusual lunch. It was being around this many people at all. She was out of practice.

"Ava will be here on Friday," Ruby said. "She's as excited as I am, but she couldn't get away from school. A bunch of her theater friends are coming up from New York to see Daphne. Same with my friends in Boston."

"Are they staying in the area?" Russ asked.

"Some. Not many options here in town, but plenty within an easy drive. But we timed the class so people could make it a day trip from New York or Boston. A longer one from New York, obviously, but doable." Ruby seemed unable to sit still, a bundle of raw energy and nerves. "We are thrilled to have Daphne here. We loved getting to know her better over the winter. I'm dying to see Hollywood and where she lives. She says Ava and I have a standing invitation to visit, but I don't know if she's just being polite."

"If she said it, she meant it," Russ said, nothing casual about him as he watched Ruby fidget and squirm.

Ruby turned to Mark. "How's everything at Moss Hill?"

"Fine. Why?"

But she swung around to Russ. "No problems with your apartment?"

His eyes narrowed on her. "None."

"That's good," Ruby said half under her breath. "Good, good."

Jess, seated at the far end of the table, leaned forward. "Is something on your mind, Ruby?"

She didn't respond at once. She took a breath and fixed her gaze on Russ. "We could have a situation brewing with Saturday."

Kylie went still. Was this why she was invited to lunch? She felt a subtle change in Russ as he studied Ruby. "What kind of situation?" he asked.

"Problems with codes, permits, fire extinguishers. I don't know. Not my area of expertise."

"Problems at Moss Hill, you mean?" Jess asked, clearly shocked.

Ruby nodded. "My mother says someone is spreading rumors around town about possible safety violations and cut corners."

Mark bristled visibly. "There are no problems at Moss Hill."

Jess gasped. "Who is spreading these rumors? Has anyone said anything directly to your mother?"

"You know Mom," Ruby said. "If a blade of grass has a complaint about a lawn mower, she'll hear about it. She's tuned in to town gossip. This will be the first event at the mill. All we need is some crank causing trouble. Ava and I aren't professional meeting planners, but we've done everything possible to dot every *i* and cross every *t*. Mark, are you sure—"

"I'm sure," he said stiffly. "You have nothing to worry about."

"What if a contractor cut a corner you don't know about?"

Jess touched Ruby's shoulder. "You're getting spooled up."

"I know. I am. I've been stewing since Mom told me about the rumors last night. I'm worried someone's trying to sabotage us."

"Why would anyone want to do that?" Jess asked.

"Because people can be jerks," Ruby snapped.

Kylie said nothing. Russ Colton hadn't said a word since his initial question to Ruby, either. The meals arrived. Ruby looked as if she regretted ordering a sandwich. Jess snatched two fries off Mark's plate before trying her soup. Kylie hadn't expected the conversation to turn to news of unpleasant rumors. Was that why Ruby had invited her to lunch? But Kylie couldn't see how she could help unravel what, if anything, was going on.

Ruby stared at her sandwich. "What if someone doesn't want Daphne here—or just doesn't want Moss Hill to host events?"

Mark lifted a triangle of his club sandwich. "A mixed-purpose space was always in the plans for Moss Hill. It's no surprise to anyone we'll be hosting a variety of events there. As far as I can see, people are excited about having that kind of space in town. There have been no problems or complaints."

"Not everyone is excited, obviously," Ruby said. "My mother says she has no idea who is behind the rumors."

"Is this sort of talk unusual around here?" Russ asked.

"Knights Bridge is a small town," Mark said. "People talk. They have their grudges. But nasty rumors like this? I'd say it's unusual."

Ruby seemed to make an effort to try a small bite of her sandwich. "I haven't lived here full-time since I started college, but I can't think of anyone who would want to sabotage a class by a Hollywood icon who's donating her time..." She put down her sandwich and sank against the back of her chair, crossing her arms over her chest. "I didn't sleep at all last night. I'm steamed, obviously, but I'm also this close to totally freaking out."

"Just because something is annoying doesn't mean it's problematic," Jess said.

Mark nodded. "I promise you, Ruby. These rumors are completely unfounded."

Kylie tried her soup. It was thick, creamy and cheesy, with chunks of fresh broccoli. She understood now why Ruby's text had struck her as off. Ruby had arranged lunch to reassure herself nothing was wrong at Moss Hill that could jeopardize Daphne Stewart's appearance in Knights Bridge. Kylie lived there. It made sense to invite her to lunch in case she'd heard or seen anything that might indicate trouble for Saturday.

Russ finished a triangle of his sandwich and wiped his fingers on a napkin as he studied Ruby. "Do the rumors include Daphne or just Moss Hill?"

"Concern about Daphne and the people attending the master class."

"What kind of concern?" Russ asked.

Ruby sniffled, calmer. "That there'll be an accident, and people will get hurt because of the cut corners or bought-off contractors or inspectors. Whatever."

Mark sucked in a breath. He seemed to take her high emotions in stride but clearly wasn't pleased with this development. His wife of less than a year was pensive. "Who's on your short list of possible jerks who could spread such a stupid rumor?" Jess asked.

"No one," Ruby said. "I haven't heard anything negative about Daphne's class. I don't want these rumors to take on a life of their own. I hope I'm not making things worse by mentioning them."

"I'd rather have you speak up than keep this to yourself," Mark said.

"Christopher Sloan said he'd stop by Moss Hill and talk to you."

"Anytime." Mark turned to Russ. "Feel free to join us."

Russ gave a curt nod. "Thanks."

"I just need reassurance," Ruby said. "I know ten-to-one this is small-town grumping and griping, creating drama where there is none—someone looking for attention. You know, the arsonist who sets a fire and then sits back and watches the flames."

Jess dipped her spoon into her soup. "In this case, the fire won't catch and spread because there's nothing to feed it. There are no problems at Moss Hill."

Kylie glanced at Russ, but his expression hadn't changed. His deep blue eyes settled on her. "What about you, Kylie? Have you heard any rumors?"

She ignored his undertone of suspicion, assuming it came with the territory of being an investigator. She shook her head. "No, but I doubt I would. I didn't know about this class until yesterday."

"Kylie keeps to herself," Ruby said, the slightest edge to her voice, if only because she was so agitated. "The artist at work. Deadlines. Am I right, Kylie?"

"Fortunately, yes," she said, forcing a smile and seeing no need to explain further.

Ruby clearly wasn't satisfied. "If you like your solitude and need it for your work, why move into Moss Hill? You had to know you wouldn't have the place to yourself. The apartments and offices would get rented, the meeting space would get booked and you'd run into Mark's staff, groundskeepers, cleaners, security guards—all sorts."

Kylie decided she'd had enough of her soup. "In a way, the activity at Moss Hill is one of its attractions after my months on my own up the road. My apartment is quiet. I can be removed from the activity around me whenever I need to be."

"I'm sorry," Ruby blurted. "I didn't mean to put you on the defensive. I sound like such a bitch. I'm really on edge, I guess. I want everything to be perfect on Saturday. I'm sure there's nothing to these rumors. Kylie, you're welcome to come to the class. You and Daphne probably have a lot in common."

"Thanks," Kylie said. "I'd like that."

"Are you on a tight deadline?" Jess asked.

"Not at the moment." Kylie didn't explain further. She appreciated the change in subject, but not to that particular subject. "It's supposed to rain tomorrow. April showers bring May flowers, though, right?"

Russ picked up his coffee. "So they say."

Kylie sensed he was aware she'd been borderline desperate to keep the subject from shifting to her work. Fortunately, the weather was ever a source of interest in New England, and everyone else at the table seemed relieved to move on from talk of Moss Hill and Daphne Stewart. Jess mentioned that it didn't rain much in Southern California, and the rest of the lunch passed amicably and innocuously. By the time they considered dessert, Ruby was calmer, if still bothered by the rumors. Kylie was under no illusions that Mark Flanagan had dismissed them, either—and she knew Russ Colton hadn't. Not a chance.

Russ Colton was riding back to Moss Hill with her. Kylie adjusted to this fact as she got in her car with him. She'd thought Mark or Ruby might give him a ride, or he'd want to take a walk in the village and check it out, stretch his legs after his long overnight flight, then find his own way back—but none of that had happened.

He strapped his seat belt on next to her in the little car. He oozed masculine confidence, but it didn't strike Kylie as deliberate. It was natural. A part of who he was. Over lunch, she'd tried to assess him as an objective observer. He wouldn't do for Cinderella's or Snow White's prince. Maybe a Badger. She could take part of his last name. Colt Badger, PI.

Now that could be fun.

She pulled onto the side street where Smith's was located and came to the intersection with Main Street, aware of her passenger's dark blue eyes on her. "You don't seem peeved at Ruby O'Dunn for implying you could be the one spreading rumors about Moss Hill," he said.

"I didn't take her comments that way. She's just nervous about Saturday."

Russ didn't respond right away. "I get the impression people around here have you pegged as a reclusive, eccentric artist. Are you?"

She eased the car onto Main Street. "I just had lunch with four people. I didn't tell you to find your own way to town. That's not being reclusive."

"We are here in your little car together, that's true. Self-interest at work? Did you suck it up and go to lunch so you could find out more information about what's going on at Moss Hill this week, with Daphne arriving and me here?"

Kylie could feel her tension rising but tried not to show it. Russ Colton was a pro. He knew what he was doing. He knew how to elicit information from people. She drove past the common, sunny and green on the perfect spring day. "It would be a simple solution if I were the reclusive, eccentric artist who doesn't like the idea of dozens of people showing up in her creative space." She kept her tone as neutral as she could manage. "If I'm the one spreading these rumors, you talk to me, reassure me, threaten to take away my crayons, and all is well. An unknown rumor-monger and potential saboteur is more worrisome. I'm not a threat to anyone."

"You weren't messing with the fire extinguishers

or something like that when I caught you at the mill this morning?"

"You didn't 'catch' me. I just happened to be there the same time you were."

"You ran when you saw me."

She glanced at him. "Wouldn't you?"

He grinned. "I'd buy me a beer."

"It was too early for beer," she said, taking the turn onto the back road to Moss Hill.

"Are you being straightforward or combative with me?"

"Maybe both." She tightened her grip on the wheel. "This is becoming one of those days I wish I could start over."

"Sorry. I shouldn't badger you when you're kind enough to drive me to lunch and back."

His tone didn't hold a single note of contrition. He wasn't sorry. He was doing his job. The apology was merely a tactical maneuver. "Why don't you just tell me how I got on your radar? Was it running when I saw you, being in the lobby in the first place—or was it lunch and these rumors?"

"Now, that's combative," he said.

"I consider it straightforward."

He settled back in his seat. "Here's my take. You were blindsided by the news of Daphne's class on Saturday and an investigator about to show up on your turf. You calmed down when you remembered Julius Hartley. Then you saw me, and I'm not Julius—not by a long shot—and Ruby O'Dunn invited you to lunch out of the blue. You guessed something was up and decided to find out what." He paused. "Am I right?"

"I don't consider Moss Hill my turf."

"I'm staying across the hall from you. I'd consider that my turf."

Meaning she was on *his* turf. His bottom line, maybe. "I'm coming up for air after a series of tight deadlines. I only expected to stay in Knights Bridge for a few months when I moved here. Now it's been ten months, and I'm trying to be more social and meet people in town."

"That's it, huh?"

Obviously he didn't believe her. "Maybe I knew you were jet-lagged, and I thought I'd be a good neighbor and accompany you to lunch. Welcome you to town. Make up for our bad start."

"Yeah. Maybe." He shifted his long legs, clearly having difficulty getting comfortable. "I've been in little seats too many of the past twenty-four hours."

"You didn't demand a first-class seat?"

"Coach is fine with me."

Kylie glanced at the river, quiet and shallow, without any steep drops away from the dam. "I haven't seen anyone sneaking around Moss Hill, in case that was your next question," she said. "I don't keep track of all the comings and goings. Probably not even most of them."

"Does Mark Flanagan have enemies?" Russ asked.

She'd expected the question. "Not that I'm aware of. It's my understanding that Mark grew up in Knights Bridge. People in town know him and like him, from what I can tell. But I'm not the best one to ask, since I'm new here."

"Where did you grow up?"

"East of here. Near Mt. Wachusetts."

"Any enemies?"

"Me?"

"You. Yes."

She attempted a smile despite his probing questions. "I don't get out enough to have enemies."

"It could be an ex-boyfriend, ex-husband, ex-friend, ex-colleague."

"I can't think of anyone in my life who would spread rumors about Moss Hill, for any reason."

"I'm not asking you to draw a conclusion. I'm asking if you have enemies." Russ's tone had softened, as if he'd realized he'd gotten intense. "You're the only resident at Moss Hill, and you're new in town. You seem to know more about the people here than they do about you. Why is that?"

"A natural consequence of being new here. I want to get to know people now that I have more free time. Everyone is busy with their lives and the people they already know."

"And you're reclusive," he said.

"Busy, not reclusive."

"Hair-splitting."

Fair point, she thought. "Focusing on me is a waste of your time, but feel free. I'm sure Ruby's taking idle talk to an extreme conclusion."

"Could be," Russ said. "Who is Christopher Sloan?"

The abrupt shift in subject caught her by surprise, but she welcomed it, could feel her grip on the steering wheel ease. "He's one of two full-time, professional firefighters in town," she said. "The Sloans are another local family. They own a construction company. There are a bunch of them. Christopher's older brother Brandon is married to Ruby's sister Maggie."

"The Sloans worked on Moss Hill?"

"Some. I don't know details. Christopher and Ruby..." Kylie didn't finish.

"He and Ruby what? They're an item?"

"I don't know for sure. You know what it's like when you're the newcomer in a small town."

"I don't, actually."

"People sometimes say things in your earshot they might not say if they knew you from when you were in kindergarten."

"So, you've heard talk about Ruby and this firefighter."

"There are sparks between them."

"Sparks, Kylie?"

She heard the amusement in his voice and instantly felt heat rise in her cheeks. She resisted glancing over at him, but was aware of how close he was in the tight quarters of her small car. "You know what I mean," she said finally.

"I'm not much on noticing sparks, I guess. Let's just say my friends don't come to me for romantic advice, at least not more than once. I ask them if they want to stay in or get out of the relationship. Only two options."

"You're a black-and-white thinker."

"When things are black-and-white. What about you? Do your friends come to you for romantic advice?"

He'd set her up, she saw now. "It depends on the friend. And I don't tend to be a black-and-white thinker. I was up for the sunrise this morning. Did you see it on your flight? So many colors. Then they all melted into the blue sky..." She slowed for a curve. "Let's say that's the kind of thinker I am."

"Is that what we call a blue-sky thinker?"

"Or the sunrise thinker, maybe."

He looked out his window. "I didn't see the sunrise. I don't sleep much on planes, but I was reading. Julius Hartley gave me a copy of *The Three Musketeers*. He said I would understand Knights Bridge better if I read it."

"One for all and all for one, or a lot of sword fights?"

"I was hoping for a scantily clad damsel in distress."

Kylie laughed as she turned into the Moss Hill parking lot. "No luck there. Still too cold. Your Hawaiian shirt with the palm trees suggests you like your warm weather."

"As I said, my brother gave me the shirt. He binge-watched *Magnum, PI* over the winter."

"He lives in Los Angeles?"

"He does."

"Does he know Daphne Stewart?"

"They're friends. I met Daphne and Julius through Marty. That's how I ended up at Sawyer & Sawyer."

Without trying, Kylie thought of a dozen questions she wanted to ask him about his life in California, his work, his past, his brother—where they'd grown up, what he'd done in the navy, why he'd become an investigator, what Daphne Stewart was like. But she didn't ask any of them and instead turned off the engine and got out of the car.

Russ met her on the breezeway, stretching his lower back. "Thanks for the ride into town."

"You're welcome. Thanks for lunch. There's a parking garage under the residential building, in case no one mentioned it. If you need anything while you're here, feel free to knock on my door again."

"I won't disturb you?"

She smiled. "Oh, you'll disturb me, but I won't mind."

"I'm going to take a look around the place."

"I won't call 911 if I see you, then. If you see anything suspicious, by the way, there's decent cell service here. You should be able to call 911."

He stared at her a moment, then broke into a slow, thoroughly sexy grin. "I'll keep that in mind, Kylie. Working the rest of the day? Should I worry if I see the lights on at 3:00 a.m.?"

"If you do, it'll be because I got up early, not because I stayed up late."

His gaze held her for longer than she found comfortable. "I might take a walk later, or settle in and have a beer on the balcony—assuming it's warm enough."

"Evenings still can get cool this time of year, but that can be nice, too. I had wine on my balcony during a snowstorm after I first moved in here in March. It was magical."

Russ raised his eyebrows. "We need to work on your idea of magical."

Kylie felt heat rise in her face. "Well, enjoy the rest of the day."

"I will, thanks. Knock on my door if you think of anything else that could help unravel what's going on with these rumors." He reached into his jacket and withdrew a card, handing it to her. "Or call or text."

"Sure thing."

Kylie took the card and slipped it into her pocket, eager to get back to her worktable.

Time to disappear.

She waited for Russ to go into the main building before she headed inside, her pace picking up the closer she got to her apartment and a locked door between her and her temporary neighbor. She wasn't afraid of him. She just didn't want him prying into her life.

And it was tough to be neutral about him. He was physical, intelligent and always on alert. No question about that.

Also, sexy.

No question about that, either.

Kylie dove into her apartment, breathing deeply as the door shut behind her. Her reaction to him wasn't going to get her anywhere but into deep trouble.

Time to calm down and get to work.

She made tea. She sharpened pencils. She cleaned erasers. She sorted crayons, dusted her scanner, changed the batteries in her wireless keyboard and checked three times to see if the ducks had returned to the river, but they hadn't.

Finally, Kylie approached her worktable as if it held classified information.

Imagine the field day Russ Colton would have if he knew about Morwenna Mills.

She frowned at Sherlock Badger. "Where were you today at lunch when I needed you?"

A little stuffed badger wouldn't have helped her case with a real investigator.

She didn't sit. She stared out at the river, concentrating on the shadows and the green of the fields rising up across from Moss Hill. But her mind didn't clear. It was cluttered with images of lunch, Ruby's fears, Mark's firm denials of problems at Moss Hill, Jess's quiet concern and Russ—questioning, suspicious and thoroughly confident.

And so damn sexy. The dark blue eyes, the tawny hair, the broad shoulders, the easy smile.

None of that was helping, either.

Kylie had to adjust her thinking, since she'd expected Julius Hartley, the investigator who'd escorted Daphne Stewart to Knights Bridge last summer. He was a good-looking man, but in his fifties and clearly out of his element in the small, rural town. Russ was closer to her age and struck her as a man who made a point of not being out of his element anywhere.

She picked a random blue crayon out of a basket on her worktable. Some days she thought she should have a studio separate from her home. She could go to work like "normal people," as her sister would say, then insist she'd been joking. But ever since Kylie had entered art school, friends, family, professors and strangers had cautioned her about the chronic uncertainties of being a freelance illustrator, especially of children's books. Even working illustrators with longtime careers had cautioned her.

By and large, people meant well. They didn't want to see her broke or hurt by rejection and the unpredictable nature of her chosen profession.

That was fine. She didn't want to see herself broke or hurt either.

From the time she was a little girl scribbling on her

bedroom walls, she'd envisioned herself taking a pseudonym, but she'd started her career working under her own name. Now Morwenna Mills was her public face—the author and illustrator who had created the Badger family, newcomers to a little town not unlike Knights Bridge.

Kylie had never written her own children's book. She'd recognized that being both writer and illustrator might not work out and hadn't shown her project to anyone until it was finished. It could have gone right into the trash heap, but it hadn't. Her agent had loved the writing and the illustrations, and so had publishers.

Taking a pseudonym hadn't been required, but it had made sense. At first, she'd continued to take on work as Kylie Shaw. Now she only worked as Morwenna.

For better or worse, she thought, picturing the California investigator across the hall. Had he already guessed she was hiding something?

She could swear him to secrecy and tell him about Morwenna.

But why tell him if she hadn't told her parents and sister and her closest friends? Why open that can of worms? Why take the chance? She was deep into her series of fairy tales. It didn't have the same pressures as her recent Badger deadlines, but she was absorbed in the work.

Always her excuses for keeping Morwenna to herself.

She didn't intend to keep her secret forever, but right now Ava and Ruby O'Dunn, two popular young local women, were excited about having a Hollywood costume designer come to town. They didn't need the distraction of her alter ego this week.

Kylie sat at her worktable and opened her sketch pad to her maple tree.

Right tree. Wrong location.

It was progress, enough to get her back to work.

Seven

"Ruby shouldn't have said anything," Christopher Sloan said as he, Mark Flanagan and Russ stood on the balcony outside the meeting room, above the Moss Hill dam. "Her mother hears all the town gossip. It's the nature of her job, and she likes it—likes being in the know. Ruby should be used to it by now. It's easy for idle talk to get turned into something it shouldn't."

Mark didn't look convinced. He and Christopher had finished their look at the renovated mill and hadn't found anything amiss. It was midafternoon, cooler by the river. Russ had settled into his apartment after he'd had his own look around the property. Not a peep from Kylie Shaw. She was hiding something, no question, but he doubted whatever it was had anything to do with fire codes or corners cut during the refurbishment of the old hat factory.

Russ sensed that he and the two local men were on the same wavelength. He hadn't expected to feel comfortable with the two New Englanders right from the start, but he could see they, too, weren't concerned about actual problems with the mill but instead with the potential effect of the nebulous rumors.

"Why would there be idle talk about this place?" Mark asked. "And why now?"

"Because a Hollywood type is on her way to town. Doesn't matter that she lived here forty years ago. She's dressed movie stars." Christopher nodded to Russ. "And there's our PI here. Ruby told everyone you were on the way, Russ. That had to stoke the fires."

"Drama," Mark said tightly, clearly disgusted.

Christopher shrugged. "Sometimes people talk out of their hats and don't realize they're stirring up trouble."

"They should be more careful." Mark stared down at the water flowing steadily over the dam, as it had since the mid-nineteenth century. "I don't need rumors going around that I did anything but a damn good job on this place. If I find out who said anything…"

"You'll tell Eric or me," Christopher Sloan said, then turned to Russ. "Eric is my oldest brother. He's a police officer in town."

Russ said nothing. He could see how frustrated and disturbed Mark was by this development.

"This will die down once Saturday's event passes without a hitch," Christopher added.

Mark continued to stare at the water. "I hope so."

Russ leaned against the rail. If the two men were lying and the place was riddled with safety issues, then the rail could give way and land him in the river. But he didn't believe the rail was anything but solid. "Mark, is there anyone with a grudge against you—anyone who'd want to make your life miserable?"

"I've fired people, if that's what you're asking. So

have the Sloans and other contractors who worked on renovating this place. I can't think of anyone who's been a real problem."

"No one you had to have escorted from the premises by police? Lawsuits? Angry letters? Threats?"

Mark shook his head. "Nothing like that."

"My brothers and my sister have had a few problems with employees they had to let go," Christopher said. "Nothing recently that I know of."

"What's recently?" Russ asked.

"Past six months. Probably the past year."

Russ stood straight. "What about the O'Dunns?"

"I don't see how rumors about this place not being safe would hurt the O'Dunns," Mark said. "Everyone in town loves Elly and her daughters. Phoebe's engaged to Noah Kendrick, of course, and he's a high-profile billionaire, but it's a stretch to connect him with this nonsense."

And nonsense it did seem to be, Russ thought.

"Ava and Ruby have stars in their eyes," Christopher said. "They're getting carried away with this notion of opening a children's theater here, with Daphne Stewart's help. They'd put on plays, offer classes and workshops—Ruby can go on forever about the possibilities. I gather Ava's just as bad. Heads in the clouds."

"Let's get past the class on Saturday first," Mark muttered.

Christopher nodded thoughtfully. "Exactly what I told Ruby."

Russ had asked Daphne how serious she was about this theater venture, but she'd changed the subject and he hadn't pursued it. He decided to make no comment about the idea of Moss Hill as a children's theater.

Christopher had to get back to the firehouse. Mark needed to get home.

Enough of ambiguous rumors for one day.

Russ walked with the two Knights Bridge men to the front of the building. He had no firm plans for the rest of the day. Since he didn't have a packed agenda and there was zero urgency, even with someone spreading rumors about safety at Moss Hill, he figured he could relax, take a nap, go for a run and maybe see if he could find out more about Kylie Shaw, children's book illustrator.

Kylie Shaw had a bare-bones website that hadn't been updated in months.

Russ found himself peering at her photo on his laptop. Since her hair was chin-length, the photo wasn't that recent. She was standing on a stone bridge but otherwise he couldn't pinpoint the location. He doubted it was Knights Bridge.

Never mind Knights Bridge—he wasn't sure it was in the US.

The site was geared to people who might hire her as an illustrator, not to readers, children in general or other illustrators. Her bio was professional but hinted at a certain artistic quirkiness. She'd grown up in small-town New England with a younger sister. Her father was a veterinarian, and her mother trained and groomed dogs—the perfect background for an illustrator of children's books.

Her list of credits included about a dozen children's books she'd illustrated, none in the past two years. She wasn't on social media: LinkedIn, Facebook, Twitter, Instagram.

If she'd been on deadline, she had to have work.

Maybe a web presence wasn't important to getting contracts.

Or maybe she was lying about the deadlines. She could have come to Knights Bridge after a setback in her career, used her retreat as a way to get back on track. That would mean she had solid savings or another income. Boyfriend, alimony, inheritance?

Russ shut his laptop. Looking up a children's illustrator on the internet was a sign he was jet-lagged, bored, taken by said illustrator's fair hair and pretty light blue eyes—or all of the above.

He saw no point in digging deeper. If he'd discovered a sabotaged fire extinguisher or scrawled threats on a wall in the meeting room, that'd be different.

Kylie Shaw was probably in her apartment drawing pictures of cuddly critters.

Not anything he needed to spend time on.

He got to his feet and decided on a run. A good one. At least five miles.

He changed into running clothes and set off up the river, in the opposite direction of the village. The river widened, coursing over exposed rocks and the occasional downed tree, mere driftwood now. The bank was steep, washed out in places but for the most part intact.

He slowed as he came to a red-painted covered bridge.

A surprise, this.

Picturesque under the April sky, surrounded by green fields and woods, the bridge could have been the subject of a New England postcard. Russ wouldn't be surprised if it had been.

He listened to the sounds of the river, and of the breeze in the trees.

"Damn, it's quiet."

His flight might have been days instead of hours ago.

He walked across the wood bridge, a single lane over a relatively narrow section of the river. A small plaque indicated the bridge had been built in 1845—more than a decade before construction of the mill down-river and generations before cars, trucks and a runner from Southern California.

Russ exited the covered bridge and followed the road uphill to a gentle stretch that ran a bit farther back from the river, along a field plowed for spring planting. He came to a house situated amid mature shade trees, rock walls and flower gardens bursting into bloom. The house's blue-gray shingles and dark gray shutters blended with the early spring landscape as clouds moved in from the west.

He paused, taking in the views, the silence.

Was this the house Kylie had rented when she'd first arrived in Knights Bridge?

He didn't have an artistic bone, muscle or cell in his body, but he could imagine crafting illustrations for children's books here.

He continued on his run, eventually coming to a cul-de-sac off his road, with three houses. School-age kids were playing softball in one of the yards. A man was working on a tractor in another yard. Laundry fluttered in the breeze on a clothesline in the third yard.

Nothing around here was as isolated as it seemed,

but he would bet Kylie had rented the house down the road. How had she chosen it? Friends, relatives, a website—a stab in the dark?

He turned around and jogged back to Moss Hill.

Another shower, a check of his messages and it was time for that beer on the balcony.

The way Moss Hill was constructed, he couldn't see onto Kylie's balcony.

Just as well, maybe.

There was no furniture on his balcony, and with the waning daylight, the temperature was dropping. He had a decent cell signal and called Julius Hartley.

"No problems so far, I take it?" Julius asked.

"Nothing serious. Small-town talk." Russ filled Julius in on the rumors. "Has Daphne been in touch with anyone in Knights Bridge besides Ava and Ruby O'Dunn?"

"Not that I'm aware of."

"You and Loretta stay in touch with Dylan McCaffrey and Noah Kendrick. They're more likely to draw negative attention than Daphne is."

"But there's been nothing," Julius said. "Loretta has concerns about their security setup, but that doesn't mean anyone's threatened them or causing trouble. Dylan and Noah aren't involved with Moss Hill."

"What about money for a children's theater?" Russ asked.

"Community support has to be there for it to work, with or without their money."

"Makes sense." Russ drank some of his beer. He could hear a bird in the distance, and the ever-present flow of the river. "How's Daphne?"

Julius sighed. "She left me a voice mail a little while ago saying she's getting cold feet."

"Is she or is this a ploy?"

"I haven't called her back. She said in the voice mail she's so nervous about Saturday she could throw up. I've never known her to be nervous, but she's never given a master class anywhere, never mind Knights Bridge."

"She's not going to throw up," Russ said. "Don't indulge her. Tell her it's too late to get cold feet."

"See why I turned her over to you?" Julius chuckled softly. "Loretta and the move to La Jolla were part of it, but Daphne knows what buttons to push with me. You have no buttons."

"Is that an insult or a compliment?"

"A fact. What do you want me to tell her?"

"Tell her Ava and Ruby are doing a thorough job, and everything's set for her arrival. She has nothing to worry about. I'll be back on Wednesday and will escort her here myself."

"She'll like that. You can be her entourage."

Russ gritted his teeth but said nothing.

"Daphne won't want to disappoint anyone," Julius said. "I'll tell her she can start packing. She told Loretta she might bring the sequined gown she wore to her first Academy Awards ceremony thirty-odd years ago. Her design, of course."

"Julius…" Russ welcomed a soft, cold breeze floating across the river. "I don't know how to say this, but—"

"You don't care if Daphne wears sequins. I won't tell her."

"You can tell her. I don't care."

"Where are you right now?"

"Balcony outside my apartment."

"That explains why your teeth are chattering."

"My teeth aren't chattering, Julius. I'm dying here, though. Baseball season has started. There's no cable."

"There's Wi-Fi."

"Helps. Did you and Loretta meet my neighbor when you were out here? Kylie Shaw. She illustrates children's books. She would have been renting a house out past the covered bridge then."

"There's a covered bridge? No, I don't recall meeting this woman. I'll ask Loretta."

"Don't go to any trouble. I was just curious."

"That bored, or is this Kylie Shaw attractive?"

"Goodbye, Julius."

By the time Russ finished his beer, it was six o'clock. Three hours earlier in California. He yawned, but he wasn't tired enough to sleep. A nap would only make adjusting to the time change worse. Not sleeping much on his flight meant it'd be easier to sleep through the night, but only if he stuck it out now and stayed awake.

He scrambled some eggs and made toast for dinner. Read some of his book, a history of the Quabbin Reservoir and the four towns lost to its creation. When he started dropping off to sleep, he went back onto the balcony. The temperature had dropped precipitously since his beer and his call to Julius.

He could hear something splashing down in the river.

It'd been a long day given his flight and the three-hour time difference, but Russ knew that wasn't the reason for his restlessness.

He was bored.

He'd never been good at being bored.

The rumors about fire extinguishers and such weren't enough to engage him. A local fight. Nothing to do with Daphne.

His phone buzzed with a text. It was from Marty. How's it going? Any snow?

No snow but it's cold enough. Daphne been in?

Just made her a French martini.

Russ pictured his brother, Daphne, the bar. A different life.

He went inside.

He read more of his book and was in bed by ten o'clock.

Russ awoke early but not early enough to catch the sunrise. He got dressed and walked down the road to the covered bridge, took a picture on his phone, and figured when he had a decent signal he'd text it to Marty in Hollywood Hills.

He walked back toward Moss Hill but his thoughts took him to a call with Marty ten years ago. Marty had been an MBA student in Phoenix. Russ had been in the navy, stationed in San Diego. He'd considered a variety of options, including becoming a SEAL, but had settled on security and investigative work. He'd always had clarity about his goals. Marty…

Russ smiled. His brother didn't have goals. He had dreams and ideas.

Lots of dreams and ideas.

He could hear his brother's voice that day. The confidence, the swagger, the frustration. All were there as twenty-five-year-old Martin Colton tried to figure out what to do to get his parents' approval.

Hey, Russ. I've been busting my ass in school but I'm taking a break to go up in a helo with Dad.

You'll have your MBA before you know it.

Yeah. I guess. I want to get my pilot's license. I could do volunteer search-and-rescue missions.

You always have a lot of ideas, Marty. Wish I were going up in the helicopter with you.

Mom's going with us.

She hates helicopters.

She wants to see Sedona from the air. It's good, Russ. All good.

Marty's standard phrase to this day. *It's good. All good.*

Russ walked back to the mill. It would be cooler today, with rain moving in by evening. He didn't mind rain. He saw he had an email from Julius. Loretta had arranged for him to have lunch with Olivia and Dylan McCaffrey tomorrow at their place in Knights Bridge. They had a house in San Diego, too.

He texted his photo of the bridge to Marty.

Four in the morning in California, and his brother texted him back. Nice. It's like something out of a Bing Crosby movie.

You working on your screenplay?

No. Doing tai chi.

It could be true. Have fun.

Russ unlocked the door to his apartment and went

inside. He had today to kill. He could do some digging into the rumors Ruby O'Dunn had reported yesterday, but he had no reason to go deep and risk causing more harm than good. He'd keep an eye and ear out for trouble. In the meantime, he could watch it rain, read his book on Quabbin or *The Three Musketeers* or do some actual work—such as check out the Knights Bridge Free Public Library where forty years ago, Daphne Stewart, then Debbie Sanderson, had worked.

Also he'd noticed on the library website that Kylie Shaw was leading story hour for three- and four-year-olds later that morning.

Eight

Built in 1872, the Knights Bridge Free Public Library occupied a shaded corner on South Main Street, across the common from the Swift River Country Store. Kylie locked her bike on the rack out front. She'd almost canceled story hour, her one regular commitment in town. She'd awakened feeling out of sorts and vulnerable.

Watched, she thought, walking up the stairs to the library's front door.

She had only a few minutes to spare before the little ones started to arrive. Having children of her own wasn't a prerequisite to being a children's book illustrator. She knew illustrators who didn't particularly like children, never mind have any, but she enjoyed kids. She'd always envisioned herself having some of her own.

But she wasn't going there now. She had enough on her mind.

She'd spotted Russ Colton walking down the road toward the covered bridge before she'd set off on her bicycle in the opposite direction. She didn't know if he'd seen her.

The man was a distraction.

She welcomed the thud of the heavy front door behind her. She loved the late-nineteenth-century character and atmosphere of the library, with its dark woods, marble fireplace and countless nooks and crannies. The land and building had been donated by George Sanderson, Daphne Stewart's great-great-grandfather. His portrait hung above the mantel in the main reading room. He was middle-aged, his demeanor stern but not severe. Now that it was the twenty-first century, his portrait added to the library's atmosphere. It had probably seemed contemporary in the 1870s.

Kylie spotted Samantha Bennett, another Knights Bridge newcomer, at a small table in the back of the main floor, a stack of musty-looking books in front of her. An expert in pirates, Samantha was a member of a family of serious adventurers. Her grandfather, Harry Bennett, now deceased, had explored Antarctica. Her parents were exploring sunken World War II submarines off the coast of Great Britain. Samantha herself had come to Knights Bridge in search of eighteenth-century pirate treasure. Now she was engaged to Justin Sloan, the second-eldest Sloan sibling, a volunteer firefighter and carpenter for Sloan & Sons, and as close to a real friend Kylie had allowed herself so far in Knights Bridge.

"Lost in the world of pirates?" Kylie asked with a smile.

Samantha laughed. "In the world of a particularly nasty pirate, in fact. No Johnny Depp as Captain Sparrow in sight today. How are you, Kylie? My spies tell me you have a neighbor at Moss Hill, at least for now."

"It was bound to happen."

"Bet you never pictured a California private investigator moving in." Samantha sat up straight, raking her fingers through her short, dark curls. "Your presence is my cue to pack up, because it means we're about to be inundated with small children. I love kids, but it's hard to study bloodthirsty pirates with four-year-olds on the premises."

"We read a pirate book last time," Kylie said. "It wasn't about your kind of pirates, though."

"I hope not. Can you imagine? You'd be banned from leading children's story hour. How's it going? This is—what, your third story hour?"

Kylie nodded. "So far, so good."

"Illustrating children's books must help." Samantha yawned, covering her mouth with the back of her hand. "Sorry. I got here first thing, and I've been at it ever since. I should set an alarm for breaks. I need coffee and a good walk before it rains. Chase out the cobwebs. How've you been, Kylie?"

"Great, thanks. Working. You?"

"The usual. On the trail of Captain Benjamin Farraday, my mysterious real-life pirate. Justin and I are setting a date for our wedding. It's going to be in England if we can work out the logistics—we know that much. You lived there for a while, didn't you?"

"I did, yes. Great spot for a wedding."

"Most of my family is in England and Scotland at the moment, and Justin's sister is there with her new husband. Talk about shockers. They'll be back in Knights Bridge, though, no doubt in my mind." Samantha waved a hand. "Lots of reasons to have an English wedding."

"I'm glad things have worked out for you and Justin."

"Love is in the air in our little town," Samantha said lightly, getting to her feet. "We'd love to have you over to dinner now that you're not as crazy busy with dead-lines. We're still out at the Sloan cabin on the pond. I'm surprised my grandfather hasn't haunted me. He trekked through Antarctica, but he lived in London and Boston. I don't think he could have stood it here, but I love it."

Helped to have rugged Justin Sloan in her life, Kylie thought. She wondered if Justin had been informed of the rumors about Moss Hill, given his prominent role at Sloan & Sons, but Kylie decided she didn't want to give fuel to the gossip by repeating it. Samantha scooped up her books and her tote bag. Kylie left her to it and said goodbye. Dinner with Samantha and Justin felt natural, not forced—not like yesterday's lunch.

Kylie headed to the children's alcove at the front of the library, where two little girls had already arrived for story hour. Clare Morgan, the library director, herself the mother of a six-year-old, greeted Kylie. "I think we have everything," Clare said. "If there is anything else you need, let me know."

"Should be all set, thanks."

Fair-haired and a gentle soul, Clare and her son seemed to have been welcomed to their new town. On her last story hour two weeks ago, Kylie had overheard an elderly man ask Vera Galeski, one of the library's few employees, if Clare, a widow, and Logan Farrell, a Boston ER doctor with roots in town, were engaged yet. Vera's "Oh, I wouldn't know" was belied by her flush, suggesting she at least guessed an engagement was in the works.

Romance was indeed in the air around here, Kylie thought, but it had taken a backseat in her own life since she'd created Morwenna, and the Badgers had taken off.

More than a backseat.

Romance wasn't even in the car with her anymore, but Morwenna wasn't the only reason.

More children and their parents and minders arrived. If they were aware Kylie was an illustrator for children's books, no one at the library, including Clare Morgan, knew she was Morwenna Mills. Kylie hadn't lied—she simply hadn't mentioned it. Her every-other-week story hour guaranteed she got herself out among her fellow townspeople. As much as she liked children and had always vaguely imagined she would have some of her own one day, it would help if she had a man in her life.

Clare got the children settled with her quiet, firm, direct manner. Kylie had selected two short books, one of them a Curious George favorite and another illustrated by a very talented friend who lived in Chicago with her husband and three young sons...and also didn't know Kylie was Morwenna.

Once she started, her misgivings about leaving her apartment that morning evaporated, and she got into the stories, enjoying the children with all their energy, variable attention spans and enthusiasm. She'd be back on her bike soon, at her worktable before the rain started. She didn't know what her PI neighbor was up to today. Would the rain throw a monkey wrench into his plans?

No matter. Russ Colton looked as if he could handle a rainy evening in Knights Bridge.

* * *

He was sitting on a chair by the fireplace, looking relaxed, when she finished story hour.

Kylie had spotted him toward the end of her session. She came to an abrupt halt in front him. "Are you spying on me?"

"Waiting for you. There's a difference."

Not much of one, she thought.

Russ pointed to George Sanderson's portrait above him. "Imagine all old George has seen since he got up on that wall. He doesn't look like Daphne. Julius teases her that she looks just like him, except for the sideburns, but I don't see a resemblance."

"Russ—" Kylie pushed back her frustration "—why are you waiting for me?"

He got to his feet. He wasn't wearing a Hawaiian shirt today. He had on a black shirt under his open jacket, adding to the air of confidence and competence about him. This wasn't an easygoing man, Kylie thought. But that made sense, given his profession, and she tried to take it in stride.

He nodded past her toward the children's alcove. "You were a hit."

"Curious George was. Do you know who he is?"

"Sure. Mischief-making monkey. Surprised?"

"Even you were a little boy once."

"Tough to picture me at four?"

She smiled. "Very."

"I was a cute little devil. I'm not as cute now." He tilted his head back slightly, giving her a frank once-over. "You look beat, Kylie. The kids wear you out?"

"In a good way. Seriously, what are you doing here?"

"I want to see the room in the library attic where Daphne worked before she moved to California. I thought you might like to join me."

"I'd love to," Kylie said without thinking. She'd never been up to the library attic, never mind to the storage room Debbie Sanderson had transformed into a sewing room and taken the first tentative steps to realizing her dream to become a Hollywood costume designer.

"Great." Russ opened his palm, revealing an old-fashioned key. "Let's go."

"No one is going with us?"

"It's an attic. We don't need a guided tour."

They took the main stairs, past the spot where a fierce late-summer storm had knocked a tree through the wall, now fixed. Kylie remembered watching the sky turn green-gray as she'd worked in her bay window in her rented house on the river, deep into her solitary retreat. She'd finally ducked into an interior room, wondering who would come look for her if she were trapped there—but she and the house had come through unscathed. She'd only had to pick up leaves, twigs and a few small branches in the yard. Other places in town— like the library—hadn't fared as well, but, despite a few close calls, there'd been no serious injuries.

She glanced at Russ, imagining him dealing with severe thunderstorms and their aftermath. Coming to rescue her. Not that she wanted or needed rescuing, but she could see him wielding a chain saw, cutting through brush and trees, lifting beams and shoving aside debris. But, in fact, he worked for a Beverly Hills law firm. She smiled at the incongruity as they came to the attic stairs, narrow and steeper than the wide, formal stairs to the main reading room.

"How long have you worked for the law firm in Beverly Hills?" she asked.

Russ pulled open the door to the stairs. "A few months. I only moved to LA in March."

"Where were you before that?"

"I was on my own in San Diego. It's where I ended up after I left the navy."

"What did you do in the navy?"

"Security and investigations."

"That makes sense."

"It's worked out okay," he said, stepping back and motioning for her to go up the stairs. "After you."

They'd gone up the main stairs side by side, Kylie aware of Russ next to her, solid, taking in their surroundings. She tried not to guess what he was thinking—or looking at as she mounted the attic stairs. She'd dressed in slim pants and a shirt that worked both on her bike and for story hour. Whether they worked for the man behind her wasn't her concern. And why was she thinking this way?

Because he's action-oriented, stuck in a small town without a lot to do.

And he was suspicious of her, she thought.

He was potential trouble, in other words.

She came to the top of the stairs. With few windows and the gray of the approaching rain, the attic was dimly lit, filled with shadows and a strong sense of the past. Kylie felt on the wall for a light switch and flipped on the overhead, not that it did much good.

Russ stepped next to her, surveying the attic's mix

of boxes, filing cabinets, paintings and a variety of furniture. "About what I expected. Did you meet Daphne when she was out here last September?"

Kylie shook her head. "I only heard about her appearance."

"Do you know her story?"

"She got her start in costume design up here, sewing in the attic of her small-town library."

There was more to Daphne Stewart's story than that. She had kept her attic sewing room a secret. She'd copied Hollywood dresses and costumes and created her own, practicing her craft, dreaming of a different life. When she'd fled New England and her troubled past, she'd left her secret attic room largely intact, taking little with her as she boarded her first bus west. Her storage-room-turned-sewing-room wasn't discovered until last summer, when Phoebe O'Dunn, then the library director, had ventured up to the attic in search of vintage clothes for an upcoming fund-raiser.

"I'm sure Miss Stewart must have a lot of memories here." Kylie hesitated before she continued. "How did she come up with the name Daphne Stewart?"

"She loves to read," Russ said. "She read every book she could get her hands on when she lived here. Daphne is in honor of Daphne du Maurier, and Stewart is in honor of Mary Stewart. Have you ever read them?"

"*Rebecca* and Mary Stewart's Merlin books."

"I can't imagine that many people around here being interested in a Hollywood fashion designer." He leaned toward Kylie with a quick smile. "Don't tell Daphne I said that."

"I won't, but Knights Bridge isn't as isolated and out of the way as you might think."

"It's already turning out to be more interesting than I expected."

Although cluttered and overstuffed, the attic had been cleaned up somewhat since Phoebe's discovery of the secret room, its door concealed behind a tin closet. Now the closet had been moved to one side and the door was easy to spot. Russ unlocked it and pushed it open, and Kylie followed him into the small room.

Neither spoke as they took in the worktable, shelves, rods and hangers in the tiny space where a young woman had honed her craft and nursed her dreams. Most of the dresses and costumes Debbie Sanderson had sewn in secret forty years ago had now been removed for safekeeping from her hidden sewing room. A few bolts of fabric, notions, spools of thread and a couple of dresses were all that remained. Even the workhorse of a sewing machine had been put away. Kylie had seen pictures of it in the local weekly newspaper, which had done a piece on Daphne Stewart's visit to Knights Bridge.

Kylie stood in front of a small window that looked out on to the common. "Daphne had a good view, at least."

Russ picked up an old pair of scissors. "Wonder what I could get for them on eBay," he said with a halfhearted smile. He set the scissors down again. "It's different being here than imagining what it was like. Daphne didn't grow up in Knights Bridge. She moved here to get away from her abusive father. I gather he was a real SOB."

"But she found herself here," Kylie said, turning back to the window. One of the four-year-old boys from story hour was walking with his mother across the common to the country store. "Daphne never married after she moved west?"

"She has three marriages under her belt. She says she's done now."

"Never shut the door to love and romance. That's what they say, anyway. She's in her early sixties. There's still lots of time." Kylie glanced away from the mother and son on the common. "But Daphne's never had kids, right?"

"No kids." Russ smiled. "Just my brother."

"He's ex-navy, too?"

"No."

Kylie expected him to elaborate, but he didn't.

He stood next to her at the window. "Daphne and Julius both warned me not to let appearances fool me— this little town is filled with secrets, and time's never stopped here. What drew you here? Family, friends, some guy?"

"Deadlines. I needed a place to hole up and work for a while. I rented a house thinking I'd stay two or three months, but that was ten months ago."

"You have a solitary career. Daphne sewed up here alone, without telling a soul, but she didn't stay alone once she got to Hollywood. She worked hard and persevered to get where she is now." Russ paused. "I looked you up on the internet."

"You didn't find much," Kylie said, beating him to it. She took a cue from him and didn't elaborate. "What about you? Does being a Beverly Hills private investigator suit you?"

"Some days more than others."

"You strike me as someone who knows what you want and goes after it. You don't drift but you don't rush, either. Am I right?"

"Uh-huh."

He moved back from the window. Only then did Kylie realize he'd read into her words. "I should stick to drawing," she said. "It's incredible, thinking about a young woman sneaking up here to sew. At least she had a window with a nice view of the common."

"Where did you do your first drawings?"

"I don't remember not drawing, but my parents would tell you I started by drawing on my bedroom wall." She realized he kept steering the conversation back to her and was relieved when she noticed Ruby O'Dunn down on South Main, crossing from the common to the library. "Are you meeting Ruby here?"

Russ peered down at the street. "I hadn't planned on it."

"Maybe she's returning a book." Ruby had a determined, rushed look about her. Kylie noticed Russ's rental car parked out front. Ruby could have recognized it. "Or maybe she has an update on the rumors her mother heard about Moss Hill."

"I'm finished here. Anything else you want to see?"

Kylie shook her head. They left the attic room, locking the door behind them. She shut off the overhead, imagining Debbie Sanderson, now Daphne Stewart, doing the same thing so many times when she'd slip up here to sew.

Russ glanced back at the attic. "I see Daphne now and think about what it must have been like for her, alone here..." He didn't finish. "Let's go."

Kylie stood back, making sure he went ahead of her down the stairs. If he knew it was a deliberate move on her part, he didn't say so.

When they reached the main reading room, they found Ruby chatting with Clare Morgan, making arrangements for Clare's son to visit with Ruby's nephews after school. "Maggie will be home," Ruby said, referring to the boys' mother, the O'Dunn sister who was married to Brandon Sloan.

The matter settled, Clare returned to work.

Ruby sighed. "I've been away at school so much that I forget what day-to-day life here is like. Maggie and Brandon used to live in Boston. I never thought Brandon would want to move back to Knights Bridge, but he loves it. It's a good place to raise kids." She clapped her hands, as if getting her own attention. "But that's not why I'm here. Kylie, I'd like to make amends for my rude, crazy behavior yesterday. Chris and I will bring you and Russ dinner tonight, unless you have other plans. Maggie's doing the cooking, so you're in luck."

Kylie, caught off guard, stammered something unintelligible, but Russ was smooth, in control. "That sounds great, Ruby. See you and Chris later this evening, then."

"I have wine," Kylie finally managed. "And wine-glasses."

"Great," Ruby said. "We'll bring everything to your place."

She dashed out of the library with the energy of a woman with a dreaded mission accomplished.

Kylie had meant she'd bring the wine and wineglasses to Russ's apartment and meet everyone there for dinner. It was furnished, but maybe it didn't have as many dishes as she did? Not that she had many. She didn't entertain. Now all of a sudden Ruby O'Dunn, Christopher Sloan and Russ Colton were coming to dinner. It didn't matter that she didn't have to cook— Kylie had no idea what she'd do with them. Was this some kind of plot? Had Ruby and Russ conspired to get into her apartment? But that made no sense, unless Ruby really did believe Kylie was behind the rumors.

Kylie forced herself to breathe. She had no evidence that dinner was anything but a friendly gesture.

Russ eased next to her. "That worked out well," he said cheerfully. "Dinner, wine and a chance to see how an illustrator works."

She manufactured a smile. "I'll go home and sweep up the cobwebs before everyone gets there."

"Sounds good. I'm across the hall if you need help with the sweeping."

He sauntered—the only word for it—out the front entrance.

Friendly gesture or not, he was definitely planning to seize the moment and turn dinner to his advantage. Even if he didn't think she posed a threat to his client, he clearly had guessed she was hiding something.

Kylie returned to the children's alcove, noting a display of the first three books in the *Badgers of Middle Branch* series. The pages were dog-eared and worn.

She touched the image of a white pine in front of the Badgers' house on one of the covers. It was a good tree. It'd come to her quickly, not like the grandmother's tree in her rendition of *Little Red Riding Hood*. It didn't mean it wouldn't be a good tree, too. It was just taking its time.

She settled down, a plan developing for the next few hours. She had plenty of time to ride her bike to Moss Hill and clean her apartment before Russ, Ruby and Chris arrived.

When was the last time she'd had company?

She hadn't had any, she realized—certainly not since she'd moved to Moss Hill. Before that, when she was in her rented house, she'd had her parents over once for brunch. They didn't live that far from Knights Bridge. Most of the time she went to them. Same with her il-lustrator friends, who lived all over the place. They'd get together at restaurants—have coffee or lunch and talk about their lives and work.

Company could be nice, Kylie thought, calming down, but she needed to get busy if she was to cleanse away any evidence of Morwenna Mills in her apartment at her renovated hat factory.

Nine

Russ took a stool at the counter at Smith's and ordered a grilled cheese with onion and coffee. He needed coffee. He'd have pie for dessert, too. He noted the options under glass farther down the counter. Coconut cream, chocolate cream, apple, blueberry. A lot of carbs in pie and a sandwich, but he could go for another run this afternoon. Maybe he'd rent a bike while he was in Knights Bridge.

None of which put his reaction to Kylie Shaw and Daphne's library attic room behind him. It had left him with a tightness in his chest.

His easy morning with nothing much to do had turned into something else altogether.

Emotion. Damn.

His sandwich arrived as a uniformed police officer entered the restaurant. Eric Sloan, the eldest of the six Sloan siblings. He bore a strong resemblance to his firefighter brother, Christopher. Russ figured he'd need a score card to keep everyone in town straight, but he was doing all right.

Eric brought up the rumors. "My family's in construction. They deal with all sorts of subcontractors. They have a steady core group of workers, but there's high turnover with new hires. There's a lot of work right now, so that's not an issue."

"Are you investigating these rumors?"

"Nothing to investigate. Just talk."

After Eric left, Russ decided on the apple pie. He was in New England. It seemed appropriate to have apple pie. Before long, spring fruits would be ripe. He wondered what grew around here. Peaches, plums, pears, strawberries? Probably all of them, but it was a short growing season.

His attempt at distracting himself didn't work, but his pie was as good as his sandwich had been—and he'd finally had his fill of coffee.

He walked back across the town common to his car. As he unlocked the driver's door, he glanced up at the attic windows of the library, picturing Daphne looking down at him as she'd hemmed an Audrey Hepburn or Elizabeth Taylor dress.

And he pictured Kylie's curves and smile, and he considered her contradictions—quick and straightforward on the one hand, quirky and funny on the other hand.

Then throw in a third hand. Vulnerable, uncertain, secretive.

Russ got in the car and yanked the door shut with more force than was necessary. He could see Daphne pulling off a secret room in the library attic. He didn't know Kylie Shaw well enough to gauge what she would be good at pulling off. He could look into what she was hiding, but did it matter? Was it any of his business? The ambiguous rumors gave him a bit of latitude, but only a bit.

Raindrops splattered onto his windshield as he headed out of the village toward Moss Hill.

A rainy afternoon and evening in Knights Bridge.

He could think of several ways to amuse himself, but not one of them was possible or wise. He was here on business, he reminded himself. He had a few non-Daphne work-related things he could do at his borrowed apartment—research, reports, calls and emails.

He could stay busy while it rained and he waited for dinner across the hall.

The prospect of company pushed Kylie into high gear. She kicked off her trail shoes, tossed her jacket on to the couch and eyed her worktable. She'd left it cluttered with sketches, notes, pencils, erasers, markers and crayons. She'd pulled out all sorts of materials early that morning, before sunrise, before coffee, before setting out on her bike. She'd doodled by drawing badgers.

Most of her serious, most Morwenna-revealing work was on her computer, which she would turn off and unplug, to help her stay calm with people in her space. It was password-protected. No one could accidentally access her files.

Or deliberately access them, she thought.

No question Russ was a thorough sort. She could see him sneaking a look at her computer while she was pouring wine.

She stacked papers and tossed drawing tools into their appropriate containers. She'd held on to her privacy

in the months since she'd moved to Knights Bridge. She
wasn't going to give it up now, when she was on edge
and feeling vulnerable. She wanted to maintain control of when and how people learned about Morwenna.

But it wasn't just Morwenna. It was her work itself,
too. She'd become accustomed to the isolation of the
past months and the uninterrupted focus on her work.
Pulling herself out of that pattern was good but not as
easy as she'd expected.

Having a sexy California investigator on her case
didn't make it any easier.

"Sexy's the word for him, too," she muttered, heading to her utility closet for cleaning supplies. She'd dust,
mop, wipe down the counters and clean the bathroom.
Fluff the pillows on the couch. "What else?"

The forecast rain had started as she'd arrived at Moss
Hill, and now fog was forming along the river, the fields
on the opposite bank lost in swirling gray. Rain dripped
off the black iron balcony rails.

By late afternoon, Kylie was satisfied. Her loft-style
apartment gleamed.

She lit a few candles on the coffee table. She didn't
want the place to smell as if she'd just whipped through
it, madly cleaning ahead of company.

Russ Colton and Ruby O'Dunn arrived together.
Kylie welcomed them with a smile and a cheerful greeting, ignoring a quickening of her heartbeat at having
company.

Ruby, wearing one of her long skirts, set a basket
on the counter next to one of the lit candles. "Food for
the evening, compliments of Maggie," she said, then
spun around to Kylie and Russ. "Chris couldn't make

it. He had a fire call at the last minute. And I'm going
to bow out. I'm all butterflies about Saturday. I'll ruin
your evening."

"Butterflies are all the more reason to stay," Kylie
said. She had butterflies of her own. She pointed at
the wine and wineglasses she'd set out. "And there's
wine. It's a good merlot, bought on sale at our own little country store."

"I'm sorry. I just…" Ruby bit down visibly on her
lower lip, her turquoise eyes shining with tears. She
rallied, giving a small laugh. "I need to go curl up in
a fetal position for the evening. I'm making myself
crazy. Daphne called this afternoon, and it was weird—
I think she probably has butterflies, too, although she's
done much scarier things than teach a class in Knights
Bridge. Accept an Oscar in front of a billion people,
for one."

"I'll talk to her," Russ said.

"It's okay. I don't want to upset her more by getting
you on her case." Ruby shifted to Kylie. "Can I take a
rain check on dinner and wine? I'm too restless to be
good company."

Kylie could feel Ruby's agitation and regret. She
smiled, putting aside her own uneasiness at being alone
with Russ. "Anytime, Ruby."

"I'll get past this. Chris and his fire calls don't help.
But that's what happens with firefighters, right? They
fight fires." She gave a halfhearted smile. "I'll see you
both later. Maggie's an incredible cook. You'll love
whatever she's put together."

Russ saw her out, shutting the door behind her. He
walked over to the counter and the dinner basket. "I can

put together a plate and take it to my apartment if you want the evening to yourself."

Ball to you, Kylie, she thought. "I lit candles. I dusted. I think I can handle company. Show you a little New England hospitality instead of letting you sit in the rain by yourself."

"You'd be sitting in the rain by yourself."

"Ah, but I'm used to it. Not much rain in LA. Also, I've already opened the merlot. If the rain lets up, or even if it doesn't, we could drink it on the balcony."

"That sounds tempting. I haven't seen this kind of rain in a while."

She noticed he was eyeing her tidy worktable. She liked to keep sketch pads and basic tools within arm's reach, regardless of whether she was working on her computer. Her other materials—scanner, computer pen tools, art board, color wheels, rulers, staplers, tape and whatnot—were stacked on shelves next to her worktable.

Russ picked up the bottle of wine. "Do you work mostly on computer?"

"Mostly, yes, but I do a lot by hand. Some of my friends work solely on computer. I know a few illustrators who work solely by hand, but not many anymore. Everything ends up on the computer."

"What was your latest project?"

"*Hansel and Gretel*. I'm working on a series of fairy tales."

"Will you get artistic credit?"

"I'm focusing on the work right now, but, yes, I'll get credit, one way or the other."

He glanced at her, clearly not satisfied with her answer. "I guess I don't need to know all the ins and outs of being a children's book illustrator."

"I'm enjoying delving into the world of fairy tales. Do you have a favorite?"

"*Beauty and the Beast*." He grinned. "Always hope for us beasts. What's your favorite?"

"That's hard to say. *Rapunzel*, maybe."

"'Let down your hair.' Not a bad metaphor for life." Russ poured wine and handed her a glass. He held up his. "Cheers."

"Cheers."

Kylie raised the lid on the dinner basket and lifted out the contents. "Grilled chicken, green salad, gratin potatoes and cookies. It all smells good, doesn't it?"

"No argument from me."

"Are you concerned Miss Stewart will back out of the class on Saturday?"

"No."

A quick, certain answer. But that was his style, Kylie realized. "It doesn't sound as if there's a huge financial commitment. People will be disappointed if she backs out at the last minute, but if she's donating her time and Mark's donating the space, it won't be a disaster."

"Ruby and Ava have invited theater people from New York and Boston."

"It'll be an embarrassment, but it won't be their fault if they do their part and Daphne doesn't do hers."

"Their judgment would come into question. They're starting their last year of graduate school. They're already thinking about what's next."

"Ah. I hadn't looked at it that way."

He and Kylie brought the food to the table. She'd set

the table for three before Ruby and Russ had arrived and Ruby had taken off. "We should eat while the chicken and potatoes are still hot," Kylie said, placing her wineglass on the table and pointing to the chair across from her. "Have a seat. Welcome."

"Thanks." He winked at her as he sat. "Much better than having dinner alone in the rain, don't you think?"

She mumbled something innocuous and neutral. They passed the serving dishes, helping themselves to Maggie Sloan's amazing way with food. Kylie had heard about how good Maggie was with everything from her sons' birthday parties to a wedding but hadn't experienced her cooking herself.

"Maybe Ruby will calm down once Ava gets here," Kylie said.

"Maybe," Russ said. "She's majoring in theater management. She might bring a different perspective. If they want to start a children's theater in Knights Bridge, it would be good to show potential supporters they can pull off a class in costume design and have contacts like Daphne—and sway with them. Not many people have sway with Daphne."

Kylie frowned. "A children's theater—in Knights Bridge, you mean?"

He nodded, his dark blue eyes on her. "They want to take over the meeting space here at Moss Hill and turn it into a community children's theater. It would serve the area, not just Knights Bridge."

"I didn't realize..." Kylie tried the gratin potatoes. "A theater here at Moss Hill. Wow. That's a huge undertaking."

"Ava and Ruby—Ruby especially—seem to have a lot of big dreams."

"Is that a knock on them?"

He shrugged. "An observation. Do you have big dreams, Kylie?"

She had the distinct feeling he was trying to trip her up. She raised her wineglass. "Oh, sure. Win the lottery, spend a year in Tuscany—"

"What about career dreams?"

She smiled. "Maybe those are career dreams."

"I'm trying to understand what a children's book illustrator dreams about."

"Right now, a wolf preying on an innocent grandmother and tricking an adventurous girl coming to visit. Not the most pleasant of dreams, I can tell you. I have quite a nasty wolf in mind. I haven't begun sketching him yet, though." She drank some of her wine. "Better to dream about Tuscany, don't you think?"

"Sure." His tone said he knew she was being evasive, but he picked up his wineglass and smiled. "Here's to that year in Tuscany."

"What about you?" Kylie asked. "Do you have big dreams?"

"I tend to live in the present."

Kylie wasn't sure if he was making a joke or if he was perfectly serious, but his comment effectively closed off that subject. They dove into dinner, chatting amiably about the town. She explained what she knew about the history of the reservoir and local people with roots in the lost towns. He'd been reading a book on Quabbin that Ruby or the Flanagans had put in his borrowed apartment and offered a few tidbits of interest Kylie hadn't known—for one, that people used to come by train from nearby towns to work in the valley mills. It was called the "rabbit train," given its number of stops over a short distance. But the water that had attracted a smattering of mill owners to the rural towns of the Swift River Valley had also attracted engineers and politicians looking for a source of drinking water for the growing city to the east.

"I should have Maggie cook for me when I'm on a tight deadline," Kylie said as she and Russ finished dinner. "I'd eat better. The country store has decent home-made food, but I can't always take the time to get there. Or I don't, even if I could."

"What are some of your staples for imminent dead-lines?"

"Whatever I can cook and clean up fast. I try to eat healthy. Sometimes I'll make up something I can eat all week. Roast a chicken, do up a pot of chili, that sort of thing."

"And when you're not on a tight deadline?"

"It's not that different."

"But you like your work," he said, studying her from across the table.

She felt heat rise in her cheeks. How had she let the subject turn back to her? She smiled. "Very much. Do you like your work?"

"It suits me. When I went out on my own after the navy, I discovered how easy it is to let your life get out of balance when you're your own boss. Is that what hap-pened to you—why you moved to Knights Bridge?"

"I guess you could say that." She kept any defensive-ness out of her tone. "You must have intense times in

your work when you can't do much else. Like now—
you're on the job, not on vacation."

He leaned over the table slightly. "I'm having dinner
with an intriguing woman."

"A woman you don't quite trust." The words were
out before Kylie could stop them.

"Only because you're hiding something," he said.

She didn't look away from him. "I'm protective of
my work," she said truthfully. "I don't like talking about
it, especially when I'm in the midst of a project. I find
that talking dissipates creative energy that needs to go
into the work."

"Does that mean I don't get to see your wolf before
it's in print?"

His eyes were half-closed, but his sardonic tone
and almost-smile helped take the edge off her nerves.
"Sometimes I'll show concepts to people—if, say, I
can't decide between two or three different wolves."

"How often is 'sometimes?'"

"Not often." She got to her feet and fetched the wine
bottle, dividing the last of the merlot between their two
glasses. "Do you talk about your work?"

"When it's necessary."

"Here's my take." She set the empty bottle on the
counter and sat back down with her wine. "I think
you focus on doing the job you were hired to do and
don't worry about the niceties. What do you think, am
I close?"

"Close. Sometimes I have to worry about niceties."

"And how often is 'sometimes,' PI Colton?"

He laughed, surprising her. "Touché, Kylie. About

as often as you're open with other people about your work."

That wasn't exactly what she'd said, but she suspected he knew it. The man had great control, and he no doubt was good at his job and knew how to pry information out of people. But she didn't bite by attempting to correct him. "It must be interesting working for a Beverly Hills law firm," she said. "Do you have good colleagues?"

"Excellent colleagues. That helps. Julius Hartley is a friend, and he has a great deal of experience with law firm investigations. I'm newer to the work."

"He has more experience handling clients like Daphne Stewart, too, I bet."

"A facility with 'niceties' comes in handy with her."

He shifted the conversation to the pair of ducks he'd spotted on the river. They'd braved a break in the rain, and the rush of water over the dam. "Wonder where they are now," he said, getting up from the table. He seemed to debate what to do next, if only for a split second. He picked up his wineglass and walked over to the tall windows. "Where's the house you rented?"

Kylie stood next to him. "You can't see it from here. It's just past the covered bridge up the river."

"The one with the gray shingles, then. I thought so. I was up there yesterday on my run. Do you have anyone you check in with on a regular basis—in case anything happens?"

"My parents and sister and I check in with each other. I leave a note on the kitchen counter when I go for walks and carry my phone with me in case of emergency. But it's not something I worry a lot about. Knights Bridge isn't a high-crime area, and I don't do extreme hiking by myself."

She noticed she had less wine in her glass than he did in his, perhaps not the best sign since she was trying to measure her words. He was already suspicious. She didn't need to give him more reasons to pry into her life. She wasn't sure how he would react to finding out she was Morwenna Mills, but she didn't need to find out. She was determined to stick to her own timetable, whatever it ended up being.

She pointed her glass in the vague direction of the river. "It was something to watch the ice jams this winter and early spring. Fortunately, they didn't cause any major flooding."

"That's good." He gave a mock shudder and grinned. "Ice. A frozen river. Not what I want to think about right now."

"You must be glad this master class wasn't in February."

"You'd have still been in your house up the road. I'd probably be staying with the goats at Ruby's mother's house. You and I might never have met."

"Destiny at work, maybe," Kylie said lightly.

There was nothing light about him as he turned to her. "Maybe." But he started for the table. "I'll help clean up the dishes and be on my way. I can return the basket to Ruby. It was decent of her sister to make us dinner."

Kylie welcomed the change in subject. Why had she brought up destiny? Pure self-consciousness, she thought. That or too much wine. "Have you met Maggie yet?" she asked.

"Not yet."

"She's good friends with Olivia Frost—Olivia Mc-
Caffrey now."

"That's what I hear. Do you know them well?"

"Just enough to say hi to."

"The busy artist," he said with a smile.

Kylie didn't detect any condescension in his tone.

He went over to the table and blew out the candles,
then collected dishes and silverware and took them to
the sink. She watched him, wondered what it would
be like to have such a man in her life—to talk to over
wine and help with the dishes. But she didn't trust herself now, with the merlot, her solitary habits. She'd en-
countered more people in the past few days than she
had since moving into Moss Hill in March. She wasn't
used to it, but she didn't object. At the same time, she
doubted prolonged solitude explained her reaction to
Russ Colton. He was perceptive, he had a sense of
humor, and he seemed sympathetic and understanding
of Ruby's jitters and even Daphne Stewart's drama. He
was tough and focused, but he wasn't prone to drama
or overreacting himself. Kylie was grateful he hadn't
brought up the rumors about Moss Hill over dinner.

But she knew she wasn't always the best judge of
people. Given her natural tendency to like everyone she
met, she could be oblivious and overlook basic facts.

Such as Russ lived in California and was going back
there.

Soon.

At the door, basket in hand, he paused, then kissed
her on the cheek. "Nice getting to know you better,

Kylie," he said, close enough that she could feel the brush of his jacket against her.

He was out the door before she got her next breath.

It was twenty minutes before Kylie noticed Sherlock Badger in his spot on her task lamp.

She'd missed him. Completely. She'd talked to him while cleaning up the place, and still she hadn't tucked him out of sight in a drawer or a box or, better yet, under her pillow, since there was no chance Russ would get close to her bedroom, quick kiss or no quick kiss.

"Sherlock," she said. "Damn, why couldn't you have spoken up?"

He was such a part of her day-to-day life that she hadn't thought of him as a dead giveaway to Morwenna. She'd made him to give herself a different perspective on her badgers, a sense of what they might look like if they were real. A lark, procrastination, a necessity—whatever it had been, she'd enjoyed the process and enjoyed having him there to talk to.

Had Russ seen Sherlock?

Of course he had.

Russ was an experienced investigator. He wouldn't need much time to discover the little badger on her lamp was an exact rendition of Sherlock Badger in a popular series of children's books created by author and illustrator Morwenna Mills.

If he decided to investigate. He might not care about a four-inch stuffed badger.

But he cared about her and what she was hiding.

Would he find out she was Morwenna tonight? By morning?

Kylie groaned. All that cleaning in an attempt to maintain control of dinner, and she'd never had control. She'd flat-out missed Sherlock. She debated grabbing him and knocking on Russ's door, telling him about Morwenna herself, but what good would that do?

She touched her cheek where he'd kissed her.

Why borrow trouble?

She was staying put.

Ten

Kylie Shaw had clearly done her best to sanitize her apartment of all specific references to her work before letting him in.

Russ turned on lights in his own apartment and set the basket on the kitchen counter. He'd wash the serving dishes later.

His apartment was larger than Kylie's but not by much. He'd noticed straight away that she'd done more than tidied and dusted before guests arrived. It wasn't just the space itself that had given her away, but her reaction when he'd taken a look around.

She must have scrambled when Ruby O'Dunn had maneuvered her into hosting dinner. Had Ruby wanted to get a look inside Kylie's apartment, too?

He sat in a leather chair by the unlit fireplace. It was a night for a fire, but he found himself enjoying the damp, chilly air. He got out his phone. He thought he might be onto what Kylie didn't want people to know. Either that or he was totally off base, wrong and losing his mind.

He checked his photos and came to the one he'd taken surreptitiously while she'd unloaded the food basket. He held it under the lamp for a good, close look.

"Yes, sir, we have a badger."

His cagey neighbor had slipped up.

He was almost certain Kylie hadn't meant him to see the cute stuffed badger standing at the base of the lamp on her worktable. It was about four inches tall and looked handmade, crafted from bits of wool fabric and who-knew-what-else. Russ's sewing skills began and ended with the occasional button, snap and tear.

The badger was dressed up like Sherlock Holmes, complete with a deerstalker hat and classic Victorian tweed overcoat.

Russ had the feeling he was supposed to recognize the little critter.

He texted the photo to Marty. Any idea who this is?

Marty's response was almost instantaneous. Sherlock Badger.

Who?

Badgers of Middle Branch. Kids books. Popular. Talk of a movie.

Thanks. Keep this quiet for now.

Daphne?

Tell no one. Her, Julius, your screenwriting pals.

Got it. Mum.

Russ tossed his phone onto the side table and got out his laptop.

In three seconds he had his answer.

Morwenna Mills was the illustrator and author of a series of books about a family of badgers in a small town called Middle Branch. Their lives centered around their veterinary office and quirky house and the town.

Sherlock Badger was the lawman of the family, but he worked in "the city" and only came to Middle Branch once in a while.

This, according to a description of the characters on Morwenna's website.

Not much on her. In fact, the "About Morwenna" section was deliberately geared to kids—short, amusing, not intended to be taken as a serious, professional description of her. Grew up in New England. Loved animals, long walks in the woods, making chocolate chip cookies and picking apples.

Morwenna lives on a river near a covered bridge, where she is deep into her next Badger book.

Not enough by itself to peg Kylie Shaw as Morwenna Mills, but in combination with the stuffed badger and Kylie's behavior—it was plenty.

Russ continued his research. He was comfortable confirming, if only to himself, that his dinner companion was the creator of the Badgers of little Middle Branch.

By the time he and Ruby had arrived with the picnic basket, he'd just about convinced himself Kylie had something really unsettling to hide.

Nope. Badgers.

The fourth book in the series had been released in November, another instant hit. The popularity of Morwenna Mills and the Badgers was still on the upswing.

He found one short interview with Morwenna, done last summer, no mention of Knights Bridge or her real name—and no photographs. The article described her as living in rural New England and inspired by her long walks in the woods.

"Well, well," Russ said, shutting down his laptop and setting it aside.

His neighbor across the hall was hiding something, just not what he'd imagined.

Should he tell Kylie he knew about her alter ego?

He shook his head, the answer obvious as soon as he'd posed the question to himself. No, he shouldn't. If she guessed or worried he'd figured out she was Morwenna Mills, let her bring it up. If she didn't—he didn't plan to tell anyone. No point. He'd be back in California soon.

He got a beer out of the fridge and went out to the balcony. The rain had stopped, but the air was raw, the river rushing over the dam, the fog impenetrable. He couldn't see the sky, never mind any stars.

Alone on nights like this, would he come up with an adventurous family of badgers?

He would not.

He went back inside and bought an e-version of *The Badgers of Middle Branch*, the first book in the series. He opened it as he sat again by the unlit fireplace.

It was true. He was reading a children's book about badgers on a dark, rainy New England night.

Eleven

Daphne decided to continue with her rose-trimming despite Loretta Wrentham's surprise visit. The sooner Loretta, aka Mrs. Julius Hartley, went back to La Jolla, the better, Daphne thought. She liked Loretta well enough, but she had one of those incisive lawyer minds, and Daphne was too preoccupied to deal with incisive. She wanted indulgent, or just nothing—just to be left alone with her roses.

"I can understand why that little town makes you nervous," Loretta said, sitting by the pool, easing off her sandals. "I don't have a secret attic room in the library and an abusive father I left behind in Knights Bridge. The O'Dunns and their goats are enough to make me nervous. And all that romance going on there."

"No wonder you ended up marrying Julius," Daphne said.

"Ha. True."

But she was obviously so happy with him, and he with her. Daphne wasn't proud of herself for not wishing them well, at least in the beginning. She'd gotten used to having Julius around. There wasn't and never had been an ounce of lust between them, but they'd become good friends.

She clipped a wilted peach rose. "My father hated Knights Bridge."

Loretta sank back in the lounge chair. "Is that why you're trying to like it?"

"I do like it."

"But it's in your past—a past you're not sure you want to stir up more than you already have. You didn't get sucked into going back because of anything particular that Ava and Ruby O'Dunn did or said. You got sucked in because of yourself."

"No one sucked me into anything."

Daphne heard the defensiveness in her voice. Loretta would hear it, too. She wouldn't care—nothing seemed to bother her—but she'd duly note Daphne's reaction. She tackled another rose branch. She wore garden gloves but still had managed to bloody herself on thorns. No doubt Loretta noticed that, too.

"I got caught up in Ava and Ruby's youthful exuberance," Daphne added. "Now, push has come to shove, I suppose."

"Then you're going to Knights Bridge this week," Loretta said. "You're not backing out."

"I promised Ava and Ruby. I might whine and moan, but I keep my promises."

"Julius and I can go with you."

Daphne shook her head. "You have things to do. I'll be fine."

"But you'd like an entourage," Loretta said with a wry smile.

"Who wouldn't?"

Daphne set her clippers on the patio table and offered Loretta iced tea. To her surprise, Loretta accepted. Daphne left her by the pool and went into the kitchen to put a tray together. A pitcher of tea, two glasses, a bucket of ice and a small plate with sliced lemons. She took a guess that Loretta didn't use sugar in her tea.

Going whole hog with playing hostess, she grabbed cloth napkins and a couple of fresh ripe peaches on her way out to the patio.

"You've got a great house," Loretta said. "This is a sweet backyard."

"I finally have everything the way I want it. I'll probably start itching to make changes in a year or two, though." Daphne smiled, taking a lounge chair under an umbrella next to Loretta. "Never satisfied."

"We're making space in La Jolla for Julius's golf clubs and antique grandfather clock," Loretta said.

"I like how you say *we* even though it's your house."

"It was my house. Now it's our house."

Daphne wondered how long that sentiment would last but decided she was being negative. If she ever married again—and she wouldn't—she would insist on them both keeping their own homes. She was too set in her ways these days to make space for a grandfather clock. Golf clubs she could manage, she supposed, but she'd always hated golf.

She and Loretta chatted about the joys and challenges of combining two longtime households, steering clear of further talk of Daphne's imminent departure for Knights Bridge. She enjoyed her visit with Loretta but knew it hadn't been without Julius's knowledge and approval—just a new friend stopping by on impulse.

After Loretta left, Daphne stayed out at the pool. She felt mildly guilty that she'd inflicted her ambivalence about Knights Bridge on Julius and Loretta. They were moving, starting a life together. They didn't need added drama from her.

She gathered up the tea dishes and took the tray into the kitchen, but she left it for later and went into her studio. She sat on the high chair at her worktable and fingered a pair of scissors she'd owned for thirty-seven years. They were her first good scissors. She remembered feeling rich and successful—feeling them cut into fabric for the first time, their glide and precision. She'd had her first few jobs working in costume design by then. She'd been living in a cheap apartment, staying up late and getting up early, waiting tables to make ends meet, and she'd thought life couldn't get any better.

Now she was one of the first designers called when a movie was coming together.

She got out a bit of fabric and cut it with her scissors. She kept them in good shape. They'd last longer than she would.

Sewing in her secret room in the attic of the library her great-great-grandfather had built had helped her figure out who she was and what she wanted. She'd been desperate to be somebody. To not be the damaged teenager she'd thought herself to be.

All these years later, she couldn't believe she'd agreed to return to Knights Bridge—first for the fashion show in September, and now for this master class. She'd let herself get caught up in Ava and Ruby O'Dunn's talk of their lives, their hopes, their dreams, their desire to give back to their small town.

And their fascination with her and her work, Daphne admitted.

She'd let her ego get involved.

She put her scissors away and left her studio, shutting the door behind her. She never took her work into the rest of the house. It was one of her few rules.

She went into her bedroom, slipped into a swimsuit and returned to her lounge chair on the patio. She stretched out and shut her eyes, feeling the sunshine on her face.

What if I'd never left Knights Bridge?

She shuddered, not wanting to imagine.

But that was what she was afraid of, wasn't it? That she'd go back now and discover she'd never left, and all this—her house, her pool, her life—didn't exist. That Daphne Stewart was a dream of a sad, unfulfilled Debbie Sanderson.

It wasn't about Knights Bridge or what she might have done if she'd stayed, whether she'd continued to work at the library or become a teacher or a landscaper or a housewife. It was about this life, here, now, in Hollywood Hills.

She sat up straight. "I should call Julius and tell him I've gone mad."

He'd either straighten her out or make arrangements for a long-term care facility.

"Colt Russell would, too." She laughed aloud, almost a giggle. "Colt Russell. One day you're going to forget his real name is Russ Colton."

She was being dramatic and ridiculous, and she knew it.

Feeling better, she eased off her chair and into the pool, content with her life, more certain about going back East…back home to Knights Bridge.

By her second martini, made, of course, by Marty Colton, Daphne had lost her resolve about her upcoming trip.

She was also convinced Marty had gone heavy on the pineapple juice.

She didn't say anything, because she'd only ordered a second drink after she'd slopped at least a third of the first one on her top. Marty must have decided she'd had too much alcohol for one evening, or she'd started early, when she'd just been clumsy.

"Have you talked to Russ since he headed east?" she asked.

"Texted."

"Did he mention if Julius told him I'm getting cold feet?"

Marty shrugged. "So what if he did? You are getting cold feet."

"I never get cold feet. It's a pejorative description for deliberate reconsideration."

"Okay, you're deliberately reconsidering your commitment to teach this class on Saturday."

Daphne lifted her glass. "You used commitment to remind me I have an obligation to these people, didn't you?

"Uh-uh. Not biting" Marty reached for a bottle on

a shelf above his head. "You're trying to pick a fight with me to keep yourself from thinking about this trip."

"That's absurd. I can hardly think about anything else."

"Rest my case."

He poured Scotch for another customer. Daphne recognized it as an expensive brand and wondered if a movie star was in the house, incognito. A fun thought. Marty would never tell her. He disappeared to deliver the drink. She resisted gulping her martini. She was in the mood to be reckless. She was reconsidering Knights Bridge. She couldn't deny it, and it wasn't anyone's fault. Picking a fight with Marty wasn't fair.

He returned with a small tray with cheese, grapes, figs and nuts. "You look glum," he said, setting the tray in front of her.

"I am glum." She nibbled on a fig. "It's stupid, wasting time on being glum when nothing's wrong. No one's died. I haven't been fired. I'm not facing a dreaded diagnosis."

"I thought you were excited about exploring new opportunities with these theater twins."

"They're fraternal, not identical, twins. I am excited about new opportunities. I just don't necessarily want them to require my presence in Knights Bridge." Daphne paused, barely aware she was speaking out loud. "My great-great-grandfather left a positive legacy there. I went there as this miserable, abused girl who ran away from home. I would see his portrait every time I went up to my attic room. I'd talk to him. He'd been dead for decades, but it felt like he was with me."

"He helped give you the courage to go after your dreams," Marty said, matter-of-fact.

She looked up at him and smiled. "That's exactly right."

"You don't have to go back there. As I said, this class isn't a prison sentence. You can cancel. You're a pro. You could pull off canceling and not look bad."

She sighed and reached for two perfect red grapes. "Tell your brother that."

Marty laughed. "I don't tell Russ anything."

"I can believe that. What will I do when Julius moves to La Jolla? He's like a neighbor. I meet him on his deck for coffee from time to time. He has a great deck. I don't think Loretta has a place for all his plants." She ate the grapes as Marty waited on another customer. No expensive Scotch this time, but that didn't necessarily mean anything. When he returned, she completed her train of thought. "I can't believe Julius wants to give up Hollywood Hills and his life here, even for Loretta. Do you think he has doubts, Marty?"

"I haven't noticed any."

"I imagine Loretta has a beautiful home." Daphne snorted. "Julius said I can come down and visit. Take a few days and laze by the pool. Visit the zoo. Sounds dreadful, doesn't it?"

Marty mopped up a spill. "You just don't like change."

"Change is a part of life," she countered, defiant.

"Knowing that doesn't mean you like it. You've had Julius doing your bidding for ten years. Time for new blood."

"Russ thinks I'm eccentric and dramatic."

Marty grinned. "You are eccentric and dramatic."

Daphne took no offense. "He assumes nobody wants to harass or do harm to a mere costume designer."

"Russ doesn't make assumptions."

"Isn't a threat assessment a glorified assumption?"

"It's a professional tool to understand risk—"

"Right, right." She waved a hand. "I get all that."

Daphne didn't know what to do to dissipate her nervous energy. Probably two French martinis weren't helping. Knights Bridge. What had she been thinking? She should have let the fashion show last September be enough. Going back a second time was tempting fate. With the date drawing closer and closer, she could feel her anxiety mounting.

"I have a dark past back East," she said half to herself. "It's a personal can of worms I shut a long time ago."

"I get that," Marty said, no hint of impatience in his tone.

"Does Russ get it?"

"Does it matter?"

She eyed him suspiciously. "You aren't going to give me platitudes?"

"I don't know what a platitude is anymore."

"I've dealt with too many narcissistic types. I don't want to become one myself." She frowned at him. "I haven't, have I?"

"It's easy to stereotype people."

"I've been thinking about my father a lot these days. George Sanderson was by all accounts a decent man with a good head for business and a good heart for philanthropy. My father was named after him. Another

George. But any resemblance ended there." She chose a fat cashew from the little bowl of nuts. "My father was a bastard, Marty."

"No doubt."

"But he's dead, and I found my way here." She ate the cashew and stared at her hands, the skin tanned, an expensive sapphire-and-diamond ring on her right ring finger. She noticed age spots. Heavens. She was getting up there in age, wasn't she? When had that happened? Finally she looked at Marty Colton again. "You're not as old as I am, darling Marty."

He grinned. "Dirt's not as old as you are."

She laughed. She wasn't ready to go home yet, but she'd had enough to drink. Three martinis would put her to sleep or, worse, drive her to tears or dancing on the tables. She ordered sparkling water instead.

And that, naturally, was the moment Julius Hartley walked into the bar.

"Sparkling water," he said, easing onto the stool next to her. "That means you're either half in the bag or wish you were."

She sniffed. "Neither. I'm rehydrating. Are you hunting me down, Mr. Hartley?"

"Not hard to do."

"Marty and I were just discussing age and true love. You're not young, but Loretta…she's your true love?"

"She is, Daphne."

He hadn't hesitated. She knew she should be pleased. "You were certain right from the start?"

"Early on. I wouldn't say from the start. Loretta thought I was up to no good at first."

"She's a smart woman. I've married a few times.

One marriage barely counted. We didn't last two years. I thought it would last forever when we said *I do*. That was my first husband. He was a good man, but his idea of fun was watching television from six to nine-thirty every single night."

"He was boring," Julius said.

"For me. Not for his second wife. They've been married thirty-three years. They have a beautiful home and three grown children. I think there are grandchildren now."

"Regrets?"

"A million but never a dull moment. My second husband liked to do things, but he was lousy with money. I'm lucky I have a penny to my name after twelve years with him."

"That's when you first hired Sawyer & Sawyer."

She nodded. "One of my smarter moves."

"You're one of the smartest women I know in Hollywood," Julius said. "You're no one's fool, Daphne."

She said nothing. She tried her sparkling water. It was horrible. She remembered why she never ordered it.

Marty set a glass of beer in front of Julius, who took a sip before he continued. "You're not Debbie Sanderson anymore."

"But I am, Julius." Her throat ached with emotion when she spoke. "Deep inside I am the teenager who ran away from home to Knights Bridge and then took a bus west, not knowing whether I'd end up dead in a gutter."

"You always knew you'd end up a wealthy, successful costume designer."

"Wished it."

"Made it happen."

"It could have gone all wrong," she said.

"But it didn't," he said quietly.

"I can't go back home. It was a mistake to think I could. It was one thing to be introduced at a fashion show. Whisk in and out of there. A master class seemed like a good idea, a chance to share my knowledge and experience..." Daphne trailed off, not sure where she'd been going with her thought. She'd been talking to herself more than to Julius. She turned to him. "Ruby and Ava O'Dunn have gotten ahead of themselves, I think, and it's affected me."

Julius drank more of his beer. "You don't have to get mixed up in their plans."

"I don't want to disappoint them."

"I know you don't, but you're afraid they're relying on you—and you don't want anyone relying on you."

"I remember wandering around out by the old Moss Hill mill as a teenager. The ghosts. I'm telling you, they were for real." Daphne shuddered. "Forget it, Julius. I'm not going."

He handed her his phone. "You call Russ and tell him he's wasted this trip."

"He'll shoot me."

"He won't shoot you."

"He'll throw me off your deck, then. I wouldn't blame him."

"He'll tell you to get on that plane when the time comes and stop with the nonsense."

She tossed her head back, miffed. "Marty just said I can cancel, and it's not a prison sentence."

Julius scoffed. Only word for the sound and look

he gave her. "Come on, Daphne. You can't cancel because of ghosts."

"You've never been to Moss Hill." She crossed her arms on her chest. "I can twist an ankle or come down with a sinus infection."

"Daphne."

"All right, all right. I hate flying commercial, though. Last time Noah Kendrick took us in his private jet, remember?"

"Not everyone's a billionaire."

She returned his phone to him. "This all seemed like a better idea in February."

"You'll get through it. The diva act aside, you're a tough old broad."

"That makes me sound like a piece of beef jerky."

Julius didn't have the courtesy to argue with her. Daphne didn't know whether to be annoyed or amused. "I'm going to miss you when you move to San Diego," she said, jumping down from the stool. She could feel the two martinis, but it wasn't too bad. She blinked back tears. "I know I'm not important in the grand scheme of things."

"You're important, Daphne." He sounded sincere. "Not only are you a valued client, you're a friend."

"You're humoring me and not doing a very good job of it."

Julius laughed. "Have it your way. But you're pleased I'm happy," he said, as if cueing her. "I know you are."

"I suppose, but I wish it didn't mean I had to suffer."

"Daphne..." He blew out a breath. "Never mind. You're in full diva mode. Enjoy yourself."

There was no joy in it. She'd only hoped to distra

herself from the uneasiness churning inside her. Butterflies, she thought. She hadn't had butterflies in a very
long time. It wasn't just the thought of doing a master
class—in fact, it wasn't that at all.

It was Knights Bridge.

Daphne left Julius muttering about her "diva mode"
and said good-night to Marty. She'd taken a cab to the
bar and took one home. Less than ten minutes later,
she was at her house. She did like Julius's deck, but
her patio was special, too. She didn't have his patience
with potted plants, and she didn't want to hire someone. It was enough to keep up with all the other main-
tenance expenses.

"Imagine if you cashed out of here and relocated to
Knights Bridge," she said aloud.

She plopped onto a lounge chair and looked out at
her small yard, filled with all sorts of plants that would
die in the long, cold New England winter.

"I wouldn't have to worry about rattlesnakes, brown
spiders, black widows or scorpions."

Not that she worried about them here. But still.

How had returning to Knights Bridge for a few days
spun her into thoughts of moving there?

"Classic catastrophizing."

She decided that was funny and laughed. Moving
east wouldn't be a catastrophe.

She *was* a diva.

She went inside, peeled off her clothes and put on
a swimsuit and a cover-up, then walked back outside.
With his small hillside lot, Julius didn't have a pool,
although she wasn't in enough of a foul, self-absorbed

mood to think he'd married Loretta Wrentham and was moving to San Diego because of Loretta's pool.

Daphne eased into the warm water, did a few laps and then sank onto her lounge chair. She was meeting friends for breakfast in the morning.

She had a hell of a good life.

She was relaxed, half asleep, when her phone buzzed on the table next to her. She planned to ignore it but peeked at the number, just in case it was someone interesting. Russ Colton. Well, he was interesting. She picked up.

"Colt Russell," she said, just to tweak him. "How's my favorite little town?"

"Quiet. Late. Do you know an illustrator named Kylie Shaw?"

"No, should I?"

"Know any Shaws?"

"I once had a crush on Robert Shaw. He was the rogue in *Jaws*. He's no longer with us, alas."

Russ sighed as if he'd regretted calling.

"Julius asked you to check in, didn't he? This question about Shaws is just cover."

"Yes. You have forty-eight hours to angst before your flight takes off."

"You're not like Julius, you know. Julius is nice compared to you."

"You got that right."

He seemed amused. Daphne didn't know whether she should be amused, too, or be annoyed, but maybe there was no "should" to it. She felt what she felt. "You two aren't taking my reservations seriously."

"We are, Daphne. We want you to do what's right for you."

"Did you say that with a straight face? I'm calling you back on FaceTime to make sure."

He was chuckling when he hung up.

"Bastard," Daphne said, realizing she was smiling.

Twelve

Russ had no trouble finding the Farm at Carriage Hill on another winding Knights Bridge road. Olivia Frost, now Olivia McCaffrey, had purchased the 1803 house and several acres of gardens and fields a couple of years ago, when she'd been working as a graphic designer in Boston, dreaming of returning to her hometown.

It's a pretty spot, Loretta Wrentham had told him. *Different from what you're used to.*

Agreed on both statements, Russ thought as he parked under the Carriage Hill sign, depicting a clump of blossoming chives, the small inn's logo. When he got out of his car, he noticed the air was warmer here than on the river. Carriage Hill Road had once led into the now-flooded Swift River Valley. Now it dead-ended at a Quabbin gate, one of more than forty gates that dotted the perimeter of the reservoir and its protected watershed.

He took a flagstone walk to a blue-painted door that, according to Julius and Loretta, opened into a large country kitchen, a later addition to the original center-chimney house, which also had a blue-painted door. Narrow, cream-colored clapboards, black shutters and mature landscaping with old shade trees and evergreens completed the classic New England setting.

Before he could knock or find a doorbell, a red-headed woman opened the door. This one would be the second eldest O'Dunn sister, Maggie, the caterer who'd supplied dinner last night and was married to Brandon Sloan. She and Olivia had been friends since child-hood and ran Carriage Hill together. Russ hadn't done extensive research on the people of Knights Bridge so much as paid attention to what Julius and Loretta had told him.

He and Maggie introduced themselves. "You just missed Olivia," Maggie said. "She's walking Buster."

"Buster being…"

"Her dog. More accurately, the dog who lives here. He adopted Olivia when she moved in a year ago." Mag-gie opened the door wider. "Please, come in. Dylan is up at the new place. You passed it—it's the house and barn up the road."

"Nice place."

"Isn't it? It's been a major project for months. Not as major as restoring Moss Hill to better than its former glory, but it's in a different category. Amazing, isn't it?"

Russ followed Maggie inside. The kitchen was homey and cheerful with its butcher-block island, honey-colored cabinets, oversize gas stove, and a table and chairs by a window. A large pot bubbled on the stove.

Maggie, dressed in jeans, a sweatshirt and running shoes, pulled off a white apron and tossed it on the back of a chair. "Dylan's looking forward to giving you the grand tour," she said.

"I appreciate that. I noticed a few construction trucks and vans parked up the road."

"That would be Sloan & Sons at work. They did the construction. It's almost finished. My husband, Brandon, is up there now. Mark Flanagan was the architect—he did Moss Hill, too. But I guess you know that. Hard to believe sometimes. I remember when he would fall asleep in the back of class in high school. He's a few years older than I am, but my sister Phoebe remembers..." Maggie waved a hand. "I'll spare you. It's enough to try to keep all of us straight in your mind."

"I should start an Evernote file on Knights Bridge."

Maggie laughed. "That's almost scary to think about." She grabbed a long-handled spoon and checked the pot on the stove. "Minestrone soup. Smells good, doesn't it?"

"Smells great."

"It's what we're having for lunch."

"Thanks for dinner last night."

Maggie stirred the soup. "Ruby told me she bailed and Christopher had a fire call. She's a bundle of raw emotions right now. I hope it wasn't too awkward with just you and Kylie."

Russ smiled. "Homemade cookies helped."

"A huge ice-breaker." She wrinkled up her face. "I think that's a mixed metaphor or something."

"Do you have guests here right now?"

Maggie shook her head. "Not until Daphne Stewart arrives."

Carriage Hill wasn't a traditional inn or bed-and-breakfast open to walk-in overnight guests. It hosted guests attending destination events held there—baby and wedding showers, girlfriend weekends, teas, the occasional small wedding. Olivia and Dylan had been married in the living room on Christmas Eve. Russ could easily picture the antique house decorated for Christmas, inside and outside, with the surrounding fields and woods covered in snow. The image was so powerful that he could see himself walking through the sunlit snow, feel the cold air on his face, as if he'd entered a parallel universe in which he lived a different life.

"I have oatmeal bread rising to go with the soup," Maggie said. "Hope you don't mind a simple lunch."

"Sounds perfect," Russ said, forcing himself back to the present and his reasons for being in Knights Bridge. He had a job to do. "Ruby mentioned you're a caterer."

"One of my multiple hats. I've always loved to cook. Phoebe always loved books, and the twins always loved theater—they started putting on their own plays when they were three. Dylan said he'd meet you up at the barn for your tour. Would you like coffee first? I don't have much to go with it. I could thaw a cranberry muffin."

"I'm fine, thanks." He nodded to the table, where a dozen paint cans of various sizes were lined up on a sheet. "Need a hand with anything?"

"Oh, that'd be great," Maggie said. "I could use some muscle to open a couple of the paint cans. I collected everything Olivia and I had left over from various winter painting projects. Now we're into spring painting projects."

Russ grabbed a screwdriver off the table and tackled one of the cans, with dried creamy white paint on the sides and top.

Maggie took a smaller can and shook it. "Doesn't feel like much paint's left in this one. I understand you're here to get the lay of the land before Daphne's arrival. I can show you the room we have her in if you'd like."

"No need," Russ said, popping open the paint can. "She's looking forward to staying here."

"I never thought she'd be back to Knights Bridge, to be honest, but Ava and Ruby can be very persuasive—and their enthusiasm is contagious, don't you think?"

"I haven't met Ava yet. Ruby is certainly enthusiastic."

Maggie peered into the opened can. "That looks good—enough left to paint something, even if I don't know what yet." She set her can back on the table. "Ava and Ruby both put a lot of pressure on themselves. They're fascinated by costume design and are thrilled to have Daphne here, but I don't think anything's going to come of this children's theater. Not yet, anyway. Ava loves New York, and Ruby's heart is set on acting. Do you know a lot of actors, Russ?"

He shrugged. "Some."

"How's Julius these days?"

"Moving to La Jolla with Loretta."

"Good for them. I never put the two of them together, not that I know them well. I'm glad it's worked out." Maggie pointed to another can. "I think that's the teal. I have a chair I want to paint teal."

Russ picked up the can. Sunlight streamed through the kitchen windows. The rain had ended overnight, and the morning had dawned bright and clear. He set the can on the table. It, too, popped open with little effort.

Maggie sat on a chair at the table and stretched out her legs. "I've been on my feet all morning. Feels good to sit down a second. How do you like our little town so far?"

He replaced the lid on the teal paint. "Quite a mix of people."

"It's been a wild ride around here ever since Olivia wrote to Dylan last March to come clean up his yard or let her do it. Imagine, he didn't realize he owned property here. Now he's discovered a grandmother he never knew existed, and he's married to one of Knights Bridge's own. Life can be strange sometimes, can't it?"

"No argument from me." He replaced the lid on the white paint, tight but not so much so it would be a struggle to reopen. "Kylie Shaw is another newcomer to town."

"I don't know her well," Maggie said, her tone neutral. "Samantha Bennett, my almost sister-in-law, and Clare Morgan at the library both know her better than I do. Mark says he was happy to have her move into Moss Hill. I think he and Jess kept an eye on her when she was renting the house up the road."

"I saw the house on my run on Sunday. It's a beautiful place, but I don't know if I'd want to be alone out there all winter."

"No kidding. They'd see her shoveling the walk—Jess says she went out there one day and found a snowman in the front yard, complete with coal eyes and a carrot nose. Kylie must have made it. I've lived by myself. I never considered making a snowman. But she's an artist, and I'm a cook."

Russ wondered if the snowman had resembled one of the Middle Branch Badgers. "Do you know much about her work?" he asked Maggie.

"Children's books. That's all I know. Phoebe thinks she might use another name. We try not to pry. Kylie came to town for a personal artistic retreat. I don't think she meant to stay this long. Her lease with Mark is month to month. I'd be surprised if she stays another winter, but you never know."

"Does she have a permanent address?"

"I think Moss Hill is it right now. The house she rented is up for sale, or will be soon. It's owned by an art professor who got a job in Iowa. I think she and Kylie are friends." Maggie reached across the table for another small paint can, this one with no label or dried paint splatters. "Mystery paint. Want to have a go at it?"

She set the can in front of Russ. He tackled the lid with his screwdriver.

"Kylie might have friends in town I'm not aware of," Maggie added. "Believe it or not, I don't know everyone in Knights Bridge. You don't suspect she's behind these silly rumors my mother heard, do you?"

"I have no reason to suspect anyone of anything."

"That's good. Kylie moved to town before any of us had heard of Daphne. A number of people remember her when she lived here as Debbie Sanderson. I wonder how many people are tucked in the hills and hollows and along the streams and ponds out here that I don't even know exist. It's easy in a small town to get into a rut of who you know and don't know. The Frosts, the Sloans, the odd person here or there."

"That's probably normal." Russ gently opened the can to a vibrant pink. He showed it to Maggie. "What you were expecting?"

"No, but it's a great color. Can't think of what we'd use it for, but we'll think of something." She grabbed the lid and replaced it on the can of pink paint, banging it down with such force that Russ figured he knew why the lids were on so tight. "On the whole, I'd say we're open to new people, but we don't want to be intrusive, either. Brandon and I lived in Boston for several years. We moved back to Knights Bridge to raise our boys and be a part of our hometown." She grinned at Russ. "That's the short version of that story."

Kylie Shaw remained a mystery, but Russ doubted it would be difficult to track down more information on her. Friends, family, colleagues, previous addresses. Boyfriends.

Did he want to go that far?

Maybe.

He found himself liking Maggie and looking forward to meeting Olivia and Dylan. Julius had described the new couple as grounded, eager to make Knights Bridge their main home. Dylan—and now his wife—also owned a home in San Diego.

"I saw Kylie a little while ago, by the way," Maggie said casually, getting to her feet. "She was on her bike."

"Out here?"

"She cruised past the house about an hour ago."

"It's a dead-end road."

"She comes out this way regularly. We wave to each other."

"Since the weather warmed up?"

"I saw her a few times last fall, too. I don't remember if I noticed her before that—I think she moved into Knights Bridge in July. Bike riding is great exercise. I should probably do more of it myself. I haven't noticed her ride by again. It's turning into a gorgeous day. She could have decided to ride into Quabbin. There's an old road inside the gate that bikers sometimes use. There are strict rules, since it's protected land. Or she could have parked her bike and taken a walk in the woods."

"Alone?"

Maggie reached for her apron. "I think Kylie does a lot of things alone."

Russ couldn't think of a single reason he should care if Kylie Shaw was riding her bike here or anywhere else.

"Olivia should be back soon with Buster. He's a great dog, but I always keep in mind this is Buster's turf."

"I'll take a walk down the road and then head up to the barn."

"Great." Maggie gave Russ a cheerful frown. "Why do I have the feeling we weren't just having a friendly chat?"

"We were."

"But you're an investigator. You know how to get people to talk."

He winked at her. "I look forward to the soup and bread."

He headed outside, noticing dozens of daffodils blooming on the border on the Quabbin side of the yard.

He could hear birds twittering in the trees, but he had no idea what kind of birds. Little ones. Best he could do.

He stood on the front walk and looked up the road, toward the new house and barn the McCaffreys were building, now almost finished. Then he looked down the road, where Olivia McCaffrey was walking the infamous Buster and, presumably, pretty, secretive Kylie Shaw, aka Morwenna Mills, was on her bike.

Russ went that way.

Bike tire tracks and the prints of a large dog in the dirt on the side of the old, narrow road compelled Russ to continue around a curve. The pavement looked as if it had taken a beating over the winter, but many of the potholes, ruts and cracks probably weren't new. On either side of the road were trees and more trees, and a stream, no doubt working its way into the reservoir.

He'd walked about two hundred yards without seeing a soul.

What a place, he thought.

Two steps later, he heard a cough and paused.

Nope.

Not a cough. Someone was vomiting. The sounds were distinct and unmistakable.

He picked up his pace, rounding the curve in time to see Kylie holding the waist of another woman as she pitched her cookies into sprouting ferns on the side of the road.

"Do you need an ambulance?" Kylie asked.

The woman—she had to be Olivia Frost McCaffrey—waved a hand no.

Then she went down onto her knees, hurling the rest of her guts out.

Russ eased in next to Kylie. "Anything I can do?"

She fixed her light blue eyes on him. "This is Olivia McCaffrey. I came upon her a few minutes ago. We were talking, and all of a sudden she got sick to her stomach."

"Buster," Olivia said between wretches. "He got loose. He still has his leash on…"

"Buster is her dog," Kylie said.

Russ nodded. "We'll find him, Olivia, but let's see about you first."

She sank onto her butt in the dirt on the side of the road. "Oh, man. That was bad. I might never eat Maggie's blueberry muffins again." She smiled wanly up at Kylie. "Thank you."

"I can get Dylan," Kylie said.

"No, it's okay. I'm fine. It's just…" Olivia wiped her forehead with the back of her hand. "I guess all first-timers hope they don't get morning sickness. I was hoping to be one of those women who sails right past that phase, but obviously I'm not."

"Morning— Oh!" Kylie clapped her hands together. "You're expecting. That's wonderful, Olivia. Congratulations."

Russ was half wishing he'd gone the other direction and was now talking construction with Dylan and the Sloans. He had zero experience with morning sickness. Puking for a whole host of other reasons, yes. Viruses, food poisoning and hangovers he could handle without skipping a beat.

"I just need a minute," Olivia said, looking as if she needed more than that.

Kylie crouched next to her. "I'll stay with you and walk with you back to the house."

"Thanks." Olivia peered up at Russ. Kylie quickly introduced him. Olivia smiled, still green and pale. "Julius's colleague. Sorry about this, Russ."

"No problem. Take your time."

She shifted back to Kylie. "I'm sorry we haven't had you over yet. You're all alone in Knights Bridge."

"The beauty and curse of being a freelance illustrator," Kylie said, obviously awkward at the shift in subject to herself. "I have friends and family not too far. I never lack for company. Now, did you see which way Buster took off?"

Olivia pointed down the road, toward the Quabbin gate. "That way. I'm afraid his leash will get caught on something and cause a ruckus. He's big, and he thinks he owns the road, but he won't bite your arm off or anything like that."

Russ saw it was up to him to fetch Buster. "You okay here?" he asked Kylie.

She nodded. Olivia tucked her knees up. "I just need another minute. Then we'll head back to the house."

That settled, Russ continued down the quiet road, alternately calling for Buster and listening for a bark, whine, sniffle, cough—anything that would clue him into the dog's location and whether he was in trouble. The best-case scenario, Buster had found his way back to the house and was now asleep under the kitchen table.

Russ paused at the yellow metal Quabbin gate, off the turnaround at the end of the road. He heard something panting in the woods on the right-hand side of the road, opposite the gate. Whatever it was, it was bigger than a squirrel. He ducked past an evergreen, discovering a big dog—what looked to be a mix of black Lab and German shepherd—lapping from the stream. He'd managed to catch his leash both on undergrowth and between two rocks.

Russ stepped on the leash, then picked it up. "Hello, Buster," he said.

Buster looked up at him, licked his chops and tried to bolt.

Tightening up on the leash, Russ reassured the big dog while at the same time letting him know who was in charge. "I'm the alpha dog here, pal."

Buster seemed good with that.

They returned to the road. Buster was muddy but otherwise didn't appear any worse for the wear for his jaunt. When he spotted Olivia, he tried to race to her, but Russ didn't think she needed a big, slobbering dog jumping on her.

She smiled when she saw Buster, though, and greeted him cheerfully, her color marginally better. She looked up at Russ. "Thank you," she said, giving him a wan smile.

"No problem. You're doing okay? It's a good walk to your house." He liked to get moving after barfing, but he knew nothing about morning sickness and what Olivia would want to do. "I can get my car."

She shook her head. "I can manage. It'll feel good to walk." She let Kylie help her to her feet. "You can finish your bike ride, Kylie. I'm fine now. Really."

"I'll walk to the house with you and then come back

for my bike," Kylie said. "I don't mind. It's a beautiful day to be outside."

"If I won't be keeping you from anything…"

"You won't."

Olivia didn't argue further. Russ kept charge of a reasonably compliant Buster as they all walked up the road to Olivia's antique center-chimney house. She wasn't too wobbly, and when they reached her front walk, she invited Russ and Kylie inside. Before they could respond, Maggie rushed outside, clearly needing no explanation when she saw her friend. "I know that green look. Come on, Olivia. I'll make you some tea and let you get your feet under you."

"I'll clean up Buster," Russ said. "Is there a preferred spot to do it?"

Maggie nodded. "There's a mudroom. You can take him in through the back door, although he's plowed through the kitchen with muddy paws enough times."

Back door it was. He tugged on Buster's leash and started across the front yard but stopped when Olivia turned to him. "Thank you for your help," she said.

"No problem."

"I'm sure dog catching isn't in your job description." She shifted to Kylie. "I can't thank you enough. I went from faintly queasy to all-out nausea so suddenly…"

"All's well that ends well," Kylie said with a smile. "I'm glad you're feeling better."

The two Knights Bridge women disappeared into the house. Buster plopped down onto Russ's foot as Kylie gestured with one hand toward the dead-end road. "I'll get my bike and head home. Good you came along when you did." She started down the stone walk. "See you at Moss Hill."

Russ watched her, trying to guess if she knew he'd seen Sherlock Badger. Maybe, maybe not. She was accustomed to hiding her true feelings, wasn't she? But keeping Morwenna Mills to herself also must have honed her skills at detecting trouble, avoiding risky situations and staying on alert. She had to know, at the least, that he wasn't satisfied with her story about herself and her reasons for being at Carriage Hill—or, for that matter, in Knights Bridge.

But not satisfied wasn't the same as suspicious, and he didn't want to screw up this place for her. It might have started out as a refuge, an artist's retreat, but he had a feeling it had turned into home.

Not that he knew what home meant, or felt like. He'd lived most of his life on the move.

All his life. Even before he'd moved to Hollywood, his apartment in San Diego had been temporary, an arrangement he'd made with a couple of navy buddies at sea.

He tugged the leash, half expecting Buster to try to drag him back down the road, but the big dog had obviously had his fill of adventures for the time being. They walked around to the back of the house, through a garden of raised beds filled with herbs popping up now that it was spring. It bordered a field marked by an old stone wall, probably constructed by farmers clearing the land long before Quabbin Reservoir.

Russ took Buster onto a stone terrace and into the mudroom.

First, see to Buster's muddy paws.

Then figure out what Kylie had been up to on her bike ride out here.

Thirteen

Russ definitely knew about Morwenna. No question in Kylie's mind. It hadn't been any one thing—a particular look or comment—but she'd detected a change in him. Even the surprise of finding her with a pregnant, vomiting Olivia McCaffrey didn't explain his subtle but unmistakable change in attitude.

Kylie tried to focus on riding her bike up the road from the spot where she'd come upon Olivia, but her head was spinning with a hundred thoughts, sensations and worries. Before setting out that morning, she'd talked herself into thinking Russ hadn't spotted Sherlock Badger after all and didn't know about Morwenna, but such was not the case.

"Oh, yes," she said aloud as she dodged a pothole. "He knows."

Russ's car was still parked in front of the 1803 house, but she didn't see anyone outside and continued on up the road. She'd ventured out this way first thing that morning, drawn by the bright, clear spring day and the need to burn off her restless energy. She'd relished jumping on her bike. She'd had a rough night, given her worries about Morwenna and her reaction to Russ's quick, unexpected kiss and all it promised.

At least she'd arrived at the right time to help Olivia, who could easily have stumbled or passed out, as violently ill as she'd been.

Kylie reminded herself she had nothing to hide, really. It wasn't as if working under a pseudonym and keeping it to herself were a crime. She wasn't deceiving anyone so much as just not talking about her work as an illustrator and now also an author of children's books.

Should she beg Russ for his silence? Let him blab to whomever he wanted? Daphne. His colleagues in Beverly Hills. The O'Dunn twins. Mark Flanagan. The Sloans. The McCaffreys.

One had to work at it to keep a secret around here, Kylie thought, trying to smile. But she felt awkward and unsettled, if not guilty.

When she came to the McCaffreys' new house and barn, Russ was standing at the end of the driveway, as if he were waiting for her. She debated pedaling past him with a quick, friendly wave, but instead she stopped, easing off her bike. "Olivia's doing better?" she asked.

"She's resting." he said. "Buster's cleaned up and asleep in the mudroom."

"A little drama for the morning."

His gaze was steady on her. "Did it blow your plans?"

"Not at all."

"What were you doing out here?"

"Olivia's house is inspiration for the grandmother's house in my rendition of *Little Red Riding Hood*. The Quabbin woods are fodder, too." She resisted going into more detail since she was working on her series of fairy tales as Morwenna. "Buster is helping me reimagine the wolf."

"He's all bark and no bite. Little Red Riding Hood's wolf eats her grandmother."

"Yes, well, there's that. There are more innocuous versions of the story. Anyway, that's what I was up to."

"You're out here doing research," Russ said.

"You could call it that." She didn't explain further, never mind the trace of skepticism she heard in his voice. "I should get going. I have a few things I need to do. I didn't expect the situation with Olivia, obviously."

"Friends and wives of friends of mine have had morning sickness. Doesn't look fun."

"No."

"What about you?"

"Me? You mean have I—" Kylie stopped herself and took a breath before she continued. "Friends and wives of friends of mine, you mean. It's come up in conversation. No direct experience until this morning."

"No one's ever thrown up on your shoes?"

"Not human."

"Now there's a provocative answer."

"I grew up around animals," she said.

"Your father's a veterinarian and your mother is a dog groomer and trainer." Russ shifted his stance, his eyes never leaving her. "I read that on your Kylie Shaw website."

As opposed to her Morwenna Mills website? Kylie pushed that thought out of her mind. "Good upbringing for an illustrator. I'll leave you to enjoy your day."

"Dylan McCaffrey is giving me the grand tour of

this place. I told him we could reschedule, but when he stopped in to check on Olivia, she and Maggie were having tea and toast and talking morning sickness." Russ smiled. "Tour's back on. You're invited."

Kylie hesitated. She could confront him about what he knew about Morwenna, or tell him herself, pretending she had no idea he'd figured it out, but she didn't want to. It wasn't the time or the place for such a revelation, but she was being stubborn, too. He was being intrusive—and he knew it. Morwenna was irrelevant to any concerns he had about Moss Hill or Knights Bridge ahead of Saturday.

Maybe they both were playing games, but so be it.

She noticed she had mud on her right hip but, with his gaze lingering on her, decided not to brush it off. "You must be bored," she said. "A little town like Knights Bridge doesn't offer the excitement of Los Angeles. You can see the night sky here. That's one thing. With Quabbin so close, there isn't much ambient light. People come out here to see the stars—a different kind of star from what you're used to."

Russ shrugged. "I'll go along with that."

Kylie held tight on to her bike. "You're not used to small-town life."

"You don't know what I'm used to, do you?"

"Not for a fact, no. You've got me there." She kept her tone light, ignoring a rush of heat at his quiet, deep voice, his steady blue eyes. "But I'm not wrong, am I?"

"I've discovered that most people don't fit in tidy boxes."

She tried not to read into his words. "What about your clients?"

"All kinds."

"I've seen the effects of success and the need for success on people in my profession. The pressures of a Hollywood career must be intense. Daphne Stewart works behind the scenes, but it's still Hollywood."

"She's grounded in her own Daphne way," Russ said, no let up in his intensity. "How do you stay grounded?"

"I finish the project I'm working on, and then I start the next one."

"That easy, is it?"

"Most days."

Kylie eased her grip on her bike. Russ would notice how tense she was. He was a man who noticed everything. He was self-confident, knowing, sexy—and well aware of his impact on her, never mind their dance around the subject of her work and success. He was clearly suspicious of her reasons for being out here. It wasn't as if he was subtle about his suspicion, either. Had to be a hard way to live, she thought, always wondering if people had ulterior motives for what they did. But it was his job, too. He wasn't here on vacation. He was working.

"Dylan wants to meet you and thank you himself for helping Olivia," Russ said. "Come on. Why don't you join me on the tour of the place?"

"I did what anyone would do. Dylan doesn't have to thank me."

"Sometimes it feels good for people to express their gratitude. First pregnancy. He's not used to this any more than Olivia is."

Kylie was tempted. Just from the outside, never mind the inside, the new barn and house were gorgeous, designed to blend into the landscape. She knew some of the background of the property. Dylan had inherited it, unknowingly, from his father, a businessman-turned-treasure-hunter. Dylan, with Olivia's help, had put the pieces together. His father had discovered that the young woman who'd placed him in adoption as an infant was Grace Webster, a former Knights Bridge English and Latin teacher now in her nineties. She'd moved into assisted living and had put her house up for sale. She'd moved into the house with her father and grandmother after they'd been evicted from one of the lost Quabbin towns. Duncan had met his birth mother and bought her old house, but he died in a fall in Portugal before he could explain his interest in Knights Bridge to his only son.

Kylie had yet to meet Grace Webster and had only met Dylan a few times, casually, in town and while out riding her bike.

Dylan McCaffrey walked down the driveway and greeted her and Russ warmly. A good-looking former NHL defenseman, he took Kylie's hand and kissed her on the cheek. "I can't thank you enough. I'm glad Olivia wasn't alone out there. She says she'd have been okay, and I'm sure she would have—but still. Thank you."

"I'm glad I was there at the right time," she said.

"We haven't told Grace about the baby yet," Dylan said, turning to Kylie and Russ. "She's my grandmother, in case you didn't realize. Word travels fast in a small town. If you could give us the rest of the day before you said anything to anyone…"

"Of course," Russ said without hesitation.

Kylie nodded. "Absolutely."

Dylan looked relieved.

Every fiber of her being urged Kylie to get out of here. She was coming off months of nonstop, if good, work, and she didn't trust herself in social settings right now. She didn't want to seem rude and standoffish. She wanted to get to know her fellow residents in Knights Bridge better. It was past time. But getting to know them under the nose of a suspicious private investigator maybe wasn't the best option.

Smarter to wait until Russ Colton was on his way back to California, wasn't it?

But Kylie found herself following the two men up the driveway.

An hour later, Kylie caught her breath, slowing as she hit a downhill stretch of road.

The "grand tour" had been grand, indeed, but also unsettling in ways she couldn't have predicted. Russ's genuine interest in Dylan's plans for his adventure travel business and his and Noah Kendrick's entrepreneurial boot camp, Dylan's love for Olivia, the possibilities of the future—they had gotten to her, made her think about her own life and what she wanted.

She couldn't tuck herself away at her worktable, talking to Sherlock Badger, forever.

But she didn't regret wandering through the spectacular house and barn with Dylan and Russ, no matter the consequences—the distractions. If she regretted anything, it was turning down Dylan's invitation to stay for lunch. She was downright hungry.

"Barn" was a loose term for the New England barn-like building that would serve as a base for Dylan's new enterprises in Knights Bridge. No cows, horses or hay were involved in the place, for one thing. It was light-filled and a surprisingly contemporary space. Like Moss Hill, Mark Flanagan's design incorporated old and new seamlessly, drawing only praise in a town that had seen little real change in its architectural landscape in decades.

The house, set back from the barn, was equally beautiful and intriguing. Both structures blended into the landscape, looking as if they belonged there, amid the rolling fields, old stone walls and woods. The kitchen window offered a stunning view of Carriage Hill, rising up across a meadow coming to life with the warm spring weather.

Most important, Olivia continued to recover well and wasn't in any danger.

Kylie couldn't shake the image of Russ walking up the road with the big dog.

He was one rugged man.

She took the long way back to Moss Hill, past the nineteenth-century cider mill where Justin Sloan had met Samantha Bennett last fall when it caught fire in a severe thunderstorm. The fire and Justin and Samantha's whirlwind romance had caused quite a stir in town, Kylie recalled. Although she was an outsider and had never expected to stay in Knights Bridge, she'd hear tidbits at the library and country store about the people in her little town.

She came to the Sloan farm and the offices of Sloan & Sons construction. A black Lab rolled in the sunlit grass. Kylie smiled, feeling her tension ease as she paused to gaze out across the fields and hills to a sliver of the reservoir in the distance, blue, quiet, seemingly untouched by humans. She suddenly couldn't imagine living anywhere else.

Once everyone knew about Morwenna, how would it change the life she had here?

The wind picked up as she cut down a dirt road and came to the river. When she arrived at Moss Hill, she left her bike at the rack out front and took off her helmet, aware she had red cheeks and tangled hair.

She didn't see Russ or his car.

Just as well, she thought.

Her apartment was warm, cleaned up from last night's dinner. She touched her cheek, almost as if she could feel the brush of Russ's kiss. The sexual tension between them might be real, but it was also inconvenient.

She sat at her worktable. She'd managed to snap a few shots of sugar maples, leafing out now that it was spring, before she'd come upon a pregnant, nauseated Olivia.

In another minute, Kylie had the photos downloaded onto her computer. Best thing she could do now was to get back to work—hide out, basically, until after Daphne Stewart's class. The Hollywood designer and her investigator would go back to California, and Ruby and Ava O'Dunn would go back to school.

Then I can surface.

In the meantime, Kylie thought, there was plenty of day left to work on *Little Red Riding Hood,* and she had several new ideas for the maple tree in front of the grandmother's house.

Fourteen

Russ joined Dylan for coffee on the stone terrace off the Carriage Hill kitchen. Lunch had been every bit as good as it had smelled. The minestrone soup and the oatmeal bread, fresh out of the oven, had been hearty, filling and just what he needed after his unpredictable morning.

Olivia had eaten a few bites before excusing herself. Maggie had left before lunch to run errands.

The air had turned breezy and cool. Russ warmed his hands on his coffee mug. He grinned at Dylan. "Loretta warned me I could regret not packing a parka."

Dylan laughed. "Sounds like her. Knights Bridge definitely isn't Southern California."

"You're adapting if we're having coffee out here."

"So I am," he said, his satisfaction with his new life obvious as he sat across from Russ at the wood table. Dylan sat straight, looking like the successful corporate executive he was. "Loretta wants me to talk to you about security."

Russ nodded, grateful Dylan had spared him from

having to figure out how to broach the subject. "I'm an investigator with Sawyer & Sawyer these days, but I know a bit about security."

"From your navy days," Dylan added.

"I'd be happy to help in any way I can."

"Knights Bridge has a low crime rate, but our new ventures will draw more people here. I don't lie awake nights worrying about trouble, but I realize we need to be proactive. Noah does, too. We're used to considering security when we're in San Diego. Here...it's a different story."

Russ got that. Winding roads, old mills, a covered bridge, a country store—it would be easy to get lulled into a false sense of security, even if Knights Bridge wasn't exactly San Diego. "How do your wife and Noah's fiancée feel about beefing up security here?"

"Phoebe and Olivia grew up here. Knights Bridge is their hometown. They like to think nothing's changed, but they know better. You probably noticed we installed an alarm system up the road." Dylan smiled. "It might be the first one in Knights Bridge."

"What about here?" Russ asked.

"Locks. No alarm system. Working on it, though."

It was a start. "Good security doesn't have to be intrusive. There's what you see and what you don't see."

"Yeah."

Russ gazed at the idyllic setting. Mulched walks marked off the raised flower and herb beds, which extended to a small garden shed. He waited, sensing Dylan had more to say.

"Phoebe's having more trouble than Olivia adjusting to heightened security." Dylan waved a hand. "She and Noah will work it out. He'd do anything for her."

As Dylan would for Olivia, Russ thought. According to Loretta and Julius, and from what Russ had learned so far on his own, Olivia Frost McCaffrey and Phoebe O'Dunn were self-sufficient, independent women, no doubt as supportive of the men in their lives as they were of them.

For no good reason Russ could think of, he wondered what kind of support system Kylie Shaw had. Who was helping her navigate her new world as Morwenna Mills? From what he'd seen, for the most part she had only herself—whether by design or not, he couldn't guess.

"Where are Noah and Phoebe now?" he asked.

"Noah's winery," Dylan said. "They'll be flying here for a few days soon. Phoebe's fallen in love with California."

"The winery's on the central coast, isn't it?"

Dylan nodded. "Noah's folks retired up there." He stretched out his thick legs, eyeing Russ. "Anything to these rumors about Moss Hill?"

"Mark Flanagan and Chris Sloan don't think so. Nothing serious, at least."

"The Sloans are a hard-driving lot in a tough business. They're fair-minded and solid, but they're bound to annoy a few people from time to time, and they often have to make difficult decisions. They did with their work for me. Mark comes across as more easygoing than your average Sloan, but he's dedicated and exacting. I don't know much about the construction of Moss Hill. Here, though…" Dylan shrugged. "I can't remember any particular altercations. A few accidents, a near heart attack. That sort of thing."

"Kylie Shaw?"

Dylan didn't seem surprised by mention of her name. "I don't know Kylie at all. No help there. You don't think she's responsible for this talk, do you?"

Russ shook his head. "I don't."

"There's worrisome talk and there's just talk. Which is this?"

"I'd be speculating."

"All right. Fair enough." Dylan set his coffee mug on the table. "We should talk more."

A broad-shouldered, dark-haired man who could only be a Sloan came out through the mudroom. Dylan introduced him as Brandon Sloan, Maggie's husband and a carpenter with his family construction firm. He was also working with Dylan on adventure travel.

"I just saw Olivia," Brandon said. "She says she'll be out soon, and you should plan to grab your shovel, Dylan, because she wants to spread the last of the bark mulch."

"Lucky me," Dylan said. "A year ago I didn't know what bark mulch was."

Brandon grinned. "I guess she's feeling better."

The conversation turned to plans for the initial adventure travel outings. It was just getting off the ground, and Russ gathered they were still working out any kinks, figuring out what the opportunities and obstacles were. Carriage Hill would provide lodging and meals for local adventure-travel outings but mostly for the entrepreneurial boot camp.

"Maggie's stretched too thin, with catering, this

place and the goat's milk soaps, and Olivia—" Brandon shrugged. "She loves keeping her hand in, but she can't do everything, either. They're planning to hire a professional innkeeper. They could use the help."

"No doubt," Russ said. "What kind of adventure travel do you have in mind?"

"It doesn't have to be physically daring or demanding," Dylan said. "We'll see how it develops. We're planning a trip to Newfoundland in August."

"Newfoundland is beautiful," Russ said.

The two men looked surprised. "You've been to Newfoundland?" Brandon asked.

Russ smiled. "Whales, icebergs and stunning scenery."

"Perfect," Dylan said.

"Before I forget," Brandon said, "Maggie says you're invited to dinner at her mother's place tonight. Six o'clock. Call if you need directions."

"Thanks."

"Maggie says Kylie's welcome, too."

Russ nodded. "I'll let her know."

"Great."

Brandon got to work, and Olivia came out, her color back. Dylan stood. Time to fetch his shovel.

Russ brought his coffee mug into the kitchen. He was struck by the contrast with the kitchen at Julius Hartley's house in Hollywood Hills. He hadn't been here a full three days, and this little town and its people had wormed their way into his system.

He drove back to Moss Hill. Mark's offices were bustling. A dozen cars were in the parking lot, including Kylie's Mini. But her bike wasn't on the rack.

Russ sat on a bench on the breezeway to wait for her.

She cruised into the parking lot ten minutes later. He noticed she almost lost her footing on her bike when she saw him. Instead, she jumped off, removed her helmet and gave him a pleasant smile, as if she'd planned what to do if she came back from her bike ride and found him sitting there.

"I thought I was done with bike rides today," she said, "but I got a firmer idea for my wolf. Thanks to Buster, of course."

"How does that relate to a bike ride?"

"I needed to let him simmer."

"Ah." Russ got to his feet. "We're invited to dinner at the O'Dunns tonight."

"We? Meaning—"

"The two of us. We can take my car this time. Yours really is little."

"Yes, it is."

Color rose in her cheeks and something else in her eyes—desire, he thought. Pure and simple. He couldn't say what was in his eyes. Desire probably was a good start.

"I was planning to work the rest of the day. I can see *Little Red Riding Hood* now. It's not bits and pieces in my mind anymore. Being out at Carriage Hill this morning helped."

"You create visual narratives with your work."

She smiled. "Exactly."

He winked at her. "I saw that on your website." Her Kylie Shaw website, he thought. "What do you say? Shall I knock on your door at five-thirty?"

She hesitated, then nodded. "See you then."

And she bolted, yanking open the door to the residential building and disappearing, as if she wanted to get away from him before she could change her mind about dinner.

Russ saw he had a text from Marty. We're out of Chambord. I'm afraid to tell Daphne.

She'll live.

How's KB?

I'm off to look at the ducks on the river.

Let me know if you need me to spring you.

Russ laughed. This place was Marty's idea of hell. A small town, a quiet river, a renovated hat factory and ducks.

He headed around back to the dam. He took a few photos and texted them to Marty. He'd have to be sure to take some pictures of the O'Dunn goats at dinner tonight.

His big brother in Hollywood would appreciate goats.

Fifteen

Kylie brought her bottle of expensive champagne to dinner. It was all she could think of in a pinch. Elly O'Dunn appraised the label with a low whistle. She was in her fifties, with graying red hair, freckles and a casual manner—Kylie could see why people told her things. A widow for ten years, Elly had managed to hang on to the house she'd built with her husband on the other side of town, out toward Echo Lake. Kylie had ridden her bike to the lake last fall, taking in the colorful foliage.

"This is the good stuff," Elly said. "What are we celebrating?"

Figuring out her plans for *Little Red Riding Hood* wasn't enough. "Moss Hill's opening and how well it's going," Kylie said. "First apartment rented, first event— worth celebrating."

"Works for me. I'll fetch glasses."

Elly went inside. She'd set up a buffet-style dinner on a table on the screened back porch, a cozy, comfort- able spot with mismatched chairs and flowerpots lined

up on the floor, ready for planting. Russ had gone out
to investigate a large vegetable garden tilled and par-
tially planted for the season. He'd managed to produce
a bunch of daffodils for Elly, probably from the country store since Kylie couldn't fathom him picking them,
never mind where he'd have found any available for
picking. He was a man of surprises.

Ruby joined him, pointing toward pens where her
mother's dozen-plus Nigerian Dwarf goats pranced.
When her husband had been killed in a tragic wood-
cutting accident ten years ago, Elly had started raising
goats to help her cope with her grief. Phoebe had told
Kylie the story at the library last summer, before Noah
Kendrick had arrived in town and swept her off her feet,
pretty much literally.

Mark and Jess Flanagan arrived for dinner, and finally Christopher Sloan. Russ and Ruby came in from
the garden, and Elly handed out glasses and poured the
champagne. "Courtesy of our Kylie," she said cheerfully.

The toast to Moss Hill seemed to go over well. Kylie
relaxed slightly, aware of Russ watching her as she sat
in a comfortable chair by the screen. It was a cool evening, but the air felt good after the long winter. The
porch was just enough shelter to keep it from being too
cold to stay outside, and Elly had brought out a stack of
blankets. Kylie imagined snuggling up under one with
Russ. She was so shocked at the turn her mind had taken
she almost shot out of the chair and excused herself—
but he was her ride back to Moss Hill.

Mark stayed on his feet, his champagne in one hand.
"Whoever the crank is who made the comments about

Moss Hill, it's got a clean bill of health. The rumors will sort themselves out."

Chris Sloan nodded. "Ruby insisted I check out the place. I hope it helped."

She bristled. "I didn't insist."

"All that matters right now is Moss Hill is set for Saturday," Jess Flanagan said mildly.

Chris helped himself to a beer out of a cooler. He'd downed the champagne in a couple of quick swallows. "There seems to be a lot of drama around Daphne Stewart."

"She's that kind of personality," Ruby said, instantly combative.

"No crime in that," Chris said.

Ruby crossed her arms tightly on her chest, her cheeks visibly flushed even from where Kylie was sitting. Chris looked as if he had no idea what he'd said wrong and would rather be anywhere else.

"I hope you weren't upset by all this, Kylie," Ruby said, her tone softening. "It hasn't affected your work, has it? You must need a certain atmosphere to get into the spirt of illustrating children's books."

Kylie resisted the temptation to glance at Russ. "No problem." She noticed Elly O'Dunn by the door. "This place is great, Elly. Are goats a lot of work?"

It wasn't the subtlest change in subject, but it did the trick as Elly launched into a description of what was involved in raising goats.

Ruby shot away from Chris, who looked as if he might seize the moment to retreat but managed to stay put. She went to the table, laid out with cold hors d'oeuvres. She grabbed a triangle of cheese and turned to Russ. "Maggie told me about this morning. Olivia was sick to her stomach while walking Buster. Gad, I hope it's not a bug. That's all we need going around town, with or without Daphne arriving."

"Food poisoning would be worse since Olivia runs an inn," Chris said.

Ruby shot him a look. "No kidding."

Definitely a little tension there, Kylie thought. But she wasn't about to break her promise to Olivia about her pregnancy. "Olivia was feeling much better when I left."

"That's good." Ruby narrowed her eyes as if she suspected there was more to the story, but she turned to Russ. "Maggie said you were there, too. You're not getting us at our best, are you? First, rumors and then this."

"I was glad to help," he said. "I enjoyed meeting her and her husband, and your sister and her husband."

"My big brother, Brandon," Chris said with an easy grin.

"He's good to Maggie," Ruby said. "Typical Sloan, it took some doing to get him to see what she and the boys meant to him."

"Ruby," her mother said. "You okay?"

"Yes. Sure. Sorry." She grabbed a slice of apple and added it to her cheese. "Olivia's place is great, isn't it? Not everything in Knights Bridge is that quaint and pretty, but it sure is."

Russ agreed, and Ruby went inside to help her mother bring out food, refusing any additional help. The conversation on the porch shifted to the Red Sox and the start of the baseball season. Kylie didn't bring up her last Red Sox game and her seventh-inning departure.

Ruby, who lived in Boston, scoffed as she set a large bowl of salad on the table. "The only baseball games I've sat through start to finish were ones my little nephews were playing in." She smiled at Russ and Kylie. "They're five and seven."

Elly came out with a bowl of steaming tortellini. "Dinner is served," she said cheerfully. "I hope you don't mind eating off your laps."

No one minded. Ruby sat next to Kylie. She seemed eager for company—an ally, maybe, in avoiding Chris Sloan and whatever was going on between them. They struck Kylie as friends who should remain friends. With Ruby's sister Maggie married to Chris's brother Brandon, their relationship was already complicated. But Kylie didn't pretend to know anything about romance. After all, her main companion was a stuffed badger.

"Tell us about yourself, Kylie," Elly said. "Did you always want to be an illustrator?"

"Once I knew what one was," she said lightly.

Mark opened a beer bottle. "Where did you live before Knights Bridge?"

Kylie noticed Russ settled back in his chair, watching her. "I've bounced around quite a bit," she said. "It's one of the perks of being a freelance artist. I'm not tied to an office, so why not work in, say, a little town in Massachusetts?"

"I think I'd work in Paris," Jess said with a laugh.

"I did for a short time, as a matter of fact."

"Good for you," Elly said. "I hope there was a handsome Frenchman involved."

Kylie sidestepped that one. "Paris is great, but I love it here. I haven't done much traveling this past year. I have business in Los Angeles that I've been putting off." She decided to draw Russ into the conversation. "You mentioned you're new there. How do you like it?"

"No complaints," he said.

"You must have interesting clients," Elly said. "We're all fascinated by Daphne Stewart and her long Hollywood career. I think deep down Ruby wants to try her hand in Hollywood. What do you think, Ruby?"

Chris Sloan's gaze was on her as she hesitated. "I can't do both Hollywood and a children's theater here."

"Maybe this theater idea is a diversion," Chris said. "It feels safe compared to Hollywood."

"Maybe I'm looking for a way to do what I love and still stay in Knights Bridge."

He shrugged. "Your decision. No one here is holding you back from doing what you want."

"I appreciate that," she said softly.

Jess Flanagan put her plate on a tray on the table and smiled at Russ. "Chris has known what he wanted to do since he was three. My mother remembers him in his little red firefighter hat."

"Works out that way sometimes," Russ said. "It's great you're doing what you've always wanted, Chris."

"I'm fortunate," he said.

"You are who you are." Ruby's voice was just above a whisper. "I need to be who I am."

Kylie glanced from Ruby to Chris, taking measure of the tension between them. If Ruby pursued an acting career in Hollywood, it was clear it would mean the end of her relationship with Christopher Sloan. He wasn't interested in being a firefighter in LA. He wanted to stay in his hometown.

He got up, thanking Elly for dinner. "If you pin down these rumors about Moss Hill, let me know."

"I will, Chris. I wish I hadn't said anything."

He shook his head. "Always speak up." He grinned at her. "Not that you need to be told." He turned to the rest of the dinner guests. "Mark, Jess, you need anything else from me before Saturday, give me a shout. Russ and Kylie, good to see you. Ruby—"

"I'll walk out with you," she said, jumping to her feet.

Elly watched them, frowning, as they went out the screened porch door, but she said nothing.

"Come on, Elly," Jess said. "Have a seat and relax with your company. Mark and I will get the dishes."

"Dishes can wait. Sit. Relax."

Which is what Jess did, snuggling next to Mark on a comfy-looking outdoor couch. When Ruby returned, she dove into the conversation, no sign any longer of her tension about the rumors, Saturday or Christopher Sloan.

Elly O'Dunn was gracious when the evening came to an end. "Thank you again for the champagne, Kylie. It was wonderful. We must find more reasons to celebrate."

Kylie smiled. "I like that idea."

It was dark when she finally sat next to Russ in his rental car. "See what I mean about the night sky here?"

"I do, indeed," he said. "It's something on a clear night."

"It was a pleasant evening. Ruby's figuring out her

life. I remember when I was finishing up art school and entertaining the possibilities. But my hometown didn't have the pull on me that Knights Bridge does her."

"No buff firefighter was waiting at home for you?"

Kylie laughed. "There was not. Would it be so bad if Ruby decided to give up her dreams of Hollywood to stay here, open a community theater, live a different life from the one she's imagined for herself?"

"Depends on the reasons, I guess."

"Chris Sloan might have fallen for ambitious, any-thing-is-possible Ruby O'Dunn, but he has no interest in giving up his job here for a life in LA."

"What if he sacrificed a solid, secure job and his life here and she hated LA?"

"Too soon for a relationship, maybe." Kylie gazed out her window at the dark landscape and the sprinkle of bright stars in the night sky. "We're all lucky to have such options in our lives."

"We are. You were fun tonight. Personable."

She turned and smiled at him. "Surprised?"

"Not really. I noticed that was one expensive bottle of champagne."

"It was good, wasn't it?"

"Very good." He was silent a moment. "Nice that Morwenna Mills can afford it."

"Sherlock did me in, didn't he?" Kylie stared out at the river. They were almost to Moss Hill. She hadn't said a word since Russ had made his comment. "I swear I could have stuffed him in a cupboard and he'd have found a way to sneak out and blow my cover. It was time. Past time."

"He's been telling you that, has he?"

"Sherlock and I have a unique relationship."

"Ah."

"How did you know he wasn't some little badger I'd picked up in Boston or Paris or wherever?"

"I could tell you'd sanitized your work area, and he got my attention—I had a gut feeling you'd overlooked him."

"Sanitized? That sounds like spies and antibacterial wipes were involved. I just grabbed anything that would invite questions or give me away." She sighed. "I swear Sherlock hid while I was cleaning up."

"He looks handmade."

"He is. I prefer drawing, but I have my crafty moments. Sometimes I have to remind him he's made out of scraps and dryer lint."

Russ slowed for a curve. She couldn't tell in the dark if he was smiling, trying not to smile, definitely not smiling. "I didn't recognize Sherlock," he said. "I don't have little kids to read to. But, it wasn't hard to figure him out."

"Don't tell him that. He likes to think he's mysterious."

"Should I call you Morwenna now?"

"No one calls me Morwenna. I suppose if I do media and events I'll be Morwenna, but my agent, editor—no."

"But you don't do media and appearances."

"Some media early on. None lately, and no appearances."

"Will this last?"

She didn't hesitate. "No." She looked up at Moss Hill, looming against the starlit sky. She wouldn't mind being at her spring now, even in the dark. "Did you Google *badger dressed as Sherlock Holmes*? Is that how you figured him out?"

"I snapped a photo of him while you weren't looking and texted it to my brother, Marty, in LA. He recognized Sherlock right away. Marty's like that. He won't say anything."

"I appreciate that. You could sound contrite about sneaking a photo of Sherlock, though."

"I could, but I'm not contrite."

"You don't do contrite, do you?"

"I can't think of a time. Maybe when I was ten."

"Were you nervous? I didn't notice you breaking out into a cold sweat. Did your heart beat rapidly?"

"Because I was sneaking a picture of a stuffed badger?"

"Because I could have caught you."

"Kylie. I wasn't worried about you catching me."

She turned to him and saw, now that they were turning into the Moss Hill parking lot and there were lights, that he was grinning. Ten years in the navy, she remembered. A professional, licensed investigator. But she didn't let it go. "I'm trying to think what I'd have done if I'd caught you," she said. "I couldn't have denied Sherlock. That wouldn't have been right somehow. But I wouldn't have told you about Morwenna and Middle Branch, because I'd have been irritated and felt violated."

"I didn't deserve the truth, you mean."

"Right."

He parked in front of the bike stand. "Do you ever lock your bike?"

"Not here. I probably should."

He turned off the engine and sat a moment in the dark, warm car. "Are you irritated now?"

"I haven't decided."

"Feel violated?"

She tightened her jacket around her. "I feel relieved," she said finally. "That doesn't mean I'm going to thank you for being a sneak."

"You don't have to thank me." He turned to her, the light on half his face, the other half lost in the shadows. "Why the secrecy about Morwenna?"

"It just happened. I'd never both written and illustrated anything. I used a pseudonym in part to help with the anxiety and second-guessing."

"In case it didn't work out," Russ said.

She nodded.

"You didn't think about what if it did work out."

"Not a lot."

"Morwenna Mills is popular."

"Right now, yes. I don't take her success—my success—for granted, and I'm immensely grateful. But I don't want to lose what's worked for me. Revealing that I'm Morwenna..." She took in a deep breath and let it out slowly. Russ waited, not jumping in to finish her thought. "It was just easier not to. I don't want it to mess up my work, my relationships with friends and family."

"You didn't create Morwenna because you have enemies—a stalker, an envious colleague, anyone you're hiding from?"

"No."

"Do you have anyone like that in your life, either

as Kylie Shaw or Morwenna Mills? Ex-husband, ex-boyfriend, enemies? I know you draw children's books, but still, everyone has enemies.

"Not that I'm aware of, and for the record, I've never been married."

"I feel like I blew your cover, but it wasn't as if you're a spy. You'd be a good one. You didn't bat an eye this morning or tonight at dinner, and you knew I'd figured you out." He paused, still next to her. "Scratch that. You knew I'd discovered you were Morwenna." He paused again. "No way have I figured you out."

"Russ…"

He touched her hair above her ear and brushed a curved finger along her jaw, then to her lips. "I'm not here to mess up your life, Kylie."

"I appreciate that."

"Morwenna Mills is exploding in popularity. How you manage the rest is for you to decide, but if you want to talk, feel free. I'm not going to tell anyone you're Morwenna, except Marty, since he's my source, but he's cool. Your identity as Morwenna isn't relevant to my reasons for being here."

"I'm not a security threat to Daphne Stewart or anyone else."

"And I'm not a threat to you or to Morwenna." He leaned over and kissed her lightly, lingering just long enough that she knew he wanted more. "Promise."

He was out of the car before Kylie recovered.

Sparks, she thought. *Talk about sparks.*

She pushed open her door, welcoming the shot of cool April night air when she jumped out of the car. He was on the breezeway, the door to the residences open as he waited for her.

"Stairs or elevator?" he asked.

"I always take the stairs."

"Thought so, but you look a little wobbly."

"It's the champagne," she said.

He grinned. "That's what I figured. The champagne."

Kylie let him go ahead of her on the stairs. All she could think about was how incredibly sexy he was, from the way he moved to the fit of his pants on his thighs, his jacket on his shoulders. The kiss didn't help. She wanted more.

Not convenient.

"What are you thinking about, Kylie?" he said as he waited for her on the landing.

"Would you believe *Little Red Riding Hood*?"

"If it was the truth."

She had no intention of telling him the truth, but she didn't want to lie, either. "I did manage to get some work done today. Did you?"

"Not sure I had any real work to do."

They continued down the hall to her apartment.

"Where did you get the name Morwenna Mills?" Russ asked.

"Mills is a family name on my mother's side. It's Welsh, and Morwenna is derived from a Cornish saint, Morwen. Some say Morwenna means *sea wave*. I like that, even if I live on a river instead of the sea. The name is often associated with creativity and self-expression."

"That appealed to you, too."

She nodded, taking out her keys. "And I just liked the name. I didn't mean to send you on some kind of grand chase. I know you have better things to do. Are you annoyed I didn't tell you about Morwenna?"

"Intrigued."

Not the answer she'd expected. "Then I'm glad we talked, so you can be intrigued no more."

"I don't think that's going to happen."

"I'd like to hold off on telling anyone else until after the class on Saturday. I don't want to be a distraction. But I will tell people."

"That's your choice. You can trust me."

"And Marty."

"Marty's a bartender. He's even more trustworthy than I am." Russ watched her unlock her door. "I have to go back to LA tomorrow."

"You'll be back here with Daphne for her class?"

"On Friday. That's the plan."

"Well, I'll see you then, I guess. Good night." Kylie left the key in the door and turned to him abruptly, touching his hand, kissing him on the cheek. "I do trust you."

He took her hand into his, pulled her closer. This time, when his mouth found hers, their kiss wasn't quick or light. Kylie slipped her free arm around him, inhaling sharply at the feel of the hard muscles in his back—and in so doing, managed to deepen their kiss. Heat spread through her, quickening her heartbeat, locking her into this moment. The months of deliberate solitude and constant work fell away.

Russ let go of her hand, swept his arms around her and lifted her off her feet. "Damn," he whispered, kissing her again.

She wanted to touch him everywhere, have him do

the same to her. Images and sensations flooded her as she responded to the wet heat of their kiss, the wet heat at her very core.

Then it was out. The thought, the question. She couldn't stop it.

"Do you think Mark has security cameras in the hall?" she asked.

"What?"

And next thing, she had her feet back flat on the floor and was adjusting her jacket and shirt, askew from the mad kiss.

She waved a hand. "Never mind."

"Small towns," he muttered. "You know everyone."

"We could have..." She cleared her throat, realized her hair had fallen out of its clip. "Who knows where we were headed."

"I do. I was about to make love to you out here in the hall and kill your reputation in town, and who knows where else if there is a security camera and someone got hold—"

"Let's not go there."

He grinned. "Hell of a kiss." He pushed strands of hair out of her face. "Let's do that again soon."

"That would be nice."

"You bet." He started down the hall to his apartment. "Be good."

Kylie didn't breathe until she was inside, her door shut. She'd left a light on. A good thing, since she was only semicoherent.

Rumors, Olivia, a tour of the beautiful McCaffrey home, a meal with other people for a third day in a row, champagne... Morwenna...a kiss...

Not any kiss, either.

She couldn't deny she felt wobbly now.

She sank into her chair at her worktable and switched on her task lamp. "Don't look at me like that, Sherlock," she said, then laughed—at herself, her crazy day, everything. Russ Colton knew she was Morwenna Mills, and it hadn't changed a thing.

Well, of course not.

He was going back to his Beverly Hills law firm.

Kylie got out a fresh sketch pad and a perfectly sharpened drawing pencil. It was on the late side for her to work, but she didn't care.

After *Little Red Riding Hood*, she would do *Beauty and the Beast*.

She loved having that clarity. The decision was made.

And she had a sudden inspiration for the beast.

Tall, ex-military, scars…and a Hawaiian shirt, possibly one that included palm trees.

In the morning, Kylie looked at her quick sketches of her beast and threw them all away.

The scars could work, and he'd be tall, but right now…

She dug one out of the recycling bin and sighed at her scribbles. Right now he looked like a guy who'd wanted to make love to her until she'd mentioned security cameras.

He even had Russ Colton's thick brow.

And the shirt was a dead giveaway.

He needed to be Belle's beast, not her beast.

She tossed the sketch back into the bin and grabbed her car keys. She'd make a quick trip to the Swift River

Country Store to stock up on supplies. She felt a few days of hibernation and decompression coming on.

Russ's car wasn't in the parking lot. He'd be on his way by now, Kylie thought.

She didn't run into anyone she knew in town. When she got back to her apartment, she put a chicken in the oven, cut up a bunch of vegetables, threw together rice pilaf and washed salad greens.

She stood with the refrigerator door open and surveyed her afternoon's work, neatly wrapped and ready when she wanted it. She could get multiple meals out of her efforts.

But she didn't go straight to work. Instead she went out to her balcony. Warm from her marathon session in the kitchen, she welcomed the cool afternoon air. She pulled a clip out of her hair, remembering Russ's touch as she watched her two ducks swoop low over the river. They stopped short of the dam, skidding into the quiet, deep water of the millpond.

She'd called her agent and told her the jig was up on her keeping Morwenna secret. *How will the people there take it?*

I don't know.

Doesn't matter. I never thought you were long for that little town, anyway. I see you in a loft in Tribeca. You can afford it now.

I like my life here.

Trade-offs. I'm glad the cloak of mystery about Morwenna is finally off. We'll make plans.

Kylie put the clip in her jacket pocket and shook out her hair. She felt cooler, more in control of herself and her circumstances.

Plans.

To the increasing frustration of her agent and publisher, she'd turned down all invitations since the *Badgers of Middle Branch* had struck a chord with young readers. Book festivals, bookstores, libraries, professional conferences, meetings with Hollywood types—she always said no and stayed home and worked. In Morwenna's early days, she'd attended a conference under her own name and hung out with her illustrator friends, but she'd felt uncomfortable with her secret identity. She hadn't attended a conference since.

Should I call you Morwenna now?

Russ hadn't seemed taken aback by her alter ego. He had to have dealt with real, dangerous treachery in his navy days, and with more volatile secrets than hers.

Kylie licked her lips, as if he had kissed her seconds ago instead of last night.

Or perhaps she'd kissed him. One of those chicken-and-egg things, maybe.

But her attempt at lightheartedness didn't quite take hold. She'd put her love life on hold when she'd moved to Knights Bridge. Not that it'd been rocking and rolling before that. Her Red Sox game with the irritable carpenter had been her one attempt at a date. It had been such a disaster, she'd been quite content putting off romance until she felt more settled and secure.

Could she find a way to have a man in her life, with her work, her quirks?

She didn't know, but she was definitely attracted to one Russ Colton.

She went back inside, made tea and returned to her worktable. She couldn't wait to crawl into her creative cocoon. She liked it there, and if her attempt at a beast had been premature, she was ready to settle on her vision of Little Red Riding Hood's wolf.

Sixteen

Russ got into LAX in the middle of the afternoon and was tired enough to think he'd misread the text he received on the Jetway.

I'm here. I'll pick you up at baggage claim. I'm in your Rover.

It was Daphne Stewart's number. Russ adjusted his duffel bag on his shoulder. Why the hell was Daphne in his Rover, meeting him at the busy Los Angeles airport?

He got out of the Jetway and texted her. On my way.

Ten minutes later, he pulled open the passenger door of his Land Rover and spoke to Daphne across the seat. "I'll drive," he said, tossing his bag in back.

"You've been on a plane all day."

"Exactly. I'm frayed. I can't handle sitting while you drive." He jerked a thumb at her. "Out, Daphne."

She rolled her eyes. "All right, all right." She shifted into Neutral and pulled on the emergency brake. "Marty didn't tell me it was a standard transmission. I'd have worn driving gloves. I've ruined my manicure." She got out and came around to the passenger seat. "This thing hurts my back. Marty said it would."

Russ ignored her and took her place behind the wheel. A day on a plane after losing his mind and kissing Kylie Shaw/Morwenna Mills, and now Daphne Stewart driving his Rover. No wonder he was tense.

"Marty had to work," she said, buckling up. "I was going to hire you a car, but I bullied your brother into letting me drive the Rover. So kill me, not him."

"Okay."

She settled back. She wore flowered leggings with a long, dark red top, flat sandals and a ton of jewelry. "It's a great vehicle. Very masculine. Reminds me of a Jeep my boyfriend had when I was a teenager. We'd go mud-bogging. That's when you drive through mud off road."

Russ knew what mud-bogging was. "You were a teenager, and you weren't in the city. Did you drive straight here from the bar?"

"I didn't go joy-riding, if that's what you're asking. I did stop at Sawyer & Sawyer, but it's practically on the way."

"Why did you stop there?"

"I had to sign something." She waved a hand, dismissive. "The receptionist offered me tea. What's her name?"

"Julie."

"Julie, right. Tea. I don't think she believed I had legitimate business. She was humoring me. Offering me tea means I'm a valued client but also a pest."

Russ grinned at her. "I'll be damned, Daphne. You are more perceptive than I gave you credit for."

"You know I'm in my prime as a costume designer,

don't you? I'm not some washed-up, lonely diva in late middle age. I didn't agree to do this master class to prove anything—to you or to anyone else."

"Who are you trying to convince?"

"No one. I don't give a damn what anyone else thinks. I don't need confirmation that I still matter. I have more work than I can possibly handle."

"Did you have tea?"

"No. Bastard."

She loved being teased, Russ thought, softening. The attention, the banter—the chance not to take herself, or be taken, too seriously. "Julie will be running Sawyer & Sawyer in five years."

"Three." Daphne twitched in her seat, as if she couldn't get comfortable. "It will be fun having you escort me to Knights Bridge now that I've talked myself out of weaseling out of going."

Russ made no comment. Traffic wasn't too bad, but it wasn't Knights Bridge.

"I'm going to need a massage after sitting in these horrible seats this long. I've hired a car for us for our flight on Friday. I'm looking forward to staying at the Farm at Carriage Hill. Will my room have a four-poster bed? I've always wanted to sleep in one. No canopy. That would make me claustrophobic."

Russ looked at her as if she'd sprouted wings. "A four-poster— Daphne, what are you talking about?"

"Do you know what a four-poster bed is?"

He gave her a curt nod.

"But you don't care," she said.

"My point."

"When I lived in Knights Bridge, that house was a wreck."

"It's not a wreck anymore," Russ said. "You can take the loft apartment at Moss Hill if you decide you don't want to stay there."

"I'd have to cook my own breakfast. I prefer to stay in separate quarters from where I'll be giving the class. It's three hours, you know. Ninety minutes in the morning and ninety minutes in the afternoon. We break for lunch. Ruby and Ava are working me to death."

The three-hour time frame had been Daphne's idea, but Russ chose not to remind her.

"And Moss Hill has ghosts I don't care to meet," she said, her tone quiet, serious. She sighed and stared out at the multiple lanes of traffic. "Old George—my great-great-grandfather—built the mill with his brother-in-law, the husband of his wife's sister. He—the brother-in-law—bought George out after a few years. Or so the story goes. By all accounts they were good men. They were benefactors in the area." Daphne was silent a moment. "But I don't want to think about the past."

Russ slowed, edging into the right lane for his upcoming exit. It was dinnertime in Knights Bridge. Was Kylie eating alone with Sherlock Badger? He glanced at Daphne. "You're in over your head with the O'Dunn twins, aren't you?"

"They appealed to the girl I used to be, with all her vulnerabilities, and to my better self, maybe—the experienced costume designer who wants to help those with the same hopes and dreams I had when I lived in Knights Bridge. I got caught up in their enthusiasm for all things film and theater."

"You were flattered by their interest in you."

"Their respect for me, too," she said frankly. She swung around at him. "I'm not taking any money for this class, you know, and I'm paying my own expenses."

"That's decent of you," Russ said.

"It's a few days. And I've wanted to go back to Knights Bridge since my whirlwind visit in September. Or I thought I did. I can't explain..." She turned back to her window. "I can do the class. It's not the problem. It's this theater that's got me tied up in knots. We'd be building it from the ground up. Ava and Ruby say Moss Hill is a perfect space, but there's so much to consider—and we don't know if it's available. The owner might have other ideas. Plus, it's new. It must be expensive, at least by Knights Bridge standards."

Russ could see Daphne had been going over the pros and cons in her own mind. A penchant for French martinis aside, she was no one's fool when it came to business. "Starting a theater, even a small one, would be a real commitment," he said.

"Ruby and Ava—you'd think I'd be inured to wild dreams, living and working out here."

"But you got caught up in this one."

"A small-town community-based theater." Daphne shuddered, smoothing her hands over her thighs as if she'd seen a bunch of wrinkles in her top. "I don't know what I was thinking. I'm afraid I led them on about my interest, my commitment."

"Nothing like a reality check," Russ said, easing on to their exit.

She shot him a look. "Are you suggesting that in reality I'm actually greedy and selfish?"

"I'm saying maybe you tuned into Ava and Ruby's hopes and dreams instead of your own."

"I deluded myself, in other words, and them, and now there's no graceful way out of it." She groaned, throwing up her hands. "I'm sorry. I'm getting myself worked up and taking it out on you. Ava and Ruby are operating on a wing and a prayer. They haven't laid the groundwork for a theater in Knights Bridge. Community support has to be there. It just won't work, Russ. I can feel it in my bones."

"Then tell them. They could be getting cold feet about this theater, too."

"It's not cold feet. It's a frank assessment of the chances of success."

Russ didn't want to argue with her. He wanted a beer, tacos and bed. "My point is," he said, keeping any edge out of his voice, "maybe Ava and Ruby keep pursuing this thing because they don't want to disappoint you, and here you are, worrying about disappointing them. You can handle this without upsetting them or doing something you don't want to do. You care about them, and you're enjoying helping them. Advise them from a stool at Marty's or a lounge chair by your pool." He navigated the maze of streets that she'd called home for forty years. "That's what you want to do, isn't it?"

She gave him a cool look. "You're very sure of yourself. Quite the know-it-all, in fact."

"You're annoyed because I'm right."

"A children's theater would be a wonderful legacy. Maybe I'll reconsider."

He could tell he'd gotten to her. "They can hang your portrait in the Moss Hill lobby with the straw-hat collection. Your great-great-grandfather gets the library and you—"

"Just stop."

Russ grinned. "There's a hat display at the library, too. Have you ever designed costumes with straw hats?"

"A few. I remember meeting elderly women in Knights Bridge who'd been home workers in the latter years of the straw-hat industry. That was a tough job. Not everything was done in the factory. To think Moss Hill has a new lease on life..." She trailed off, staring out at the residential street as if reminding herself she was in Southern California and it wasn't forty years ago in Knights Bridge. "I can donate money for a theater. I don't have to be directly involved."

"Great. You can retire to Orcas Island or stay in Hollywood and go to lunch at the Polo Lounge with your friends."

"I hear condescension and disdain in your voice, Mr. Colton."

He gave an exaggerated yawn. "I'd have to be more interested in your dilemma for that."

"You really are a bastard," she said with a laugh. "My dilemma doesn't interest you?"

"Let's just say it's not eliciting a lot of sympathy from me."

"You mean none."

"Correct."

"By the way, you can relax. I won't talk all the way to Knights Bridge. I'm getting it out of my system now."

"Good." He turned onto her street, pulled up to her sunshine-yellow bungalow. "By the way, do you know many people who take pseudonyms?"

"Not as many as I used to. Why?"

"I was thinking about how Debbie Sanderson became Daphne Stewart." Which was true. But he'd also been thinking about how Kylie Shaw had become Morwenna Mills. "Never mind. Did you see Julius and Loretta before they headed to La Jolla?"

"I did. I'm starting to feel a little lost." She shifted to open her door but frowned at him, narrowing her green eyes. "There's something…" She bit her lower lip. "I'm not going to lose you, too, am I?"

"You're a good friend, Daphne."

"Damn. Julius and Loretta. Now you and…it's a woman, isn't it? You've met someone?" But when Russ didn't answer, Daphne swore under her breath and pushed open her door. "At this rate I'm going to have to join the garden club."

After he dropped Daphne off, Russ drove straight to Marty's Bar. It was early, but his brother was working, cleaning up and prepping while it was quiet. He dumped a bucket of ice into a container behind the bar and stood straight. "Russ. Brother. You look as if you've been on a plane all day. What are you drinking?"

"Irish whiskey. Pick one." He settled on a stool at the empty bar. "You let Daphne drive my Rover."

"She stole your keys when I had my back turned. I swear."

It was total BS. Marty's sense of humor. "I wouldn't put it past her," Russ said.

His brother got rid of his ice bucket and grabbed a bottle of Redbreast and a glass, his movements quick, sure. "She said driving your Rover was on her bucket

list. I don't believe she has a bucket list, but I went with
it. How was Knights Bridge?"

"Small."

"Pretty women?"

"A few." Russ immediately pictured Kylie, her translucent skin, the desire in her eyes when he'd kissed her.
Kissing her might not have been one of his smarter
moves, since it pulled them both deeper into something
that seemed totally impossible, but he had no regrets.
He pushed the image aside, or tried to, and focused on
his brother. "What have you been up to?"

"I holed up and worked on my screenplay today. I'm
in the zone."

"Is it a movie I'd want to see?"

"You bet."

"Even if it wasn't, I'd go because you wrote the
script."

"You'd go because of the red-carpet treatment."
Marty poured the Redbreast. "Not that screenwriters
get the red carpet, but in my fantasies we would. The
Colton brothers." He pushed the whiskey across the bar
to Russ. "Right, Russ?"

Russ raised his glass. "To the Colton brothers."

Marty tipped two knuckles onto Russ's glass.
"Cheers, brother." He got a distant look, one Russ hadn't
seen in his older brother in a while. "That was my last
thought, you know."

"Marty…"

"When I knew the helicopter was going down, I
thought of you and me, a couple of army brats. I didn't
want you to be sad because we'd all died. Dad, Mom,
me. I didn't want our deaths to change you. My last

thought…" Marty blew out a breath. "It's all good, brother. All good. That was it. What I expected to be my last thought in this mortal world."

"Damn, Marty."

"Yeah. Then I lived through the damn thing, and look at me now. Anyway, I don't know where that came from. Bitch of a last thought. You know? Thinking about my baby brother instead of the buxom girl back home." Marty put the Redbreast back on its shelf. "New subject. Are you planning to stay at this law firm?"

Russ welcomed the change in subject, too, but he'd have talked if Marty wanted to talk. Always. Which his brother knew. "It's a good job. Easy. But I haven't decided."

"Don't tell Daphne. Hell, she'd hate being easy." Marty unloaded glasses from a tray, lining them up on a shelf where he could reach them. "You always said you wanted to be your own boss after the navy."

"A steady paycheck has a certain appeal."

"I don't want you doing something you hate because you're worried about me."

"I could do something I hate for a lot of worse reasons, Marty." Russ tried his whiskey. Triple-distilled, no peat, smooth. Marty had picked a good one. "But I don't hate my work."

"You could put out your own shingle in LA. You like it up here?"

"I like it fine. No complaints."

"That takes care of your work life. Your romantic life—"

Russ shook his head. "Not going there. Can you put in an order of fish tacos for me?"

"It's on its way." Marty finished unloading the glasses. "You got burned by a woman late in your days in the navy." He held up a hand. "I know this to be the case, because I'm your big brother and I know things, not because you told me."

"She told you."

"*Relished* telling me. She looked me up in Phoenix. She knew I didn't like her and wanted to rub it in that she'd dumped you."

"It was a mutual parting of ways."

"Best kind." Clearly Marty believed his own version. "No residual effect on you?"

"None."

Marty snorted in disbelief, but he had another customer and moved to the other end of the bar. Russ settled in with his whiskey. His tacos arrived, but he wasn't that hungry. He could hear Marty laughing with the customer, a guy in his fifties or sixties, apparently another aspiring screenwriter.

When he returned, Marty put the empty glasses tray away under the bar somewhere. "Trying to save me when I don't need saving gets in the way of saying yes to opportunities and possibilities for yourself."

"I don't know what you just said, Marty, but I'm not trying to save you."

But Marty was in a serious mood. "I know you want to be there for me, and I appreciate that, but not at the expense of doing what's right for you and your life."

"You've sacrificed and suffered a lot," Russ said, picking up one of the tacos.

"I didn't sacrifice anything. I have suffered, though."

"You still do suffer, Marty."

He shrugged, touching his left arm, broken in the crash—one of his lesser injuries. "Not as much. Being here helps. I don't think about the pain. I get lost in what I'm doing. The work here."

"You love it," Russ said.

"Yeah. I barely survived a bad helicopter crash that killed our father and traumatized our mother, even if she won't admit it. I had a long, difficult recovery. It was a life-changing, utterly negative, lousy thing to have happen, but there was no sacrifice involved. You were the one who got shot at on behalf of our country. I've never paid your bills. I pay my own bills, and I've said yes to possibilities and opportunities even if they haven't all said yes back. I don't know if they ever will, but I'm happy." Marty breathed, hit the bar with his palm and grinned. "So there."

"So there," Russ said with a smile.

"I don't think I've said that much at one time in ten years."

"It's because I'm eating a taco and couldn't interrupt you." Russ picked up his second taco. Hungrier than he thought, maybe. "Do you have a woman in your life?"

"Other than Daphne, you mean?"

"Oh, man. I never even thought that. Hell, Marty.

"You can relax. I'm not Daphne's or anyone else's boy-toy. She gives me advice, even when I don't want it. She thinks I'm like her and will like working behind the scenes. Says to ditch the acting auditions. She's offered to read my scripts, but I can tell she expects me to know I'm supposed to say no, thanks."

"Smart man," Russ said.

"It's a good story if I do say so myself."

"Do you want me to read it?"

"Hell, no. It's a thriller. You'll think the tough guy is based on you." Marty pointed at Russ's glass. "Another whiskey?"

Russ shook his head. "One's good. Julius is in La Jolla. I'll have the place to myself."

"His daughter—the one buying his house—has been in with him a few times. She's a gin connoisseur. I know you're not interested, but…" Marty rubbed the back of his neck. "He'd kill me?"

"Slowly and painfully."

Marty laughed and grabbed Russ's empty glass. "No more worrying about me, brother. Do your own thing and let me do mine."

"As if I could stop you."

"Now you're getting the picture."

Russ ate half of his second taco and left the rest. Marty wanted desperately to succeed in a business that often chewed people up and spit them out, including the best. But it wasn't just success he was after. It was doing the work, being here in Hollywood, seeing what he could accomplish. Russ got it, intellectually, but he couldn't get past his fear that Marty was going to get hurt.

Another hard, bad landing.

"Russ, here's what I know." Marty rubbed the back of his neck again, near another of the places that had taken a beating in the helicopter crash. "I know if I'd stayed in Phoenix, I'd have failed at working in Hollywood—because I'd never be here, I'd never have tried."

"You don't sleep," Russ said.

"I sleep odd hours when I'm into a script."

That wasn't all. Marty had coped with insomnia since the crash. He seldom talked about it. Russ respected his brother's privacy and appreciated his positive attitude—his ambitions, his dreams—but he worried. He wanted to do right by his only brother.

Marty sighed. "I'm saying I don't need your protection, Russ."

"You can damn well take care of yourself. Right, Marty. I get it."

"Not can. Am. I am taking care of myself."

"I know you are."

Russ meant it. Or maybe he didn't. He'd just spent the better part of a day on a plane dreaming about making love to a woman who drew cute badgers for a living. Maybe he didn't know what the hell he meant.

"When do you head east again?" Marty asked.

"Thursday red-eye, arriving early Friday morning." Russ got to his feet. "I'll see you again before I leave."

He paid for his whiskey and said good-night to his brother.

Russ stopped at Sawyer & Sawyer's expensive, elegant offices in Beverly Hills, the lights still on at six-thirty. He didn't stay long. Julie, the young, very smart receptionist, was packing up for the evening and vowed she hadn't meant to be patronizing when she'd offered Daphne tea. Russ told her to put it out of her mind. Daphne was looking for distractions, anything to keep her from thinking about Knights Bridge. That was why she'd talked Marty into letting her pick Russ up in the Rover.

He checked mail and his inbox and lined up real work he needed to get to.

Fifteen minutes, and he was back in his Rover. It was a quick drive to Julius's place, but traffic was miserable. The house was quiet, but it felt as if Julius had stepped out for the evening instead of a few days. Russ found a bottle of Loretta's sparkling water in the refrigerator and took a glass out to the deck.

The bright city lights drowned out the stars. It was a warm evening, warmer than Knights Bridge would be tonight. He could see Kylie out on her balcony, looking at the stunning night sky. She was visual, a woman who noticed everything, took it all in—sometimes, he suspected, getting overwhelmed and needing to withdraw, tuck herself at her worktable with her little stuffed badger.

Russ drank some of the water. It hit the spot after hours in a dry plane and the whiskey.

There'd been no sparkling water on the menu at Smith's.

He couldn't hear a river flowing over a nineteenth-century dam, and he didn't have a blue-eyed blonde across the hall. He could see the shock on her face when she'd spotted him in the Moss Hill meeting room on Sunday. She'd taken one look at him and gotten moving.

A quick thinker, Kylie Shaw/Morwenna Mills.

He could be a rigid SOB. Everyone told him so. He worked hard. Not much play but played hard when he did play. Kylie needed to cut loose.

Marty was having a hell of a time. Why worry about him? Because he didn't have a career and a pension?

Because I wasn't in the helo that day.

His father, a retired army helicopter pilot, had been at the controls. He'd died on impact. His passengers—his wife and their older son—had survived. Janet Colton had sustained minor physical injuries, but the emotional trauma of her ordeal had changed her. She'd bought a house in Scottsdale and had little to do with her sons. She wasn't unpleasant, just remote.

Marty had suffered multiple broken bones and lacerations. Russ had tried to be there for his brother during those tough, miserable weeks—months—in rehab, but it wasn't easy, given the demands of his navy career, and Marty wouldn't hear of him quitting. *You have a future in the navy, Russ. You can't abandon it because of me. I won't allow it.*

Marty's long recovery had scuttled his plans to get his MBA and to become a helicopter pilot himself, flying volunteer rescue missions. He'd gotten into product design instead, but he'd changed jobs frequently, never fully committed to—or happy—in his backup profession. It wasn't the work. He knew great people in his field and it paid well. It was that he wanted something else, and he'd finally realized he needed to do it—burn the boats, so to speak, and move to Hollywood.

Russ finished his water, remembering the first time he'd walked into the hospital and had seen his older brother, broken, uncertain he had the willpower to recover.

I should have died with Dad.

No, Marty.

They say it was mechanical failure, but I don't care what went wrong. It's done.

Dad would have done anything to protect you.

Go away.

Russ went inside the dark, quiet house. He'd drunk half the sparkling water. Not his thing.

He pictured himself drinking champagne on Elly O'Dunn's back porch, with Kylie taking it all in—the people, the dogs, the goats, the gardens. Him. Guessing what he knew about her.

He hadn't lied when he'd told her he'd been intrigued by her dual identities.

By her.

He headed upstairs to his borrowed room. Growing up with a father in the army and then a decade of his own in the navy, he was accustomed to moving, keeping his possessions limited to the essentials, but he wondered what it would be like to have a place of his own.

It was the whiskey and the long flight talking.

He would spend tomorrow catching up on his non-Daphne work. He debated getting someone else to escort her east, but he'd signed up for the job.

He'd see it through.

Seventeen

Daphne turned on the overhead light in her studio. Most of the time she relied on task lighting, but not tonight. She switched on her desk lamp, floor lamp and table lamp. Tonight, she thought, she wanted as much light as possible.

She opened the French doors, letting in the smell of her roses.

Julius was a great guy to have in her corner and a friend, but Russ was something else altogether. She had to admit she'd wanted to preen a bit when she'd picked him up at the airport. He was good-looking, not classically handsome but a man with a strong presence. Sexy. Confident. He knew who he was, but she knew him well enough now to see that sometimes he could get very rooted in that self-knowledge, to the point of rigidity.

He'd looked faintly impatient and annoyed when he'd pulled open the passenger door to his Rover.

"Not faintly," Daphne said with a laugh.

He'd made no secret of his response to finding her behind the wheel of his beloved Land Rover. That only made him sexier.

Probably not the most evolved thought she'd ever had, but there it was.

She'd noticed how he'd carried his duffel bag. No effort.

Marty was sexy and knew himself, too, in a more tortured way.

Daphne fought a yawn. She couldn't help herself. She felt like an overstimulated toddler. She'd been enthusiastic about the class in February. The closer she got to the day and to Knights Bridge, the more butterflies she felt.

She stood at her large, counter-height worktable, set up in front of the windows and French doors to take advantage of the views of the patio, pool and her roses.

She'd loved roses as a little girl.

It was one hobby her father hadn't minded. Proper, elegant girls and young women could appreciate roses. He'd wanted her to be like his grandmother, the beautiful daughter-in-law of the late, great George Sanderson. Daphne had a photo of just the two of them—her great-great-grandfather in his formal Victorian suit, her great-grandmother in her graceful Edwardian dress.

No photos of the rest of her family. Her feckless grandfather. Her mother, living in her own world, unable and unwilling to deal with her circumstances—to protect her only daughter.

Her father. Handsome, tortured, alcoholic and mean.

Daphne had taken only the one photo with her when she'd fled her childhood home for Knights Bridge. She'd kept it with her on her long trip across the country. She'd bought a frame for it, and now it was on the dresser in the guest room. It might have been a vintage photograph she'd picked up in an antiques store. She couldn't see herself or her father in the faces of her long-dead relatives.

She liked to believe her great-grandmother had tended her own roses, something she herself loved. She'd take books out of the library on roses and study them, then apply what she learned to the three rose-bushes in her backyard. She was painstaking, exact. She'd lose herself in the work. She was convinced now, in hindsight, that her work with roses had helped her with her work in costume design.

Her father had grabbed her by the wrist one day, when she was about thirteen. *What did you do to yourself?*

I caught a thorn when I was working on the roses.

Why were you working on the roses?

Because they needed trimming.

Trimming? What are you talking about? Leave the roses to the gardeners.

But there were no gardeners.

He'd been drunk, living in the past—before the Depression, bad luck and entitlement had done in the last of the Sanderson money. Before alcoholism had robbed him of his ambition, self-restraint and purpose.

Your father doesn't mean to hit you, Debbie.

She shut her eyes, smelling the roses here in her home in Hollywood Hills. They weren't meant as an homage to her past, a reminder of her roots. She loved roses and most days could sit here, looking out at them, smelling them, and not think about her father at all.

In the morning, after toast and about a gallon of coffee, since she hadn't slept well, if at all, Daphne dragged her suitcase out of the hall closet into her bedroom, plopped it on her bed and packed for Knights Bridge.

"Hell," she muttered. "I'm going."

She decided against sequins and such for her Saturday class and settled on a black jumpsuit—her own design—with Manolo Blahnik flats, gold jewelry, a diamond watch and a colorful Hermes scarf. She'd make a statement while looking professional.

Satisfied, she threw in jeans, a couple of simple tops, walking shoes and wool socks. Damned if she was showing up in New England in April without wool socks. She remembered seeing daffodils covered in snow. It could happen, although the forecast for the next few days was promising—in the sixties, zero chance of precipitation of any kind.

She wheeled her suitcase to the entry and left it by the front door.

Done.

She changed into a cute retro swimsuit she'd designed for herself and a cover-up and was on her way to the pool when her doorbell rang. Russ? The mailman? Not Julius or Loretta. They were in La Jolla. Annoying, but there it was. She had friends but not many who'd ring her doorbell on what ostensibly was a work day.

She opened her front door to Noah Kendrick and Phoebe O'Dunn. A San Diego high-tech billionaire and his Knights Bridge librarian fiancée, two lovely people who, in a way, were responsible for Daphne boarding a flight for Boston tonight. Phoebe was the one who'd discovered Debbie Sanderson's secret attic room in the Knights Bridge town library.

Daphne couldn't help but smile as she greeted them. "Please, come in."

"We won't stay long," Phoebe said, stepping inside. "We're driving to San Diego from the winery and wanted to stop by and wish you luck in Knights Bridge."

"Thank you," Daphne said, genuinely taken aback.

Noah eased into the small entry behind Phoebe. "We're sorry we can't be there."

"Well, it's not like you need a class in costume design." Daphne motioned toward the back of the house. "Won't you have a seat on the patio, stay for coffee?"

Phoebe shook her head. "We don't want to take up your time, and we have to run. We wanted to be there on Saturday to support my sisters, too. Ava and Ruby are so excited about this weekend. They remind me of my mother. Always a million different things going on at once, all of which they're confident they can handle with ease—and usually do. It's great, such energy and enthusiasm."

"Contagious," Daphne said, smiling, feeling slightly guilty at her uncharitable thoughts toward Phoebe's twin younger sisters during her tossing and turning overnight. She'd splashed cold water on her face and scolded her reflection in the mirror for sounding like her father. "I'm looking forward to seeing Ava and Ruby. We've talked on the phone and emailed over the winter, but it's not the same as seeing them face-to-face."

"So true," Phoebe said. She had long, softly curling auburn hair and kind turquoise eyes—her sensitive, quiet nature a contrast to her more exuberant younger sisters. Noah, lithe and fair, moved closer to her. She hooked her arm into his arm, color rising in her cheeks.

"We credit you for bringing us together, Daphne. I hope my finding your attic room has brought you more positives than it has—" she hesitated "—than it has negatives."

"You mean did it open a big can of squirmy, nasty worms?" Daphne laughed. "Well, it did, but it needed opening. I'm glad my neurotic ways did some good, though. You two look happy as clams."

"We'll be in Knights Bridge again soon," Noah said.

Phoebe flushed. "I'm going to be talking to my mother about wedding plans."

"You're not having your wedding at her place with the goats, are you?" Daphne waved a hand. "Sorry. I shouldn't have said that."

Noah laughed. "It would be fun. Imagine Julius and Loretta."

"I am," Daphne said.

"We're having it at the winery," Phoebe said. "Trust me, my mother will be hugely relieved."

Of that, Daphne had no doubt, given Noah Kendrick's circle of friends, colleagues and acquaintances who would expect to be invited to his wedding.

"And of course we hope you can be there," Phoebe added.

"I'm so glad. I wouldn't miss it."

After they left, Daphne went out to the pool. She'd order herself a nice lunch and have it delivered, and that evening, she'd board a plane with Russ Colton. Life could be worse, even if he was flying coach and she was flying first class.

Eighteen

Kylie stayed in her fairy-tale world until Thursday afternoon, with limited breaks for walks, stretching and one torturous session with weights in the exercise room. She saw no people, but she did talk to her sister once, for five minutes, because any longer and Lila wouldn't just be suspicious Kylie was holding back, she'd know. And Kylie wasn't ready to tell her sister about Morwenna, and she was too raw and uncertain about her reaction to Russ to even breathe that a Beverly Hills private investigator had found her out. Lila would want all the details of why Kylie was telling her about Morwenna now.

Anyway, Lila was deep into her veterinary studies and didn't need distractions right now, either.

Best to hold off, Kylie thought as she headed outside to her bicycle. As far she knew, Russ hadn't told anyone about Morwenna. She trusted he wouldn't, but she also knew the time had come to let the word out. She had a list of people she needed to tell herself, before they heard through other means.

She snapped on her helmet and climbed onto her bike, lured by the spring sunshine and warm temperatures to take a good, long ride up the river. She needed some serious aerobic activity. Short walks, stretching and light free weights were great, but she could feel her hours at her worktable in every muscle in her body. She'd lost herself in her work, sketching ideas for dense woods, a greedy, clever wolf and a trusting girl yearning for adventure as she set off through the woods to visit her grandmother.

The photos Kylie had taken on her phone out past the Farm at Carriage Hill had helped solidify her thinking, and helped with light and unexpected details—such as dead lower branches on evergreens, perfect for *Little Red Riding Hood*'s dense, spooky forest. Most of her photos were of maple trees and stone walls. She wouldn't take photos of Olivia and Dylan's antique house without permission.

"Imagine if Russ had caught me snapping pictures of the McCaffreys' property," Kylie said aloud as she set off on her bike. But she'd never do such a thing, and she didn't blame him for wondering what she'd been up to—even without knowing she'd taken pictures of anything out on Carriage Hill Road.

She didn't need photos of Dylan and Olivia's 1803 house. She had a concept she liked for the house where Little Red Riding Hood's grandmother met her untimely fate.

Kylie pushed aside her noisy thoughts and focused on the sunlit river, the clear, coppery water coursing over rocks and boulders, a tree hanging by a few thready roots to a washed-out section of the bank.

She came to the house she'd rented from July until a few weeks ago.

She sighed, missing this place, as much as she loved her loft apartment at Moss Hill.

She jumped off her bike, leaning it against a stone wall that ran in front of the house. She faced the river across the road, the deciduous trees leafing out, creating dappled shade on the shallow water and chunks of granite. She'd loved watching the changes in the landscape during her months living out here, from the long, hot days of summer to the short, frigid days of winter. She'd never paid such close attention to light as she had during her retreat in this simple, lovely riverside house.

I hate to sell the place, Kylie, but there's no point holding on to it.

Intellectually, Kylie understood. She'd never intended to fall in love with Knights Bridge, or her friend's house.

Emotionally, she didn't want to give up the house. She'd joked with her friend that she should get to approve the buyer. Her friend had laughed.

Decent of her, Kylie thought with a smile as she walked across the front yard above the stone wall, the spring grass soft under her feet. Painters would be here soon. They'd paint all the interior walls and woodwork Dover White, fresh and neutral for the upcoming open house. The front door would get a fresh coat of deep yellow paint, a cheerful shade her friend was convinced would aid in a quick sale.

Kylie stood on the simple stone steps and touched the brass front-door latch. Most of the time she'd used the side door. She still had a key, in case her friend needed her help in any way, but she didn't go inside.

She hoped a family would buy the house. She could envision children, dogs, cats, a clothesline with sheets fluttering in the breeze.

She jumped down to the stone walk and took it to the driveway. But as she headed to her bike, she noticed a For Sale sign by the mailbox and gasped in shock. It didn't matter that she'd known this would happen. She'd moved to Moss Hill for that reason—her rented house was going on the market because its owner had moved to Iowa and had no use for it. But she'd thought it wouldn't happen until after the painters had finished, and they hadn't started yet.

Fighting tears, Kylie ran to her bike, grabbed her helmet and put it on. She could afford to buy the house, but she'd been through all that in her head. She still didn't know how long she would stay in Knights Bridge. She'd moved into her apartment in Moss Hill to get through the last of her tight deadlines and give herself as much time as she needed to figure out what was next, with no pressure.

An unfamiliar truck rolled to a stop on the road in front of her. At first she thought it was someone asking for directions, but she recognized the driver—Travis Bowman, the carpenter who'd taken her to the Red Sox game last summer.

He waved to her as he got out of the truck. He was a big man in his early thirties, with short-cropped dark hair and a casual, friendly manner, despite the chip on his shoulder. He'd been so burned out and negative on their day together that she'd left him early in the seventh inning and gone to visit her sister. She'd found her own way back to Knights Bridge. Travis hadn't asked her out again. Kylie didn't know if he'd gotten the message or she hadn't interested him.

"Hey, Kylie," he said as he came around the front of his truck to her. "Long time."

"Hi, Travis. Good to see you. I didn't know you were in town."

"Just passing through. You don't rent this place anymore? What happened?"

"I moved out last month. It's on the market."

"So I see."

"It's getting fresh paint, but might as well put up the For Sale sign in the meantime." Kylie heard the emotion in her voice but doubted Travis would, if only because he wouldn't be paying attention to anyone's emotions but his own.

"The Sloans and Mark Flanagan aren't involved?" he asked.

"I don't know. There's a lot of construction going on in town right now. I imagine they have their hands full. I don't think the owners need an architect, and it's a simple paint job—" She stopped, catching herself. Travis had worked briefly for Sloan & Sons. He'd left on his own, but she wasn't going to indulge any lingering grudges he might have, given his tendency to see the dark side of everything. She smiled at him as she held her bike, ready to be on her way. "How are you, Travis?"

He shrugged. "Great. I moved out to Syracuse to be closer to my kids. They're four and six now. My ex is there. I came back here for my uncle's funeral. Cancer. Where are you living?"

"Moss Hill. I'm on my way back there now."

"Meeting a friend?"

"As a matter of fact, I am. I promised Ava and Ruby O'Dunn I would take a look at the meeting room. They're setting up for an event this weekend."

Travis grinned at her. "You have friends in town now, Kylie?"

"Imagine that." She faked a laugh. His chronic negativity grated on her nerves. "I'm sorry to hear about your uncle. I should get rolling. See you around."

He didn't budge. "How do you like living at Moss Hill?"

"It's great."

"If I lived alone, I think I'd want to be closer to the village, but to each his own. Glad things worked out for you. Still illustrating children's books?"

She nodded, climbing onto her bike. The bit about meeting Ava and Ruby was an exaggeration, if not an outright lie. Ruby *had* invited her to stop in anytime today. Ava had arrived from New York, and Kylie had noticed them carrying various mounted Hollywood posters into the meeting room, in anticipation of Daphne Stewart's arrival.

"I love to read to my kids," Travis said. "They're into these badgers right now. Have you heard of them? *The Badgers of Middle Branch.* Middle Branch is a little town on a river in a valley. Reminds me of small towns in this area. Maybe Greenwich or Dana before they were flooded for Quabbin. Not that I remember them, of course, since I wasn't born then."

Kylie didn't breathe. She felt her grip tighten on her bike, automatically, a visceral self-defense reaction to Travis's words. It was no coincidence he'd brought up the Badgers. She said nothing. Let him tell her where he was headed with this one.

"It's okay, Kylie." He settled back on his heels, conversational, seemingly easygoing. "I know you're Morwenna Mills. I've known for a while."

"Let's talk at Moss Hill," she said.

"Hey, I'm not making you nervous, am I?" But he didn't wait for an answer. "I'm not after anything. Money, favors—nothing like that. Nothing at all, in fact. I swear. I know Morwenna's a secret."

"Travis..." Kylie made herself breathe. "I'm glad you and your kids enjoy the Badgers. I do, too, but I can't—I need to go."

"Sure, sure. I'll be off, too. Tell Mark I said hi. I don't know Ava and Ruby well. I drove past Moss Hill coming out here. I haven't been inside, but the place looks great. Mark and the Sloan boys are exacting bastards. Baby sister Heather Sloan, too. I'll say that for them. Screw up with them, and they'll hand you your head." He grinned suddenly. "In fact, I screwed up, and they did hand me my head. Learned my lesson. I didn't get fired—I quit first."

"No hard feelings, then?"

"None, at least not on my part. All of them—the Sloans and Mark, and Jess Flanagan, too—gave me more chances than I deserved. My ex had moved to Syracuse by then, and I was missing my kids and didn't realize how it was affecting me. I'm not making excuses. It's all water over the dam now, anyway. Good to see you, Kylie." He waited a moment, then grinned. "Morwenna."

Kylie waited for him to get back in his truck and

rattle up the road. She exhaled, her heart pounding, her hands clammy. A couple of weeks after their Red Sox game, Travis had run afoul of the Sloans, Justin in particular. She didn't know the details—she didn't *want* to know the details—but Travis had left Sloan & Sons voluntarily a week later. She'd never asked anyone if it had been a case of quit or be fired and hadn't heard anything in town. Travis wasn't from Knights Bridge. There was no reason for him to be a major subject of gossip.

In their day together in Boston, he'd never mentioned an ex-wife and children. Too painful, maybe? It could explain his negativity. She hoped he'd been truthful about getting on a more positive track and that venturing back to Knights Bridge wasn't causing a setback for him.

She started down the road, in the opposite direction he'd gone.

Was *Travis* responsible for the rumors about cut corners at Moss Hill?

Kylie debated calling Russ. She had his card. But why bother him with what amounted to speculation on her part? Even if Travis was the source of the rumors, there were no safety or legal issues with Moss Hill, and he was on his way back to Syracuse.

Thinking about Russ didn't help Kylie calm down after her encounter with Travis. For all she knew, Russ had decided not to accompany Daphne Stewart east, or he'd run into more urgent issues that required his attention.

But Kylie doubted that would be the case.

Whatever had bubbled up between her and Russ

early in the week might go flat once he was back in town, but he'd do his job.

He'd be here for Saturday.

Mark Flanagan's truck was the only vehicle at Moss Hill when Kylie cruised into the parking lot on her bike. She jumped off, left her bike and helmet on the rack and headed into the lobby of the main building, catching Mark coming out of the meeting room. He and Christopher Sloan had gone through the place. She was confident it was safe, but if she were putting on the first-ever event there, she'd want to know Travis Bowman was in town and potentially the source of the unfounded rumors.

She poked her head into the meeting room. "Mark, do you have a sec?"

He frowned at her. "What's on your mind, Kylie? You look as if something's troubling you. Is something wrong?"

"I wanted to let you know I ran into Travis Bowman just now, up at the house I rented."

"Travis? He's in town?"

She nodded. "I wasn't sure if you'd remember him—"

"Excellent carpenter with a bad attitude. What did he want?"

She'd decided while biking back to Moss Hill not to mention Travis's comment about Morwenna. Leaving out only that part, she related her encounter with him to Mark. "Do you think he's responsible for the rumors?" she asked.

"I can't say for certain—I don't have any more details than I did on Sunday when Ruby mentioned the rumors—but it wouldn't surprise me if Travis had a hand in them. It could be inadvertent on his part. He bad-mouths everyone and everything. Just how he's wired. It would be easy for his usual grousing to get turned into something more. I doubt he's trying to get anyone into trouble." Mark paused, studying Kylie. "He didn't give you any trouble, did he, Kylie?"

She shook her head. "I don't have a problem with him. He's just a negative guy."

"Justin didn't fire Travis. He quit. That much I know." Mark sighed heavily. "I'll talk to Justin in case I'm missing anything, but this is all making more sense. Thanks, Kylie. By the way, how's your apartment working out?"

They chatted amiably for a few more minutes. He was hiring a property manager and would start interviewing next week. He didn't like being a landlord, but that distaste was compensated for by how much he liked not having a landlord himself.

"I should get back," he said, nodding toward the meeting room. "Ruby and Maggie are stopping by soon to discuss refreshments for Saturday. Ava promised not to second-guess them. I'm not betting on that one."

Kylie laughed, feeling calmer and more centered as she headed up to her apartment.

There.

She'd told Mark, the main target of the unpleasant rumors. She didn't need to call Russ. She was off the hook—Mark could take it from here. Travis's mention of Morwenna was personal, and she didn't regard it as a veiled threat—more like his way of telling her he was in the know.

She eyed her cluttered worktable, a sign of a productive two days. She'd worked on paper and on computer, her version of *Little Red Riding Hood* taking shape not just in her mind and bits and pieces but as a whole story, a visual narrative.

Sherlock Badger watched her from his perch on her lamp. "I see you didn't clean up the place while I was out," she said, gathering scattered pencils and crayons.

But she didn't have the attention span for cleaning up, either.

She tossed the pencils and crayons in their appropriate bins, shut down her computer and went into the bathroom. She turned on the water in the tub. It was early for a bath, but she didn't care. New and architect-designed, the bathroom was energy-efficient, water-efficient and luxurious, with a separate tub and shower. Kylie had bought fluffy, oversize white towels and a spa robe, hung on a hook on the back of the door.

No one was around, but she closed the door, anyway.

She added a healthy scoop of the Farm at Carriage Hill lavender-scented goat's milk bath salts to the steaming water. The Swift River Country Store offered a limited quantity of Carriage Hill spa products, and she'd bought soap and bath gel on one of her trips to town.

A bath and cheese, fruit and vegetables for dinner… and champagne on the balcony, since she'd slipped a new bottle into her basket on her quick trip to town yesterday.

A perfect way to spend the rest of the day.

Except she couldn't drink an entire bottle of champagne herself, and she didn't feel like drinking—celebrating—alone.

"You could invite Travis to join you, since he knows about Morwenna and you won't have to clean."

Kylie groaned at her lame attempt at humor. She'd never had Travis to her rented house. They'd spent one day together. *Part* of one day. They'd never had a relationship. She'd been procrastinating, struggling with a concept, and he'd seemed like a nice enough guy—going out with him would be refreshing, fun.

That hadn't worked out, had it?

As she peeled off her biking clothes, she had a mad urge to book a flight somewhere. She could have champagne and take a luxurious bath in Paris or London or Amsterdam—or Hawaii. She'd never been to Hawaii.

She thought of Russ's palm-tree shirt and smiled.

She eased into the hot water, smelling the lavender, feeling the softness of the goat's milk against her skin. The muscles in her neck and shoulders ached from her work marathon. She shut her eyes, wondering what it would be like to take a bath with Russ…

We'd have to skip the lavender.

She laughed, hoping he didn't have telepathic skills and wasn't reading her mind right now. She would relax, have her bath, eat dinner, skip the champagne and go to bed early. She wanted to be up for tomorrow's sunrise. Daphne Stewart would give her master class and go back to Southern California—along with Russ Colton. After that, Kylie would tell people she worked under another name.

Then she would go on a trip.

Not Paris, she thought. Not this trip.
Paris would only remind her of her bad luck with men.

After walking up to the spring to catch the sunrise,
Kylie, feeling restless, took herself to breakfast in town.
Smith's was crowded with Sloans, a diplomat now retired to Knights Bridge, the ER doctor engaged to Clare
Morgan and several residents of Rivendell, the local
assisted-living facility, who were indulging a "hanker-
ing" for blueberry pancakes.

Kylie sat at the counter. It wasn't as isolated as her
usual corner booth. She ordered blue-cornmeal pancakes, sausage patties, coffee and fresh-squeezed orange juice. It was rare for her to have breakfast out,
but she loved it.

As she drank her coffee, she overheard the Sloans
mention Dylan McCaffrey and realized word was out
that he and Olivia were expecting a baby. Olivia's parents, Louise and Randy Frost, were en route to Hol-
land and, according to Chris Sloan, had promised to
celebrate on a canal trip in Amsterdam. Eric Sloan indicated he liked that idea.

When Chris finished his breakfast and headed out,
he stopped to say hi to Kylie. That he didn't mention
Travis Bowman either meant Mark hadn't told him
about his presence in town or Chris didn't consider it
a problem, either.

It was also possible Mark hadn't mentioned her name
when he'd told Chris.

Or Chris didn't want to trouble her about Travis
while she was eating pancakes.

Mind reading wasn't going to get her anywhere, she decided. Travis's past and any problems he had with the Sloans and Mark Flanagan were no longer her concern.

Clare Morgan and Logan Farrell said a quick hello as they headed out.

Eight-thirty in the morning and Smith's breakfast crowd was already thinning, just the seniors lingering over coffee and a discussion of various goings-on in town. Kylie wouldn't be surprised if a few of them showed up at Daphne's class.

She was mopping up a pool of pure maple syrup with the last of her pancakes when Russ Colton arrived with a petite, copper-haired woman who had to be Daphne Stewart. "This was an actual house when I lived in town," she said, taking off a lightweight leather jacket. "I didn't get here in September. Oh, my. Brings back memories." She pointed a red-tipped finger. "We'll take that booth there."

While she got settled, Russ eased between Kylie and the stool next to her. "I thought that was your bike outside," he said.

"The mud's a dead giveaway." She noticed he wore a canvas jacket over a denim shirt, dark cargo pants and trail shoes. He'd taken off sunglasses when he'd entered the restaurant. She smiled, acknowledging a slight weakness in her legs that she couldn't fairly attribute to her hike and bike ride. "Welcome back."

"Thanks."

"How was your flight?"

"Long. Daphne requested breakfast here. I'll get her settled at Carriage Hill."

"She'll love Carriage Hill," Kylie said.

But Russ made no comment, his eyes serious as he narrowed them on her. "Then I'll stop by Moss Hill and you can tell me about Travis Bowman."

"How—"

"To quote Ruby O'Dunn, Knights Bridge is a small town. People talk."

He joined Daphne in her booth.

Kylie paid for her breakfast and got out of there, glad she had ridden her bike to town. Not only did she have pancakes to burn off, she had her reaction to Russ Colton to get under control.

Nineteen

"I'm impressed you didn't bring the steamer trunk," Russ said as he set Daphne's bags—one she'd checked and a small one she'd carried on board—on the throw rug on the wide-plank floor of her bedroom at Carriage Hill. He'd offered to carry them. She hadn't asked. He didn't know if she hadn't thought to or he'd jumped the gun. Either way, he had to establish boundaries with her. Bad enough she regarded him as something of a bodyguard as well as an investigator, but he wasn't her damn manservant. He didn't mind carrying her bags, but he wasn't as loose with the parameters of his job as Julius obviously was, at least with her.

She'd gone into the room ahead of him. "You need to free yourself of your preconceived notions about me," she said, peeking out a window overlooking the Quabbin side of the yard.

"How hard was it to get everything in these two bags?"

"Almost impossible. I had to leave my sequin Oscars gown at home. I packed some horrible little roll-up jumpsuit thing that promises not to wrinkle. I can't see myself ironing, but I can't see anyone else here ironing, either." She turned to him, her green eyes bright and alert despite the overnight flight. "You wouldn't consider—"

"No, Daphne. I'm not ironing for you."

She gave him an impish grin. "It would be sexy as hell, you with an iron and an ironing board."

"This is why you have three ex-husbands."

"What, you don't believe men should iron?"

"No, I think men ironing is fine, perfectly normal. I just don't think they're sexy when they do it."

"It depends—"

He stopped her right there. "Daphne."

"It's so much fun to tease you, even more so than Julius and Marty. They're both more sociable than you are. Marty, in particular, is a people person. His job requires a certain conviviality where yours doesn't. You can get away with that clamped-jaw, no-sense-of-humor demeanor you've had since you arrived back in Los Angeles on Wednesday. Some of your clients probably like it. Julius has a softer way about him."

"I've done a lot of flying this week."

"Is that a change of subject or an explanation?"

"Take it as you will. What time do you want to see Moss Hill?"

"Give me a couple of hours. I want to take a nap and freshen up. The red-eye has lost its charm, if it ever had any." She glanced around the attractive corner room, decorated with hand-painted furniture and colorful bed linens. A second window overlooked the front yard. "The memories I have, Russ. Grace Webster, the Sloans, the O'Dunns, the Frosts. I'm holding my breath until I get through this weekend. Maggie and Olivia are as lovely as ever. They make their own goat's milk soaps for the bath amenities, you know."

"I do know. There are some in my apartment."

"Nothing too girly-smelling, I hope."

"You're on a roll, Daphne," Russ said. "See you in a couple of hours. Call or text if you need me before then."

She yawned, covering her mouth with one hand. "I'll be lucky if I'm awake in two hours, but I'm looking forward to seeing Moss Hill." She winked at him. "How's that for the power of positive self-talk?"

"Keep it up."

She rolled her eyes as he left her to her nap and unpacking and went downstairs. No one was in the kitchen, but he could hear Olivia and Maggie in the backyard. They'd invited Daphne to join them, but she'd opted for getting settled. Buster was sprawled across the threshold of the mudroom. Anyone trying to get out of or into the kitchen through the mudroom would have to step over him. The ruler of the roost, Russ thought with a smile. The big dog didn't stir, either because he accepted Russ or was dead to the world.

He returned to Moss Hill and parked by the bike rack, Kylie's muddy, unlocked bike in its usual spot. He took his own bag up to his borrowed apartment. He had no interest in a nap, but he hadn't slept much on his flight. He could sleep anytime, anywhere—except on planes.

Kylie didn't respond to his knock on her door.

Avoiding him?

But when he went back downstairs, he noticed her

bike was gone from the rack. She must have slipped out while he was in his apartment, dropping off his bag. She'd have seen his rental car but might not have realized it was his.

Or she could be avoiding him.

He walked up the road toward the covered bridge and the house Kylie had rented until her move to Moss Hill. She'd already been to town. It made sense she'd take off in this direction.

He found her on the old, single-lane wooden bridge. "It'd be easy to lose track of time standing here watching the river," he said, easing in next to her. She had her hair pulled back in a tangled ponytail, her bike tucked next to her as she stared down at the water. "The sound is soothing, isn't it?"

"Especially after a long flight, I imagine."

"How've you been, Kylie?"

"Good, thanks. Working and enjoying spring. And you?"

"Working and flying." He placed his arms on the bridge rail and looked down at the river, Kylie next to him. "I'd like you to tell me about Travis Bowman."

"I understand." She looked out across the river to a green field rolling out from the bank. "I met Travis when he worked on Moss Hill last summer. I hadn't seen him since then."

Russ listened without interruption as she related her encounter with this guy yesterday. She was clear, concise and calm. From her point of view, she'd run into a harmless carpenter who hadn't liked his job or Knights Bridge and had been in a bad place in his life and had moved on, relocating to Syracuse to be closer to his small children.

"Did he threaten you?" Russ asked when she finished.

She shook her head. "I didn't take what he said as a threat. I think he just wanted me to know he'd figured out about Morwenna."

"To be the big man or to get something out of you?"

"Blackmail me, you mean? No, nothing like that. There's no way I would pay or do a favor for him or anyone else to keep Morwenna secret."

"You didn't tell Mark that this guy brought up Morwenna."

"No, I didn't."

"Thank you for telling me," Russ said quietly.

"I haven't told anyone that I work under a different name because it was convenient for me, not because it's something I want or need to hide. Travis must know that. He doesn't have any leverage." She paused, tracing a fingertip on a rough knot in the wooden rail. "It's hard for me to believe figuring out I'm the author and illustrator behind a series of children's books would make anyone feel important. I'm proud of what I do, and I appreciate that my badgers are popular…" She shrugged. "I don't know what was on Travis's mind."

Russ stood straight. "You two…"

"We went to a Red Sox game together. I left early and made my own way home. He was negative but not what I'd call angry or bitter—just unhappy."

"Let me know if you see or hear from him again."

"I will."

He turned around, leaning his back against the rail. "Feels good to be outside."

"It sure does. I love spring. I was looking to see if there are any ducklings yet. Ducks often congregate near here." Kylie stood on her toes, leaning over the rail as if she was trying to see under the bridge. She settled back on her heels. "A bike ride and now a walk—I'm not going to get much done today."

A breeze caught her hair. Russ noticed pale blond strands against the dark maroon of her jacket. She brushed hair off her cheek, squinting at him. He itched to touch her but didn't. Not here, not now. "You've been putting in the hours since I left."

"*Little Red Riding Hood* came together. It took me by surprise. I never know what will crystalize my thinking, but once I had the setting, I was off and running. Lots yet to do, but it's helpful to take a break. Plus it would be hard to work today."

"Which is harder to draw, animals or people?"

"I don't think in terms of hard or easy when I'm in the middle of a project—I just focus on the work at hand. But standing back from it..." She considered a moment. "I still can't say. Figuring out new characters can be demanding whether they're animals or human, but it's fun, too. Characters I know well also have their challenges."

"Do you work one way as Kylie Shaw and another way as Morwenna Mills?"

"I've never thought of it like that. No, I don't think so."

"Are you more Kylie or Morwenna?"

"There's no daylight between the two of us. The only difference is that most people don't know I'm Morwenna."

"I still haven't told anyone."

"I've no doubt." She smiled unexpectedly. "You're a steely-eyed private investigator."

Russ laughed. "Tell Daphne."

"I look forward to meeting her."

He realized a car hadn't crossed the bridge since he'd arrived. He felt his long night in his scratchy eyes, his tight muscles. Best thing, he knew, was to keep going until he fell into bed tonight. "Are you annoyed I was suspicious you were hiding something and dug in, found out about Morwenna?"

"It's not like you discovered I'm in witness protection or a bank robber on the lam."

He smiled. "Imagine Sherlock Badger's reaction."

"He'd have turned me in if I were a bank robber. You're perceptive, Russ, and having an investigator on the premises got me worked up—it's no wonder you were suspicious. I didn't have a grand strategy for dealing with Morwenna. It just seemed easier not to say anything."

"You were working hard and just didn't tell anyone."

She dipped both hands into her jacket pockets and produced fistfuls of what he saw were small stones. She lined them up on the bridge rail and picked one, cupping it in her palm. "Pretty much. Next thing, it's this big secret, and then you show up, the California PI staying across the hall."

"Things moved fast after that," Russ said.

She licked her lips. "You could say that." She spun

and tossed her stone into the river. It hit a large, flat boulder and bounced into the water, creating a small splash. "But you don't need to worry about my little secret. I'm holding off telling anyone until after you and Daphne are back in California."

"Are you tempted to run—move out of Moss Hill and go somewhere else? The anonymity of a big city must be tempting right now."

"I enjoyed city life, but I love it here. Sometimes you can't run." She handed him two of her stones. "I can see you're dying to throw stones in the river. It's addictive."

"Do you aim or just wing it, see where it lands?"

"Depends on my mood. I didn't aim just now."

He flung a golf ball–size stone into the river. It dropped into a pool of water among the boulders directly beneath the bridge. He aimed the second stone, targeting a craggy granite boulder near the riverbank. It went wide, splashing into reeds.

"Missed," Kylie said next to him.

He laughed. "By yards."

"Out of practice."

"I can't say I've ever thrown stones into a river."

"But am I right, it's addictive?"

"It could be if I had a covered bridge and a river, and someone to collect stones."

"I always keep my eye out for good stones."

He looked at her, saw the color in her cheeks—wind, sun, emotion. He couldn't say for sure what she was thinking, feeling.

She cleared her throat, grabbing another stone and flinging it into the river. "Do you have plans for the evening?" she asked him.

"I'm picking up Daphne and taking her to Moss Hill to check out where she'll be teaching tomorrow, but she wants to have a quiet night. She's going to ground until her class. I'll come back to my apartment." Russ flicked a tiny stone into the river, but lost it and didn't see where it landed.

Kylie pointed. "There, by the driftwood."

But it was too late, any ripples dissipated by the time he saw the driftwood, which looked to be a tree branch of some kind. "You and I can have dinner at Smith's, or we can cook. I like the idea of cooking, don't you? My place this time."

"I'll bring wine," she said, taking the last and biggest of the stones, rearing back and throwing it hard. It landed on the opposite bank. She clapped her hands. "Did it!"

Russ could have hugged her, kissed her—made love to her right there on the covered bridge, but a car made its way onto the narrow span. Kylie grabbed her helmet, snapped it on and jumped on her bike, promising to see him soon as she started back toward Moss Hill.

He watched her, getting himself under control. "Kylie, Kylie." He exhaled, wishing he had more stones to toss into the river. Big ones.

Daphne would know all about secret identities, Russ thought as she huddled with Ruby and Ava O'Dunn in the Moss Hill meeting room. Ava, also red-haired and turquoise-eyed, was quieter and calmer than her fraternal twin, but she wasn't involved with a Sloan and local firefighter. That had to help. The three women seemed to hit it off, confirmed when Ruby and Ava volunteered to drive Daphne back to Carriage Hill and she accepted.

"You're tired, darling Russ," Daphne said, kissing him on the cheek. "You should have let me upgrade you to first class."

Ava and Ruby bit back smiles as they showed Daphne out to their car.

Russ was more than happy to go up to his apartment, unpack and take a shower. Daphne was artistic, visual and dedicated to her work. She and Kylie had common interests and talents, but Daphne relished playing the diva. He couldn't see Kylie breezing into Moss Hill the way Daphne had, squealing in delight, kissing Ava and Ruby on the cheek, all in with her role as the local girl who was now a Hollywood icon.

It was all another world from the one Russ knew.

He probably needed to back off, get a good night's sleep and let the heat between him and Kylie cool, but he had a dinner to plan.

Fortunately, Maggie Sloan and Olivia McCaffrey had presented him with a picnic basket filled with food, which, combined with the basics in the apartment refrigerator and pantry, made dinner easy. He could cook, but he appreciated not having to tonight.

Kylie arrived, dressed in a long, casual skirt and a silvery gray sweater that outlined the shape of her breasts and fell loosely to her hips. He hadn't noticed her wearing jewelry earlier, and she wasn't wearing any now—no rings, earrings or necklace. But she looked put together, her hair brushed and gleaming, pulled back loosely.

"You forgot your shoes," he said, realizing she was in her stocking feet.

She raised the hem of her skirt a few inches and wiggled her toes. "Daring, don't you think? My new look. Actually, the only shoes I have that go with this skirt are uncomfortable. I ordered them online last fall and should have sent them back, but I forgot. Now that it's warm enough again to wear them, I put them on—" she smiled, lowering her skirt "—and I remembered."

"Good thing I'm across the hall."

"Isn't it, though?" She'd set the wine she'd brought—an Oregon pinot noir—on the counter and pointed to it now. "Do you have an opener? I didn't think to bring one."

"Mark said the place was stocked with the necessities—"

"And a wine-opener is a necessity," Kylie said, pulling out drawers until she produced a corkscrew. "I'll do the honors."

If she was nervous or self-conscious about having dinner with him, she didn't show it as she uncorked the wine and brought it to the table, where she poured it into two glasses he'd set out.

"I'm glad we're having dinner here," she said. "One meal a day at Smith's is enough, and I think Sherlock Badger has doubts about you."

Russ picked up his wine. "What kind of doubts?"

"Professional. He's a protect-and-serve lawman and you're a private investigator. You have a bit of a sardonic Humphrey Bogart look about you."

"Ah, I see. So, Sherlock thinks I fit a certain PI stereotype and bend the rules."

"It was probably the palm-tree shirt. He must have noticed it when you knocked on my door on Sunday. I didn't tell him about it. Promise." Kylie grinned and clicked her glass against his. "Cheers."

"Cheers." Russ sipped his wine, watching her as she tried hers, noticing her throat as she swallowed. "Sherlock's kind of a stud for a badger."

"I think so, too."

"Why did you do a little stuffed version of him instead of the vet badger?"

"Because my father's a vet," she said without hesitation. "He's not like Dr. Badger, but still. No, it had to be Sherlock or... I don't know. A real lawman, maybe."

"Tough to find one who'd fit at the base of your lamp."

She laughed, and together they set out the simple dinner of chicken casserole, green beans, bread and sliced cucumbers and tomatoes, with fresh fruit for dessert.

"Was your work in naval security dangerous?"

"Sometimes. Short answer."

"Do you have family besides Marty?"

"My mother. My father died in a helicopter crash ten years ago. He was at the controls. My mother and Marty were passengers. He was severely injured but recovered. She suffered only minor injuries."

"Is she in LA, too?"

"Arizona. Scottsdale. She lives with three miniature poodles."

"She's never remarried, then."

"No." Russ didn't elaborate. "Marty quit his job a while back and moved to Hollywood. I hung out my shingle in San Diego after I got out of the navy. I thought I'd stay there but moved up to LA in March."

"Do you like San Diego?"

He smiled. "What's not to like except traffic?"

"All that sunshine might get on my nerves after a while," Kylie said lightly. "But you didn't stay in San Diego. If Marty's your older brother, he's what— thirty-five, thirty-six?"

"Thirty-five. He's old enough to make his own decisions." Russ pushed back his chair and got up, taking the casserole dish to the counter. He didn't know how he'd gotten to talking about his family. "I couldn't be there for Marty as much as I wanted to be the months he was in rehab after the accident."

"And you want to be there for him now." Kylie stood up with her wine. "How does he feel about that?"

"Mixed."

"Well, I think it's sweet."

Russ grabbed more dishes off the table. "Sweet? I think that's a first."

She laughed and took a quick sip of wine, then set her glass on the table and gathered up silverware. "I bet that's not true, but I imagine your work often requires you to put on your kick-ass face."

His kick-ass face. He set the dishes in the sink. "You've been talking to Sherlock too much."

"*Way* too much." She dumped the silverware in the sink and swung around at him. "Shall we have wine on the balcony?"

Russ grabbed the wine bottle and a throw off the back of the couch, and Kylie took the glasses. The temperature had dropped with nightfall, and it was a chilly evening. The sky was clear and starlit, the millpond and waterfall reflecting light from the renovated hat factory. He unfolded the shawl and draped it over Kylie's shoulders.

"Thank you," she said, catching the ends of the throw with her fingers. "I love the smells of spring. Grass, flowers, leaves—everything's coming to life."

"I smell mud, too."

"Dirt. A great spring smell."

He laughed and added more wine to the two glasses. "It's a great spot."

"We can't see the house I rented from here. The For Sale sign has gone up. The push won't happen until after it's been painted and spruced up. My friend who owns it as a country home agrees it needs a family."

"The Badgers could move there."

"It's fun living on a river after creating a fictional family that lives on a river. They'd do well here, but they're committed to Middle Branch."

"Were you nervous when you ran into this Travis Bowman yesterday?"

She shook her head. "There's no animosity between us."

Russ drank some of his wine. "You go all over town on your own, don't you?"

"Mmm. Seeing how I live alone, work alone and don't know many people here."

"And enjoy your solitude."

"I haven't been alone as much as usual this week."

"Is that a good thing?"

"I've enjoyed it. I moved to Moss Hill in part because I wanted to stay in Knights Bridge while I figure out how to emerge from my prolonged artistic retreat or whatever you want to call it. It's been good, but it's not sustainable."

"Sherlock has his limits as company."

"Don't tell him that," she whispered, as if Sherlock Badger could hear her. "He's tough but sensitive."

"You're good company, Kylie Shaw." Russ set his wine on a side table and then took hers and set it next to his. The throw had drooped, catching in the crooks of her arms. He drew the soft fabric up again, feeling the cool air as his fingertips brushed her warm skin, the contrast downright sensual. "Very good company," he said, his mouth finding hers.

She responded instantly, wrapping her arms around him, letting the throw fall. He didn't catch it, and it dropped onto the balcony rail and nearly went over the side. He slipped his arms around her, lifted her off her feet, deepening their kiss. The thin, soft sweater rode up, and he could feel the warm, bare skin of her lower back.

A thousand different sensations rolled over him at once, and he might as well have been a leaf that had fallen into the millpond below, pulled inexorably toward the waterfall and oblivion.

This woman, this funny, clever woman…sexy, vulnerable, strong…

"Kylie."

He didn't know if she heard his hoarse whisper between kisses, or if she was beyond hearing anything. He felt her fingers digging into the muscles in his back. He lowered his arms to her hips, lifted her higher, her skirt riding up, only the flimsy fabric and his pants between them as she drew herself hard against him.

He had his hands on the smooth, bare skin of her thighs, his fingers easing over her bottom, between her legs. He felt her wet heat, heard her gasp as she opened for his touch.

Her arms were over his shoulders now. She raised her head, her pale hair shining. "You're direct, aren't you?"

"I can be," he said, his thumb touching just the right spot. He knew because of the change in her eyes, the way she fell back into their kiss. He let his tongue match the rhythm of his thumb. She moaned, lost now. He could feel it. "Don't hold back."

As if she could, he thought with satisfaction. He didn't stop. He ignored his own driving need and got caught up in hers, until she clutched him, digging hard into his shoulders as her release came.

When she sank back onto her feet, she placed her palm under his belt, stroked him under his pants. He pushed against her touch, but at the same time, he tucked his fingers under her chin and tilted her head up. "One night I hope you'll stay," he said, his voice ragged. "I want you to stay now…"

"But it's a small town and you're on duty with Daphne."

He smiled. "And Sherlock Badger is a tough little bastard. He could kick my ass."

"He might anyway."

"Because of what just happened. He could also give me a high five."

"Ha."

His eyes held hers. "If I went too far—"

"You didn't." She gave him the slightest of knowing smiles. "That was obvious, I would think."

Russ scooped up the throw from the rail. She wouldn't need it now. He tossed it onto the table with their wine and wineglasses. "I think there's some Sherlock Badger in you."

"He's his own self, as are all my characters."

"Uh-huh."

"I might get myself a deerstalker hat, though."

"Thus confirming your reclusive, eccentric artist image. How's *Little Red Riding Hood*'s woodsman shaping up?"

"He's adventurous, reliable and true. Not all versions of the story have a woodsman, but mine does. I'm thinking he should have scars on his hands." She ran her fingertips over the scars on Russ's hands. "Don't all adventurous, reliable and true woodsmen have scars?"

"I wouldn't be surprised." He kissed her on the forehead. "Good night, Kylie."

By the time she went across the hall to Sherlock and all the critters and characters that percolated in that mind of hers, Russ was hopeless. He couldn't fall in love with Kylie Shaw. He didn't have the kind of life that would mesh with her life, her sensibilities.

She wanted the Badgers of Middle Branch.

He practically lived out of his duffel bag, and he had his dreamer brother, his remote mother and the memory of a father who'd liked nothing better than to fly helicopters.

Russ texted Marty. Daphne is holding her own in KB. No one to make her a French martini.

His brother responded immediately. Good. She needs to take a break. You?

I've got a handle on the rumors.

And your artist?

Russ didn't respond right away. His hesitation would be enough for Marty to figure out what was going on. Reminded me I'm on duty.

Heh. Good for her.

See you soon. How's it going there?

It's good. All good.

Russ smiled and went back out to the balcony, the throw rippling in a cold gust of wind. He gathered it up, noticing the soft wool was still warm from Kylie. He saw there was a splash of wine left in the bottle. He poured it into his glass and stood at the balcony rail, listening to the river and looking at the night sky as he finished off the wine.

An hour after leaving Russ's apartment, Kylie sat at her worktable but didn't turn on a light. The only light was from over the stove in the kitchen, and from the stars, sparkling pinpricks spread out against the black night sky. She'd changed into her spa bathrobe, leaving her clothes in a heap on the floor.

"Don't look at me like that," she told Sherlock. "Seriously, you tell me how was I supposed to resist a little romance with our neighbor?"

She smiled to herself. Having Sherlock Badger to talk to was a lot of fun, even if her parents and sister wouldn't get it. Most of her friends, either, including her illustrator friends.

Did Russ get it?

She had a feeling he did. He'd probably seen stranger things during his days in the navy.

Not that talking to Sherlock was strange, of course.

"I know, my friend," she said. "If I'd worn shoes tonight, my PI and I wouldn't have gone as far as we did."

A matter of practicality and physics, she thought. Her shoes would have flown off when he'd lifted her, probably going over the side of the balcony, but just falling off would have jerked her back to her senses. She remembered the feel of her almost-bare feet against Russ's legs, sensual, intimate.

But she'd known what she was doing and could have stopped herself, asked him to stop—he would have, no question—but she hadn't, and now she had to face the consequences. The raw need he'd stirred up in her. The swirling emotions. The yearning for something else, something more, in her life.

Was Russ sitting in his apartment running through a similar litany of thoughts, or was he thanking the stars because he'd sucked up the grace and willpower to send her on her way?

Kylie knew she didn't have the answers.

"I know you don't have the answers, either, Sherlock," she said. "I wish you did."

She got up from her worktable, turned off the light

over the stove and went to bed, slipping into her winter flannel pajamas and grabbing a book on fonts she'd been meaning to read. Her way of hitting the reset button on her life and returning it to normal.

Twenty

Daphne awoke too damn early in her pretty room at Carriage Hill. The sun was sort of up, but whatever time it was on the East Coast, it was three hours earlier at home in Hollywood Hills. But she wasn't going back to sleep, given her nightmares and her nerves, and she moaned and groaned as she threw back the covers and stood on the hand-hooked rug at the side of her bed. The chill of the early-morning air didn't make her any happier about being awake.

She was not a morning person.

People kept telling her that her natural clock would tilt earlier as she got older, but they must have meant when she was a hundred.

She tiptoed into the en-suite bathroom and forced herself into the shower. The goat's milk products were nice. She'd never had a desire to milk a goat, but she was glad there were people like Elly O'Dunn in the world who loved that stuff.

She returned to the bedroom, wrapped up in a bathrobe that was so fluffy she got lost in it. She finally dared to look at the clock.

Eight-thirty.

"What the *hell*?"

She'd expected five-thirty, max.

She jumped into the leggings and oversize sweater she'd packed for lounging and easy walks. In five minutes, she was downstairs, hoping she didn't have to be sociable before she had at least a pot of coffee.

Olivia and Dylan greeted her warmly, offering her coffee and whatever she wanted for breakfast. Such a lovely couple, worth over a hundred million and here in their country kitchen with their coffee, toast and eggs and their big dog flopped at their feet.

Daphne accepted a mug of coffee but urged them to go about their Saturday routines.

"Do you need Russ for anything?" Dylan asked.

She frowned. Russ? She realized now she didn't need him here in Knights Bridge at all. Maybe she'd known it all along, and she'd sent him here, then dragged him with her, as a way to manage her anxiety—and he'd indulged her, if not as politely as Julius would have. They'd both been frank with her, but she hadn't listened, hadn't *wanted* to listen.

Or she'd simply refused to acknowledge and deal with what was going on with her. The fear, the obsessing, the mind-reading. Looking back to the past, looking to where it had led her—where she was now, the good, the bad, the ugly. And where she was going.

Sixty might be the new forty, but it was still sixty.

What did she want to do with her life in the next five, ten, twenty years? Where did she want to die? Where did she want her ashes spread—she'd decided on cremation, so at least *that* was settled. She joked with her friends that she'd never be able to choose what outfit to wear in her coffin.

Gallows humor. On his good days, her father'd had it, too.

She didn't have a stalker. She'd never had one in her forty years as a professional costume designer, and she didn't now.

Anyway, Knights Bridge had enough rugged types to see to anyone who got out of line. She didn't need Russ.

But no one would get out of line.

Olivia and Dylan seemed to sense she was lost in her thoughts and went out into the garden—as far as Daphne could tell, they were discussing chives.

She helped herself to toast with strawberry-rhubarb jam—both homemade—and more coffee. Once she chased away the cobwebs, she put on her tennis shoes and slipped out through the front door, hoping the bright sunshine and a good walk would help smooth the uneven edges of jet lag, jitters and melancholy.

She walked all the way to the Quabbin gate at the end of the road. The spring undergrowth sprouting up, the leaves budding out, the soft, damp ground and the trickle of a stream over rocks and sodden, browned leaves combined forces and took her back in time, to those strange, awful, wonderful days when she'd lived in this little town.

She'd come out here at nineteen and imagined herself in forty years. Where did she want to be? *Who* did she want to be?

You'll never amount to anything. You're a small-town girl.

Be happy with what you have.

A family gets one chance. We've had ours. Be grateful.

Who do you think you are?

What makes you think you're better than anyone else?

Her father at one time or another, cautioning her, belittling her—fearing for her.

"A pipe dream," she whispered, quoting him—and everyone else who'd guessed she'd wanted to escape and start fresh.

Some had tried to protect her from disappointment and warn her about the hardships she would encounter. Loneliness, failure, long hours, insecurities of all kinds—financial, emotional, career. Others had projected onto her their own ideas about women, especially young women, and what they could and should aspire to accomplish. Succeeding in what they imagined to be the dog-eat-dog world outside of home and hearth seemed risky and impossible, with nothing but rejection and heartache at the end.

But what could have been more dog-eat-dog than life with her father?

He'd dismissed her hopes and dreams because he dismissed her, but it was deeper than that. He'd given up on his own hopes and dreams.

She stood just inside the gate, imagining life here before Quabbin. Grace Webster, now in her nineties, had grown up in one of the lost valley towns. Her family had been displaced, forced out of their home. Even the graves of departed family members were moved to a cemetery specially created on the south side of the reservoir. Everything Grace had known growing up had been obliterated. Travel hadn't been as easy or common in those days, and as close as Knights Bridge was to her hometown, she'd never stepped foot here until she'd had to move as a teenager.

A pregnant teenager, as it turned out.

That one had stunned Daphne when she'd learned about it last year.

But Grace had survived and made something of her life. Unmarried, her British pilot lover killed early in World War II, she'd let a loving couple adopt her baby—Dylan's father, Duncan—and set about becoming a trusted, respected teacher in her new town.

Pull back the drapes of a seemingly perfect, easy life, Daphne thought, and there were always mistakes, struggles and fears. She considered herself fortunate to have taken charge of her own life, despite the odds and the lack of encouragement. She'd had a vision for herself. It hadn't all worked out as planned, but if she'd stayed put in New England—if she hadn't left…

You think you're so high and mighty, Debbie, but you're not. You're my daughter. You can't escape that fact, no matter how far you go.

There's no running away from who you are.

Her father had smacked her on occasion, but his abuse had been more in word than in deed. She saw now how deeply miserable he was with his own choices and where they'd led him, the lack of control he'd felt at his circumstances. Easier to blame, lash out at others—his own daughter—to make himself feel better, however futile, however wrong, however much it sealed him in the cycle of self-recrimination and self-justification.

"Poor bastard," Daphne whispered, shivering more from the onslaught of memories than the April morning chill. It wasn't as bright and clear as yesterday, but it wouldn't rain—it would be a good day for her class.

She turned back toward the gate and the road. She hadn't come from a family like the Sloans, the Frosts or the O'Dunns. Her great-great-grandfather's portrait might hang in the library he'd built, but his forward-thinking, entrepreneurial mind-set hadn't been handed down through the generations. Her father had tried, in his own way, to live up to his ideas of what the Sanderson name meant. He'd inherited some money. It hadn't been so much that he didn't have to earn a living, but it had been enough that he could raise his children in middle-class comfort. He'd dropped out of law school and worked at a midsize regional bank, eventually rising to vice president.

But it hadn't been enough to smooth his sense of entitlement and his deep, abiding self-hatred.

Nothing, Daphne saw now, would ever have been enough. Her father's life had been a black hole of need and entitlement, and she'd determined at an early age that she would work hard not to be like him.

She splayed her fingers in front of her, noted the expensive rings and the excellent manicure she'd had in Beverly Hills—and the lines and discoloration. She could see her hands of forty years ago, callused from sewing, nails split and uneven. She'd learned how to give herself a manicure from a library book. Knights Bridge had its own salon these days, but not back then.

Tears welled in her eyes. She blinked them back, but they spilled down her cheeks. She gulped in a breath, desperate to stop this nonsense. Crying, wallowing in the past.

He'd come to visit in California once.

Her father.

The memory was like an assault, almost knocking her over with its force, the surprise of it. She'd just celebrated her thirtieth birthday and had started seeing the man who was to become her second husband, a sweet guy, a whiz at special effects in movies. He could get lost for days in figuring out minute technical things—how to make viewers think they were seeing a real bomb explode, a real spaceship landing on a faraway planet…stuff like that. She'd needed to talk to him once in a while, but he'd get a glazed look, and she knew his mind was doing algorithms or some damn thing. He and Noah Kendrick, an MIT grad, would probably get along.

But she wasn't distracted. The memory was still there, taking her back, back, back.

Daphne…that's what you are now? You know we named you Debbie because your mother loved Debbie Reynolds? Funny you ended up in Hollywood.

What do you want, Dad?

To see you.

That hadn't been all, of course. He'd told her he had lung cancer and less than six months to live. He hadn't asked for anything. Money, forgiveness, understanding.

When he'd left for the airport, to go home to his latest girlfriend and his death, he'd given her a sardonic grin. *I know I could be a real bastard when you were a kid. I hope it helped you more than it hurt you.*

His last words to her.

She hadn't come east for his funeral. She'd been on the tail end of a project and would have been replaced if she'd left for any reason. She'd slipped into a bathroom on the set and had a good cry, and she'd donated money to cancer research and the Knights Bridge library, in honor of the man her father had wanted to be.

"A nice passive-aggressive touch on your part, Debbie, dear," she said aloud, laughing, sniffling back her tears.

It would have been easier if her father had been horrible all the time, but life was seldom as neat and tidy as that. People didn't fit into airtight boxes.

She went around the yellow-metal gate and back out to the road. On a Saturday morning at home, she'd have breakfast alone on the patio amid her roses and bougainvillea.

"That's where you'll be next Saturday," she said aloud, feeling much better as she walked up the quiet road to the Farm at Carriage Hill. What a transformation it'd had since she'd lived in town. Nobody around here had had much money back then. A lot of people had assumed Knights Bridge had gone underwater in Quabbin like the little towns of Prescott, Dana, Enfield and Greenwich. But it had survived the massive water project, and now it was a thriving, desirable place for people who had reason to live here.

"I don't want a place here," Daphne said emphatically, somehow needing to articulate that fact clearly to the trees, rocks and streams around her.

She met up with Olivia and Buster on the road and walked back with them to Carriage Hill, enjoying the moment and letting the past fall away.

Twenty-One

People from Boston to New York—professionals, students, teachers and the curious—had signed up for Daphne Stewart's presentation at Moss Hill on her long career as a successful Hollywood costume designer. Once most of the attendees had seated themselves, Kylie slipped into the back of the room, taking a seat third in from the aisle in the last row. She planned to stay for the more informal, general morning session, then cut out. She'd skip lunch and the intensive, hands-on afternoon workshop for a smaller group.

Although Kylie was by no means an expert, costume design was part of her work as an illustrator, even if her costumes went on the fictional animals and people she drew. She was fascinated by the display Ava and Ruby had put together along the perimeter of the room, showing the progression of Daphne's work from her early days in Hollywood to the present, and found herself eager to hear what she had to say.

Ruby and Ava sat in the front row, both dressed professionally and obviously nervous and excited about this

long-awaited day. Their sister Maggie had volunteered
to stay with Daphne in the small setup room. Nothing
seemed to bother Maggie Sloan. Kylie assumed that as
a caterer, Maggie had dealt with numerous situations in
which she had to be "on" and could relate to Daphne,
but she was also good with people.

Samantha Bennett, seated in the row in front of
Kylie, turned around and grinned at her. "No way was
I missing this. I thought Justin was going to drop me
off, but he's in the lobby with Mark. Hovering, the two
of them. It's those stupid rumors. Chris is here, too, but
he would be since this is a big deal for Ruby."

It was a nice show of support, but Kylie also suspected the three men had a genuine interest in Daphne
Stewart and what she had to say.

At the same time, Kylie knew Mark and the two
Sloans wanted to be on hand in case Travis Bowman
or some other disgruntled type turned up.

Russ came in from the lobby and sat next to Kylie as
Ruby and Ava got up to introduce Daphne. He crossed
one leg over the other, sitting very close. Kylie tried to
ignore her reaction to him—the ripples of awareness,
the rush of sensations—and focus on Ruby and Ava's
short PowerPoint presentation on their guest of honor
and her forty years in Hollywood.

Finally, Daphne took to the podium, in her full public persona as a Hollywood icon. She was addressing
an audience who appreciated her contribution to movie
history and her talents as a costume designer, and she
obviously loved it. "I designed this little number for
myself," she said, gesturing to her simple black outfit.
"I chose it for today because it didn't require an iron or

a steamer trunk, and I wouldn't freeze to death. I lived in Knights Bridge for three miraculous years. I know how cold April can be."

Everyone laughed. Kylie thought Russ smiled, but he was clearly on duty. The ninety-minute morning session was divided into two sessions with a fifteen-minute break—refreshments courtesy of the inexhaustible Maggie Sloan.

Kylie settled back, watching, listening, as Daphne dove into her talk. She was engaging, forthcoming and practical—no question she was a professional who demanded a great deal, not just of everyone else but also of herself, probably especially of herself.

When it was time for the break, Kylie jumped to her feet but waited to see if Russ planned to get up. She wasn't about to try to go over or around him and risk tripping on his feet and landing in his lap. He smiled, as if he knew what she was thinking, and rose, stepping into the aisle. She started past him. He leaned in close. "I need to check on Daphne," he said.

"Of course. Do your thing."

Kylie headed out to the lobby, where tables were set up with drinks and snacks. She grabbed coffee, but as she added cream, she spotted Travis Bowman coming up the stairs from the lower level.

She shot through the crowd, spilling hot coffee on her hand as she came to him. "Travis, hi—I didn't know you'd be here."

But his eyes didn't connect with her. She followed his gaze, saw Russ and two of the Sloan brothers—Justin and Christopher—converging on her and Travis. He swore under his breath, but he didn't have a chance to do anything else. Russ and the Sloans quietly maneuvered him outside. Kylie noticed Daphne coming out from the meeting room, happily chatting with Ava and Ruby and two other young women, probably fellow graduate students. None of them seemed to have noticed Travis and the quick reaction by the Sloans and Daphne's investigator.

Kylie abandoned her coffee and scooted outside, finding the four men at the breezeway between the two mill buildings.

Travis had his palms up, more in submission than self-dense. The Sloan brothers and Russ had him encircled. "Sorry," he said. "I wasn't heading for Ms. Stewart. I swear. I'm not a threat to her or anyone else. I just wanted to see inside Moss Hill now that it's finished."

"Bad timing," Russ said.

"Yeah—yeah, I see that." He appealed to Kylie, standing between and just behind Russ and Chris. "I'm not here to make trouble. You know that, right, Kylie?"

"I'd like to think that," she said.

Russ kept his gaze on Travis. "You could have waited until after the class to talk to any of us."

"I just thought…seize the moment, you know?" Travis went pale and shrank back, although he had nowhere to go. "Before I chickened out."

He looked more pathetic than a threat. He was unarmed and outnumbered, and he'd never hurt or threatened anyone that she knew about when he'd worked for Sloan & Sons.

Kylie noticed Russ's stance relaxed slightly. Justin Sloan, however, remained rigid. "Travis," he said. "What's up?"

Travis cleared his throat and seemed to summon his nerve. "I don't work for you anymore, Justin."

Justin gave no visible reaction. "Have you been talking BS about Moss Hill, Mark Flanagan and us?"

"I had some questions. No big deal." Travis shrugged. "Easy for things to get blown out of proportion."

"Why sneak around behind our backs?" Chris asked. "Why not come to any of us directly?"

"I don't know what you're talking about. I haven't been sneaking around, talking trash, if that's what you think. Things get exaggerated in this town. I left on not-so-great terms. I worked hard on this place and wanted to see it now that it's open. And I guess I wanted you to know I'm not a loser."

"You could have sent a letter," Justin muttered.

Travis shook his head, almost laughed. "Don't ever change, Justin. Come visit me in Syracuse anytime. I'll buy you a beer."

A muscle tightened visibly in Justin's jaw. He turned to Russ. "You got this?"

Russ nodded. "No problem."

The second-eldest Sloan about-faced and went back inside.

Chris Sloan crossed his arms on his chest, not looking as combative as he had fifteen seconds ago. "It's a good job in Syracuse?"

"Yeah," Travis said. "It's great."

"Justin gave you a decent recommendation. It's more than I'd have done. We know you're responsible for these rumors. Time to let go of the past, Travis."

Chris didn't wait for Travis to respond and followed his brother back into the building.

Travis blew out a breath. "Obviously coming here wasn't one of my better ideas. Man. But Chris is right. I got caught up in the past. Maybe I said a few things I shouldn't have, but nothing really bad. I didn't mean to get anyone worked up. I worked hard on this place and wanted to see it, and I convinced myself the only way was to just show up." He turned to Russ. "I'm not a disgruntled former employee looking for trouble— I'm sorry if it looked that way."

"But you came with an ax to grind," Russ said, not backing off.

"The past crawled up and bit me. I thought I could handle it. Just being back here…" Travis grimaced, sighed. "I screwed up a lot of things when I was working for the Sloans. I'm doing fine now. Great new job, spending more time with my kids, being their dad— stepping up. I've made a few friends in Syracuse. It's a fresh start." He gave a halfhearted grin. "Nothing like getting your ass kicked by a Sloan to help you see the error of your ways."

Russ didn't smile back at him. "You're not from Knights Bridge. Your uncle's funeral wasn't in town."

"That's right. Coming here was deliberate. I guess I wanted to feel like I could be one of them, you know? A Sloan, a Flanagan. I saw I couldn't. I got it in my head that people in Knights Bridge don't let you in if you weren't born here."

"It became a self-fulfilling prophecy," Kylie said, her day with him in Boston, with all his relentless negativity, making more sense to her.

Travis nodded. "I had a chip on my shoulder, and I had problems that had nothing to do with anyone but me. Looking back, I'm surprised the Sloans gave me as many chances as they did. I got into some therapy—it was part of the deal if I wanted to see more of my kids. Being self-destructive and aggressive isn't healthy. I had these big plans…dreams…" Travis shrugged his big shoulders. "I make a good living, and I get up every day with the intention of doing the right thing, being a better man. It's enough. Being angry at the world, blaming everyone else for what I didn't have—it was no way to live."

"Hold that thought," Russ said. "You slipped up this week. You used the class today to get inside Moss Hill because you assumed Mark would never let you in if you knocked on his door and asked him."

"Not assumed," Travis said. "Knew."

"Based on your own preconceived notions about how you're regarded here."

"Yeah. My point on my mind-set." Travis glanced toward the front entrance to the main building, where several people who'd come out for a bit of fresh air were going in again. "I'm glad I got to work on this place. It came out great." He bit down on his lower lip and turned to Kylie. "I'm really sorry. I let myself get steamrolled by the past. I'm glad you moved in here, and you're not alone in that house out past the bridge."

"I am, too," she said.

Russ's gaze hadn't softened. "Why did you bring up Morwenna Mills?"

"She told you that? I was being a jerk. Plain and simple. I cop to it." Travis shoved his hands into the pockets of his frayed denim jacket. "I knew you ditched me in Boston, Kylie. I was replaying that tape in my head.

It was stupid. I'm sorry. Your secret is safe with me. It always has been."

She smiled. "No harm, no foul."

"Yeah. Thanks."

He apologized again and left, heading across the parking lot to his truck. He ducked into the driver's seat and pulled out of the parking lot, turning right, back toward town.

Russ watched until the truck was out of sight. Then he turned to Kylie. "You actually went out with that guy?"

"He had Red Sox tickets."

"That's all it takes, huh?"

"I came to my senses by the third inning and ditched him in the seventh."

"Were the Red Sox winning?"

"Tied."

"Tied and you left in the seventh? That bad a date?"

"It wasn't really a date. We just went to a ballgame together."

"What constitutes a date in your mind?"

She felt a surge of heat as she remembered last night. "A candlelit dinner. A movie. Splitting a bottle of wine at a Paris cafe, although I did that with this French sculptor who was also a mistake."

"We've had a candlelit dinner and split a bottle of wine. Next I'll have to take you to a Red Sox game and then Paris. I won't be a mistake."

"There were no candles at dinner last night," she said, teasing him.

"In my head there were." He leaned in close to her. "And there were other things that made up for candles."

"Have you ever dated the wrong woman?"

He laughed, slipping an arm around her. "Yes, ma'am. But it's a good thing we've kissed a few frogs that have turned out to be real frogs, or we wouldn't be here now. I bet you can draw a mean frog. Think the Badgers need to meet a frog family?"

Kylie smiled, finally relaxing. "It could be fun."

Daphne's class had restarted when Kylie returned to the Moss Hill lobby with Russ. Not wanting to interrupt, they joined Justin and Christopher Sloan and Mark Flanagan at the refreshment tables. Kylie tried again with coffee and poured herself a fresh cup. Justin and Chris had filled Mark in on Travis's visit, "a dumb-ass move," as Justin put it, helping himself to a molasses cookie, one of three different kinds of cookies his sister-in-law had made for the occasion.

Brandon Sloan tiptoed out of the meeting room, shutting the door quietly behind him. He shuddered as he approached the refreshment tables. "Once Daphne mentioned corsets, I was out of there," he said. He helped himself to a chocolate-chip cookie. "Thank God there was a problem with her microphone, and I could seize the moment and sneak out unnoticed."

No way had his departure gone unnoticed, Kylie thought, amused.

"Ruby would kill me if I did something like that," Christopher said.

His two older brothers grinned. "Yeah, she would," Brandon said.

Justin narrowed his eyes on his youngest brother. "You need to tell her, Chris."

Chris heaved a sigh, staring at a clump of red grapes he'd just picked up. "I know. I'm not doing her any favors. I didn't want to be a distraction this week." He grimaced. "Hell."

"Relax," Brandon said. "Everyone will be relieved when you two stop dancing around each other and call it a day. It's like when Maggie and I were separated. People knew we were supposed to be together before we did. With you and Ruby, it's the opposite."

Justin grinned at his youngest brother. "Don't you like your big brothers giving you advice?"

"I'd rather run ten miles bare-assed in a cold rain," Chris muttered. "Sorry, Kylie."

"That's okay. I can sympathize."

"Do you have brothers?" he asked her.

"A younger sister."

"What about you, Russ?" Justin asked. "Any siblings?"

"An older brother. He's only eighteen months older, though."

"It counts," Chris said. "Is he full of advice for you?"

"Other way around."

Justin and Brandon pounced on that one—the younger brother as the pest instead of the picked-on. After a few minutes, Mark rolled his eyes at Russ. "All we need now are Eric, Adam and Heather Sloan, and you could see what it's like around here. I grew up with these guys. Where does your sister live, Kylie? Around here?"

"Boston. She's in veterinary school at Tufts. Her name's Lila."

"A vet? No kidding."

"My father's a vet," she added. "My mother runs a dog training and grooming business."

She didn't remember ever saying so much about herself—not that she'd had many opportunities, given her solitary ways.

When the morning session ended for a short lunch break, Daphne headed straight for Russ. "Did I have an actual stalker?" she asked him in a loud whisper.

"No, Daphne," Russ said. "You didn't have a stalker."

"I saw you big guys go all tough and mean and wondered. Was he after you, Kylie? Of course I don't wish such a thing on anyone, but being rescued by Russ and a couple of Sloans can't be a bad thing."

Kylie bit back a smile. "It was just a guy who worked on this place and wanted to see it now that it's finished. I recognized him."

"There was no rescue," Russ added.

"Well, it was exciting while it lasted," Daphne fought a yawn. "I wish I could help myself to wine now, but I'd better wait until after the master class this afternoon or who knows what I'll say that will get me into trouble. Olivia and Dylan promised to make me a French martini tonight. I should have Marty send them his recipe. This first session went well, I think, but I'm drained. A potential stalker, though. That will be enough to re-energize me."

Ava and Ruby eased in to either side of Daphne, whisking her off to introduce her to more of their friends and professors.

Russ stood close to Kylie, his own cup of coffee in hand. "My guess is Daphne's giving this her all because she's never doing it again. How would Morwenna handle a public appearance?"

"She'd channel Daphne Stewart. What a pro."

"That she is. I doubt anyone else has a clue what this is taking out of her. What would you do if Morwenna had a stalker?"

"Call in Sherlock Badger," Kylie said lightly. "He's not in every book. He only visits Middle Branch once in a while. He'd be available."

"Is Middle Branch named after the Middle Branch of the Swift River?"

She tried to hide her surprise. "Yes, as a matter of fact."

"I've been reading that book on Quabbin in my apartment."

And he'd really read it, she thought. The damming of the Swift River had allowed the valley to flood, creating the reservoir and forever changing Knights Bridge.

Daphne wandered back, iced-tea in hand. She was visibly more subdued. "You're an artist," she said to Kylie. "You must have ways you protect your work. Even if you're just starting out—maybe especially if you're just starting out—you have to keep your focus where it belongs."

"It's easy to get distracted," Kylie said, neutral.

"Mmm." Daphne eyed her as if she suspected she'd hit a nerve. "Well. I suspect you and I aren't that different. I love what I do as much as I did when I was hiding in the library attic. I thought I'd love teaching, but I don't. Other people are better suited than I am. I'll get through the afternoon class—it's more hands-on, more about what I do day to day now versus the past.

But I can share my knowledge and experience in other ways. I'm glad I did this today, but I truly don't need to do it again. I put my dear Colt Russell through his paces because I couldn't face my own ambivalence."

Kylie smiled. Russ ignored her.

Daphne grinned, a mischievous glint in her deep green eyes. "Don't you think he looks like a Colt? He told you about his brother, Marty? I called him Colt Martin and almost got a martini in my face. They're a tough pair. You wouldn't think Marty's tough because he's such a dreamer and a nice guy, but he is. Not that Russ isn't nice. But you know what I mean."

"Quit before you dig your hole any deeper," Russ said.

She laughed. "I always take your advice."

Kylie doubted that was true. Ava and Ruby joined them as the crowd dwindled. "Where's your fire-fighter?" Daphne asked.

"He left with his brothers," Ruby said.

"Good," her twin sister muttered.

"I remember their father as a young man," Daphne said. "He was quite the stud, too. It's so easy to get caught up in love and romance and put aside our own plans for the future. I almost quit the business and moved to Copenhagen with my third husband. Lovely city, but can you imagine?"

Kylie had no idea if that was a true story and clearly neither did Ava and Ruby, but Daphne seemed satisfied when Ruby smiled. As the twin sisters chatted with Daphne, Kylie could see that Ruby especially had stars in her eyes about Hollywood.

"I can see why you two want to start a children's theater here," Daphne said. "It's a great location."

"It has potential," Ava said. "But, I'm not sure we're ready."

"Knights Bridge or you and Ruby?"

"All of the above."

Ruby nodded. "I get excited thinking about the possibilities, but when I bump up against reality, my stomach twists right into knots. My ambivalence about the theater didn't help me see what was going on between Chris and me. I'm sorry so much of that played out in public. I've been a little high-strung lately, I know."

Daphne waved a hand. "I've been married three times. You don't have to explain."

Ava kept her gaze on Kylie. "I think Ruby and I pushed Daphne to do this. Come to Knights Bridge again, teach a class, talk to us about a children's theater."

Daphne cleared her throat pointedly. "No one pushes me into anything."

"But this isn't your thing, is it?" Ava asked. "Russ, you're skeptical, too, aren't you? About this theater?"

"I don't know enough about getting a community children's theater up and running to be skeptical," he said.

"I don't either," Daphne said. "Ava and Ruby probably know more than I do—"

"No," they said simultaneously and emphatically.

Ava recovered first. "We have a lot to learn and experience before we can pull off our vision for a theater here."

"I thought I wanted to come back to Knights Bridge after I get my master's," Ruby said. "Now... I don't know."

"You need your time in the bright lights and big city," Daphne said cheerfully. "I knew I didn't belong in Knights Bridge forty years ago."

Kylie wondered what Russ's life was like in Southern California. Nothing like the one he was witnessing now, in Knights Bridge.

"Well." Daphne clapped her hands together. "No point dwelling on this. Today is a good day, and soon it will be done. People enjoyed my talk this morning. Now, some food then on to the afternoon session." She smiled at Kylie. "And I did bring Russ Colton to town. I think he fits in, myself. Rugged, tough, good with the locals. The *Magnum, PI* shirt doesn't quite fit, but Marty will find an alternative."

"That's what scares me," Russ said.

Daphne winked at him. "We're not fooled, Russ. Nothing scares you."

Kylie laughed, and Ava and even Ruby seemed to relax. Daphne made plans to ride back to Carriage Hill with Ava. "I'll go with you," Ruby said. "Chris was going to join us for dinner, but he had to go to the station and canceled. I think I'm going to buy a clue."

"I've always preferred the quick-but-painful lopping off of a relationship to the slow, miserable bleed," Daphne said. "Be sure to come to dinner tonight, Ruby. I'll introduce you to the joys of a French martini."

Twenty-Two

Russ wasn't in Knights Bridge to mess up Kylie's life.

It was his singular thought as he arrived at the Farm at Carriage Hill.

She'd told him she would drive herself to dinner. He suspected she wanted to give herself a chance to change her mind. She had a thousand reasons to stay home, including her stubborn, ill-fated attraction to a certain private investigator—that being him—but the truth was, she wanted to go. He'd seen it in her eyes when she'd ducked up to her apartment.

Maybe her life could use a little messing up.

Dylan welcomed Russ into the house and offered him a beer. The dining room was set for dinner. Maggie and Brandon Sloan were spending the evening with their sons, but the Flanagans and Justin Sloan and his fiancée, Samantha Bennett, were gathered in the living room. A low fire in the center-chimney fireplace was taking the chill out of the evening air.

Daphne had changed into a simple black dress, with gaudy earrings that suited her over-the-top personality—

or at least the over-the-top personality she liked to embrace as her own. She was seated by the fire, nursing a drink. "Marty better watch out," she said as Russ stood next to her. "Dylan makes a damn good French martini, too."

Ava and Ruby, sitting cross-legged on the floor in front of the fire, each had martinis. Ruby dove right into hers, but Ava discreetly set hers aside.

Daphne, of course, noticed. "We'll try again when you visit me in Hollywood, dear," she said. "Russ's brother is better at making drinks than I am, but I'll bet you'll like my version of a French martini when we're sitting out by my pool in the Southern California sun. I've been freezing to death since the sun went down."

The twin sisters both smiled, more because of Daphne's invitation to visit than the prospect of trying another of her martini concoctions.

Kylie entered the living room. Russ hadn't heard her come in. Olivia greeted her warmly. "I hope I look better than the last time you saw me," Olivia said with a laugh. "I decided not to push myself today, with our dinner tonight, but I'm sorry I missed Daphne's class."

"My first, last and only master class," Daphne said, tucking her feet up under her on the chair. "I'm debating whether to stay here another couple of days or go back right away. I'm considering several new projects. I had this fantasy of slowing down a bit when I turned sixty, but I hate to turn down work."

"You're in your prime," Olivia said.

"How nice of you to say so. We had quite a number of movie people in the crowd today. Word's leaking back to Hollywood that I used to live here. I managed to avoid a lot of that sort of gossip when I was here in September. Egad. People are going to find out my real name is Debbie Sanderson and there's a portrait of my great-great-grandfather in the local library. He looks a bit like George C. Scott as Ebenezer Scrooge, don't you think?"

Russ didn't think so at all. From her expression, Kylie didn't, either. Ruby and Ava said George Sanderson reminded them of Colin Firth in *Pride and Prejudice*. "Older, of course," Ruby said, "but just as handsome."

"And as rich," Ava added with a grin.

Daphne scoffed. "Well, I hope Darcy's wealth lasted longer than old George Sanderson's did. I've had to work myself to the bone my entire life. What do you think, did I show a lack of gratitude in changing my name to Daphne Stewart? I was always more of a Mary Stewart fan than Daphne du Maurier, but I do like the name Daphne."

"I'm sure your great-great-grandfather would understand," Olivia said.

"I hope so. I don't know why, but I do." Daphne sipped the last of her martini. "Do you work under more than one name, Kylie?"

Russ felt Kylie's gaze on him, but he didn't come to her aid, change the subject or deny that he'd said a word to Daphne, which, of course, he hadn't. Finally, she nodded. "Yes, I do."

"Really?" Ruby set her martini glass on a tray on a small table by Daphne's chair. "I had no idea."

"Can you tell us?" Olivia asked, clearly intrigued.

"Yes, Kylie, please," Jess said. "Tell us who you really are."

She told them she wrote and illustrated children's books under the name Morwenna Mills. She was matter-of-fact, and she didn't explain her reasoning, her success or any details.

Samantha clapped her hands together. "Morwenna is the one who created *The Badgers of Middle Branch*, right?"

Kylie nodded without comment.

"I read them to Justin's nephews. They love them. They identify with the little badgers who are always plotting their next adventure. And they love Sherlock Badger. He reminds them of their Uncle Eric."

"That's great," Kylie said. "Thank you."

"This is so cool," Ruby said, swooping up her martini again. "Calls for one more sip of this thing."

Laughter ensued, and in a few minutes, Olivia said it was time for dinner.

Russ edged closer to Kylie as she started into the dining room. "That wasn't so hard, was it?"

"It wasn't, but I think I'll try one of those French martinis."

Dylan overheard and saw to it himself.

Russ suspected that Dylan McCaffrey, of everyone in the room except maybe Daphne, most understood what it had taken out of Kylie to admit she worked under another name, and a very successful one at that. Dylan had been a professional athlete and, after the premature end to his NHL career, had succeeded beyond anyone's expectations when he'd joined his best friend, Noah Kendrick, at Noah's fledgling NAK, Inc. Dylan's quick thinking and his instincts about people had helped tip the scales in NAK's favor. The company had gone public about the same time Morwenna's badgers had taken off in popularity, changing its founders' lives, putting them at a crossroads they were still trying to sort out.

"Today was a wake-up call," Dylan said after he handed Kylie her martini and she and the other guests were taking seats in the dining room. "I have a family now— a baby on the way. I can't fool around. I talked to Noah. We'll set up a meeting."

Russ nodded. "Anytime."

"I rather like this," Kylie said from the table, as she sipped the martini.

Daphne beamed. "There." She gave Russ a victorious look. "I told you Kylie and I had things in common."

"You're scaring me," Russ said, grinning at her as he took his seat at the table. He noticed that Olivia and Dylan had put him next to Kylie. From the color in her cheeks, he guessed she'd noticed, too.

After dinner, Daphne started out to the terrace. She nodded to Kylie. "Join me, why don't you?"

It was a friendly command, Kylie thought. How could she refuse?

On their way through the mudroom, Daphne grabbed a barn jacket that must have belonged to Dylan. Kylie had already grabbed a throw from the back of a chair in the living room, trying not to think about last night's throw on Russ's balcony and how it had almost ended up in the river. She wouldn't have cared. She'd gone quickly past the point of caring.

"I do miss the night sky here," Daphne said, looking up at the stars as she spoke. "I took a pseudonym when I moved to California because I was deliberately reinventing myself. George Sanderson was a generous and solid citizen but his great-grandson—my father—was a hard, abusive man." She turned to Kylie. "But you're not escaping a troubled past, are you?"

"Fortunately, no. I created the badgers before I decided to use a pseudonym."

Daphne sank onto a chair at a round wooden table. "And Morwenna just fit?"

Kylie nodded, sitting across from her. "That sums it up. I'd never both written and illustrated a children's book, and I didn't want to interfere with my regular work under my own name."

"You hedged your bets. Makes perfect sense. Are you worried envy will be an issue when your artist friends find out?"

"It would be patronizing to assume anyone would be envious of me."

"But professional jealousy exists even among people who draw cute, chubby animals for a living," Daphne said. "Easy to think you're all in it together, but then one of you rises to the top. It can throw off the balance of friendships. It's not just when you blow past them. It's also when they blow past you and you get accused of envy when you couldn't care less."

"Maybe so." Kylie tightened the warm throw around her. "It's not something I like to think about."

"Not everyone wishes you well in life. I learned that early on in Hollywood. Creative people aren't exempt from envy, jealousy and ambition and competitiveness carried too far. That includes those of us who don't get the major headlines."

"You're very wise."

"I've been around a long time. I've seen it all."
Daphne made a face. "I can't believe I just said that.
Did Russ figure out you're this Morwenna Mills?"

"He did," Kylie said.

"He's a suspicious and tenacious sort. I think he got
shot at more than once while he was in the navy. Beverly
Hills is a big change for him from San Diego. Knights
Bridge is an even bigger change. It was my idea to
drag him out here. He all but told me I was being stupid." Daphne draped the barn coat over her shoulders.
"I almost wish this guy today'd had it in for me. Well,
no, I don't, but Russ can be annoyingly smug. Worse
than Julius."

Kylie laughed. Daphne obviously adored both men.
"Do you think you'll ever come back to Knights Bridge?"

Light from the house hit Daphne's face, deepening the green of her eyes, the lines at her mouth. She
looked tired, emotionally as well as physically drained
by her appearance. "Everywhere I go there are ghosts.
If you've lived here all your life or move back within
a short time—or come and go…" She looked up at the
night sky again. "But to be away for decades and then
return, you can't escape the memories."

"And they aren't all good memories, are they?"

"No one has only good memories." She leaned back,
eyed Kylie knowingly. "You and Russ—I noticed the
way he looks at you. You don't have a man in your life?"

"I've been busy—"

"That's what we always say, isn't it? I keep saying
I'm through with men. I don't want to marry again,
that's for sure. Creatively, single is a great way to go.

You get in the zone and stay in it unless you want to come out."

"There are always distractions."

"You're not going to tell me we have to find balance, are you? There's no such thing."

Kylie wasn't sure if Daphne was serious.

"What about kids?" She waved a hand. "Don't choke. I say what's on my mind. A man like Russ will want kids. Mark my words. His brother agrees. Marty's a hunk, too. Ever been to Hollywood?"

"For a long weekend."

"A private investigator and a children's illustrator. Not exactly your everyday couple."

"Daphne…"

"Jumping ahead, am I? Blame the martini." She sprang to her feet with a sudden burst of energy. "I hope you feel better for telling your friends here that you're Morwenna. I haven't told most of my friends about Debbie Sanderson. Maybe it's time." She inhaled deeply, as if she wanted to take in the night air, and maybe all the memories of her Knights Bridge past. "I'm not staying. I'm not doing the children's theater. The timing is all wrong for Ava and Ruby—I think they'll be relieved when I tell them. Right now the theater they have in mind for Knights Bridge is a lovely dream. It's not a realistic goal and might never be."

"And you don't want to do it, regardless."

Daphne sniffed. "You sound like Russ now. He knew I'd bail before I did. Maybe I stuck with it longer because I wanted to prove him wrong. But I hated to disappoint Ava and Ruby—I hope I didn't look too happy when I saw how relieved they were that this wasn't meant to be. They need to finish school and experiment, figure out what they want, what they're good at."

As if on cue, Ava and Ruby joined Kylie and Daphne on the terrace, followed by Olivia, Dylan and Russ. Olivia explained that the Flanagans and Samantha and Justin were cleaning up the dinner dishes, refusing any and all offers of help.

Kylie vacated her seat at the table. She was aware of Russ's eyes on her as she mumbled a good-night and slipped into the mudroom. She took her martini glass into the kitchen. She'd only had a few sips and wasn't worried about driving back to Moss Hill in the Knights Bridge dark.

It was time to make her exit.

Twenty-Three

Russ awoke with the sunrise, which hadn't been his plan or, certainly, his desire after last night, but the vibrant streaks of color drew him outside, downstairs to the front of the building. He had a long day ahead of him. Bundled up in her barn coat, looking tiny and lost, Daphne had followed him among the chives at Carriage Hill. He'd been contemplating Kylie's abrupt exit, the effect of her and her adopted town on him, when Daphne had hunted him down.

She wanted to go home. Today. *It's been great, but I need to be back to work on Monday.*

She'd claimed she'd been so preoccupied with this trip that she'd agreed to a must-do, in-person meeting on Monday without realizing it was *this* Monday, then forgot about it altogether. She'd realized her oversight when she'd received an email confirmation.

I never forget meetings. Never.

Russ figured she was making up an excuse, but he hadn't called her on it and wouldn't. He'd expected to have today, at least, to relax, maybe go for a bike ride or a long walk with Kylie, just for fun, no pressure. He didn't regret their overheated encounter on his balcony, but they'd moved fast for a woman who'd spent much of the past year alone, her primary company a four-inch stuffed badger.

Fast for him, too, but not too fast.

He walked across the parking lot, taking in the early morning colors and smells, the glow of the sunrise on the river and green fields. He'd go up to the covered bridge and back, get his bearings, breathe in the fresh air, enjoy the picturesque surroundings. Then he'd pack for his and Daphne's flight to LA.

As he started up the road, he noticed a movement in the woods at the base of Moss Hill.

Kylie, up at sunrise.

He trotted across the road and called to her. When he reached the woods, he saw there was a narrow trail. He ducked under a low-hanging pine branch and called for her again.

"Up here," she said, close but out of sight.

He continued up a steep section of trail. It curved around a chest-high boulder, and there she was, waiting for him on an exposed tree root. "You're up early," he said.

"Not as early as you are since it's three hours earlier in California."

"Good morning, Kylie."

She smiled. "Good morning, Russ. Do you want to see my spring?"

What was he supposed to say to that? Only one answer. "Sure."

She led him up the trail, through the woods, along a

stream—Russ figured he didn't need to keep track of the exact route. Kylie picked up her pace as they came to a wet spot on the hillside, presumably her spring.

She dropped to a small boulder and scooped sodden, dead leaves and debris out of a small pool. She dumped the debris to one side and pointed at a cluster of rocks. "See that water trickling from the rocks? That's the spring."

"I see it," Russ said, sitting next to her on a flat rock.

"It's safe to drink."

"Is this where you meditate, or do you sit quietly and wait for badgers?"

"I haven't seen any badgers." She scooped up more muck and tossed it aside. "A squirrel bonked me on the head with an acorn when I was up here the other day."

Russ noted the clear pool as the spring fed it fresh water. "You could walk past this spot a hundred times and never realize a spring was here."

"That's part of what makes it special."

"Am I ruining it by being up here?"

"No." She brushed her muddy hands off on her thighs. "Justin Sloan told me as I was leaving last night that he'll make sure Travis Bowman gets back to Syracuse."

"Does Travis worry you?"

"Not really, no. I never saw anything in him—he just asked if I wanted to go with him to a Red Sox game and I took a chance and said yes."

"The guy in Paris was more your type?"

"The sculptor. Lucien. He's full of himself, but he's also a very good sculptor. He was condescending to me about my illustrations. I don't think that was his intention, but we never got past sharing a bottle of wine in a Paris café."

Russ watched the flow of the spring water. "Maybe Travis was your anti-Lucien."

"I didn't have a relationship with either Travis or Lucien." Kylie shifted on her rock, the toes of her trail shoes covered in mud. "You see what my life is like. I work and I go for walks and bike rides. I'm sorry Travis disrupted Daphne's class, first with his reckless talk that got the rumor mill going and, then, showing up yesterday."

"Mark and the Sloans were on the lookout for him. He never would have had a chance to disrupt the class, but Daphne would have dined on it for months if he had. She told the guys she was sorry they missed her discussion of Victorian bloomers."

"That's when Brandon made his escape. Did she really discuss bloomers?"

Russ shrugged. "I wasn't there. She said afterward she was making a point about considering undergarments, seen or unseen, in costume design." He noticed the spark of humor in Kylie's eyes. "She wanted to hit a lot of different points. That's what she told me, at least."

Kylie grabbed a stick and flicked her pile of muck away from the edge of the pool. "She's fun, savvy and professional. She loves playing the diva, doesn't she?"

"To the hilt."

"I wonder if she practiced being a diva in her library attic room."

"She's decided to leave today," Russ said, watching Kylie for her reaction. "I'm going with her. I need to head to Carriage Hill soon to pick her up."

Kylie tossed her stick aside. "Had you planned to leave today?" she asked without looking at him.

"Tomorrow. I have a meeting I need to be at on Tuesday and work I need to clear up." And decisions to make about his future with Sawyer & Sawyer, and his future in general. He kept his voice steady. "I'm meeting with Dylan and Noah. Travis wasn't a threat, but the next guy might be. It was a wake-up call for them."

"At least it wasn't a scary wakeup call." She turned to Russ, her nose and cheeks slightly red from the cool early-morning temperature. "Noah and Dylan have more than their own safety to consider. They're starting new businesses. Dylan and Olivia have a baby on the way, Noah's getting married—they can't pretend Knights Bridge isn't part of the real world. Even I can't, and I do a pretty good job of it. Could your law firm take on Noah and Dylan as clients?"

"First things, first." Russ smiled. "Right now I have to steel myself for the drive to the airport with Daphne."

"Do you like living in Los Angeles? Would you be there if your brother wasn't there?"

"I doubt it but no complaints. San Diego's my city, though. Ever been to San Diego, Kylie?"

"Once. I didn't get to the zoo. I've always wanted to visit the San Diego Zoo."

"I'd love to show you San Diego sometime and take you to the zoo."

"I'd like that."

He looked out at the trees, the sunrise blended into the sky now, high, white clouds moving in from the west. He turned back to Kylie, noticing how at ease she was out here in the woods, next to her spring. "San

Diego is a long way to go for a date. Can you get work done on planes?"

"I don't even know anymore. I haven't flown anywhere in over a year. It's easy to slip into boxes of our own creation. Mine's been that I need to work all the time and be alone and not tell people what I do. If I do, somehow it will throw everything that's been working for me out of whack. What's your box?"

"You tell me."

"Competent, confident, responsible. They are positive qualities, and I imagine they're assets in your line of work."

"They can be. They can also turn me into a rigid jackass."

She smiled. "Are you quoting someone by chance?"

"My brother. Marty has a variety of colorful alternatives for jackass."

"My sister worries about me, too. But I don't think you're a rigid jackass. With what you see and know, what you've done, two round-trips across the country in a week and taking on a potential stalker must seem easier sometimes than it would be to let your guard down…" She went red, grabbed her stick again. "Never mind."

"Easier to take on a stalker than to take you to the zoo? Allow other people to crawl out of their boxes?" Like Marty, Russ thought. But Kylie smiled, and he decided not to think about his brother right now, no doubt in his mind Marty would have approved. "You've found a home here in Knights Bridge."

"Working on it. We'll see how people here react to Morwenna. I'm guessing they won't care. No one seemed to mind last night." Looking calmer, she put her stick aside and ran her fingers in the spring water. "Maybe it's not so much about finding a place but making a place your own."

"This spot does make you think about possibilities."

"Yes, it does. Not many people come up here." She gave him a sideways look. "I keep my phone handy in case I fall."

"Good thinking." Russ scooped up water in his hand and took a drink. It was cold, clean, no trace of muck that he could taste. "This is so different from the life I know, it's hard to describe."

"Good different or bad different?"

"Just different." He shook the excess water off his hand and touched two fingers to her cool cheek. "Except for the company. That's definitely good different."

"I appreciate that."

He tapped her lips with his fingertips, then sat back. "Bet you were glad it was me coming up the trail."

"I was prepared to hide if it was Travis being weird."

"Good thinking."

Kylie didn't respond. Russ felt her going quiet, thoughtful, in this place that soothed her soul. "Do you get ideas here?" he asked finally.

"Sometimes. Not on purpose. Mostly I try to stay in the moment and appreciate the surroundings."

"I hope I'm not ruining it for you."

"Not possible."

"A lot's changed for you this week." He kissed her on the top of her head, breathed in the smell of her hair. "For me, too. I have to get Daphne home and take care of business, but I won't forget you."

"See how you feel when you get back to LA."

"You're used to being alone."

"I'm alone a lot because of the work I do, and because of the life I lead—the choices I've made. Complete solitude isn't a necessity."

"You could have a puppy, then?"

"Puppies, cats, chickens."

He noticed she'd left out a husband and children. "That would give you lots to draw. You didn't mention a man."

"I've decided to illustrate *Beauty and the Beast* next."

"A lot of inspiration around here for the beast. Kylie…" He paused before he went too far. "Come out and see me in LA. Meet my brother. Morwenna needs to see Hollywood." He got up, dusted off his hands and his pant legs and looked at her sitting by her spring. "I'll see you, Kylie."

She smiled up at him. "Are you sure you don't need me to get you back to Moss Hill? You didn't leave a bread-crumb trail."

"I have my phone. I'll text you if I get lost."

But she'd been through the woods between the spring and the trail so many times, she'd created something of a trail, and he had no trouble finding his way back down to the road.

Daphne had her bags packed and out on the doorstep, courtesy of Dylan, when Russ arrived at Carriage Hill. She'd already said her goodbyes and gave her thanks to her hosts, and he did the same.

"I'll be seeing you soon," Dylan said quietly, walking

with Russ to his rental car. Daphne had already tucked herself in the passenger seat.

"Anytime," Russ said.

He got in behind the wheel and watched Dylan head back into the house, Buster greeting him at the kitchen door. "Not a bad life," he said.

"I'd go insane," Daphne said with an exaggerated shudder. "To each his or her own."

Russ grinned at her. "What would get to you first?"

She didn't hesitate. "Buster. My door didn't latch last night, and he tried to get into bed with me. For a second I thought it was my third husband. He was hairy, too."

"Daphne."

"Let's go," she said, buckling up. "I'm ready."

Russ thought he heard a catch in her voice, but he said nothing.

They were out on Route 2, heading east toward Boston, before Daphne broke the silence. "Did you notice I'm wearing a neutral travel outfit and almost no jewelry?"

He hadn't, but he did now. "Looks comfortable. Long day ahead."

"I want to blend in," she said. "I don't want anyone at the airport or on our flight looking at me and thinking I might be someone they know. Let them think I'm a grandmother who flew east for her little guy's piano recital. Did you ever play piano, Russ?"

Russ grimaced, but she was flying first class again and he was flying coach—he wouldn't have to listen to her all day.

"You didn't," she said. "Marty did?"

"I don't remember."

"I can see Marty at the piano as a little kid." She stared out her window. "I hope he makes it in Hollywood, but he's having fun doing the work, going for it—that's part of the dream, too. It's the best part, maybe."

"You're not going to start crying, are you?"

She shot him a look, biting back a smile. "Bastard. I'm glad you're flying coach." She sank back into her seat. "I want to get home to my patio and my pool. I swam in the streams in Knights Bridge a few times. It was always cold. The water warms up for three days in August, but it's still not what I'd call warm even then. I like my heated pool."

She drifted into silence again. Russ concentrated on his driving and pushed back any images of Kylie jumping into a cold New England stream. Tried to, anyway.

After another twenty miles, Daphne yawned, sitting up straight. "I had a light breakfast. I hate traveling on a full stomach. Did you eat?"

"Coffee, eggs, toast."

"Alone?" She waved a hand. "None of my business, I know. I'll whine if you open an office in that old hat factory and leave me, but I'll have Marty to visit—until he gets rich and famous. And there's a guy interested in me. I haven't told you about him. He's been to the bar a few times. He's about my age. Always pays in cash. I don't think he's using his real name, but you don't need to investigate."

"That's good."

"I think I worked with him when I first came to Hollywood."

"Actor?"

"Director. I think he's got his eye on Marty as talent. If I recall correctly, he's been married a few times himself. I don't need true love at this stage in my life. I want a guy who likes to travel, laugh and doesn't need me." She was quiet a moment, her deep green eyes narrowed on Russ. "That's Kylie, isn't it?"

"She's not an old Hollywood director with a bunch of ex-wives."

"I didn't say he was old and I didn't say 'a bunch.' My point is that Kylie doesn't need you. She knows who she is, she can support herself, and she has a circle of friends and family—even if she also enjoys and needs solitude for herself and her work. What she wants is to allow herself to say yes to falling for you and for you to do the same."

"Say yes to falling for myself?"

She rolled her eyes. "Say yes to falling for her and working out the issues you face. Knights Bridge, California, those badgers of hers."

"We've only known each other a week."

"You both were ready for love. A week is a start."

"It is," he said, then winked at her. "Be satisfied with that, because it's all you're going to get out of me."

As the Boston skyline came into view, Knights Bridge farther and farther behind them, Russ could see that Daphne had shrunk into her seat and was pale, clutching her hands tightly in her lap as if she might fall apart if she let go.

Damn. She *was* going to cry.

He eased the car from the left lane to the middle lane. "Marty and I both took piano lessons. He lasted longer than I did."

"How many years?" she asked him.

"Years?" Russ grinned. "Marty lasted three or four months. I lasted two lessons."

"You were incorrigible little boys, weren't you?"

"Just not cut out for piano lessons. Marty took trumpet in high school. He got pretty good at it. I've never been…creative."

"I believe we're all creative. It just comes out in different ways. For you…" She hesitated. "It comes out in the way you approach your work. You wouldn't be half as good at what you do if you weren't creative."

"If you say so."

"I do. And I say you're a damned decent sort. You threw me a lifeline just now. I was sinking, going deep."

"You were Debbie Sanderson again."

"I'm Debbie Sanderson every day. That's what I realized being back here. I never banished her. I never became anybody else. As Marty would say, it's good." She shut her eyes, some of her color coming back into her cheeks. "All good."

Twenty-Four

After her encounter with Russ at the spring, Kylie rode her bike out to Echo Lake without stopping. When she arrived back at Moss Hill, she was breathing hard, sweating and closer to sorting out her feelings about revealing she was Morwenna Mills. That surprised her. She'd thought she'd need more time. She'd kept the secret for months and months, but now that it was out—it was fine. Simple as that. She didn't feel aggrieved that she'd basically been forced into it. It was bound to happen, and now it had. She'd sent out emails last night, after dinner at Carriage Hill, and she had a few calls to make today.

She might be closer to sorting out Morwenna but she was no closer to sorting out her feelings for Russ Colton.

She climbed off her bike, pulled off her helmet and acknowledged a surge of emotion. The wind and cool air on her bike ride had whipped tears out of her eyes. She could feel them on her cheeks and fought an urge to cry.

Would she ever see Russ again?

She wiped her tears with her fingertips. Yes, she would see him again, she thought. Somehow.

She mounted the stairs to her apartment. Instead of tears, she could feel Russ's fingertips on her cheek that morning. She smiled, letting her mind drift to the feel of his hand in hers, his strong thighs under her fingertips, the taste of his mouth—his erotic touch.

She groaned. How was she supposed to work?

When she reached her apartment, she noticed a small package at the base of the door—a sheet of Moss Hill letterhead folded around an acorn, with a quick note:

Your squirrel pelted me, too. I think he was jealous. Soon, Russ.

Kylie laughed as she went inside and placed the acorn next to Sherlock Badger. She made tea and sat on her new couch, looking out at the river as she called Lila, her parents and a few close friends. She had to leave a voice mail for Lila to call her back, and her parents took the news about her pseudonym in stride—her work as an illustrator was a mystery to them, anyway. So long as Morwenna was good for her, fine with them.

Her illustrator friend in Chicago wasn't surprised. "You were on my short list of people who could be Morwenna. It's awesome, Kylie. I love those badgers. A loft in a renovated hat factory in a little New England town suits you, too, more so than a loft in Paris, even."

Kylie thanked her, and they moved on to other things.

Afterward, she was able to work. It helped that she had a good feel for what she was doing with *Little Red Riding Hood.*

When her phone rang that evening, she assumed it would be Lila, wanting more information about Morwenna, checking on her older sister, but it was Russ. "Marty and I just dropped Daphne off at her house," he said. "She was happy to be back home. How are you, Kylie?"

Just hearing his voice stirred her, as if he were there with her, touching her in all the right places. She jumped to her feet and stood at the slider onto her balcony. She cleared her throat. "Great, thanks. A little bleary-eyed. I've been working. And you, Russ? How are you?"

"Marty's buying me a beer."

"He's a good big brother."

"Yes, he is." Russ paused. "It was a long flight. I kept thinking about you. Tell Sherlock hi for me."

"Will do."

And with a soft chuckle, Russ said good-night and was gone.

Kylie went out to her balcony and breathed in the chilly evening air, listening to the river rush over the old dam, imagining—trying to imagine—Russ in California.

When she went back inside, she sat at her worktable. She wouldn't sleep for a while yet.

She sighed at Sherlock. "Russ Colton, PI, says hi."

And it was as if Sherlock shook his head, wondering what she was getting herself into this time.

On Monday morning, Kylie biked into town, arriving at the library as it opened. Clare Morgan had already heard about Morwenna from Maggie Sloan, who'd heard it from her twin sisters, now back at school in Boston and New York. "But we'll all keep Morwenna a secret if that's your wish," Clare said with a smile.

"It's not a secret any longer," Kylie said.

"This will be a good opportunity to explain pseud-onyms to the older kids. I'm not sure the younger ones will get it, but they love the Badger family and their friends. If you're interesting in doing a presentation…"

"I'd love to."

"We'll talk more, then."

Clare returned to work, and Kylie joined Saman-tha Bennett at her favorite table with her pirate books. "If you decide your badgers need some pirates, buried treasure and sunken ships, we'll have to talk," Saman-tha said.

"I'm sorry I didn't say anything until now."

"It's okay. We're still getting to know each other. I have lots yet to tell you about the eccentric Bennetts and their adventures. I get why you didn't say anything about Morwenna at first. Then you painted yourself in a corner. You really love your work, don't you?"

"I do, Sam."

She shut a book on pirates. "Speaking of *I do*, Justin and I have finally set a wedding date. We're still work-ing on having the ceremony in England, but I think we can pull it off. You're invited, of course, and not be-cause I now know you're a famous children's author and illustrator."

"I'm so happy for you and Justin."

"Thanks. If you'd told me a year ago I'd be sitting here in this little library, engaged to a carpenter, I'd have told you that you were out of your mind. Life can take the strangest twists and turns, can't it?" Saman-tha didn't wait for an answer, leaning in to Kylie. "Did

I notice something between you and Russ Colton, or is that none of my business?"

"Maybe. It could have dissipated now that he's back in Los Angeles."

"You were a momentary distraction, you think?" Samantha sounded skeptical. "That's not what Justin says. Not that we should trust a Sloan on matters of the heart, at least under ordinary circumstances, but Justin is tuned in these days. I'm meeting him for lunch at Smith's. Join us?"

Kylie smiled. "I'd love to."

When Kylie returned to Moss Hill late that afternoon, she found her sister waiting for her at the front entrance to Moss Hill. Lila explained she'd driven to Knights Bridge from Boston to make sure Kylie was okay now that she'd revealed that she was Morwenna Mills.

She held up a bottle of champagne. "Let's grab two glasses and celebrate."

"Celebrate what?"

But Lila insisted on waiting until they were in Kylie's apartment. Her younger sister's hair a darker shade of blond, her eyes a deeper blue, and she was a marathon runner and a top veterinary student, but she was without question Kylie's best friend.

Lila nodded to the balcony. "Let's have our champagne out there."

Kylie grabbed glasses and a corkscrew and followed her sister outside. Clouds had moved in, and Kylie could see where a few drops of rain landed in the millpond. There'd be more rain as the evening wore on.

Lila opened the champagne and splashed some into the glasses. "It was almost shirtsleeves weather in Boston today," she said. "It's chilly here, but I imagine we'll be getting this rain, too. Anyway…" She raised her glass. "To Morwenna and the Badgers of Middle Branch. Congratulations, big sister."

They clicked glasses, and Kylie smiled. "Thank you, Lila."

Her sister looked out at the view. "Wow. Pretty. I could get used to this lifestyle. I love Boston, but I'm a country girl at heart. Have you thought about buying a place here?"

"The house I rented is for sale. I could have gardens, dogs, chickens."

"And a guy and kids?"

Kylie's mind went straight to Russ—who was in Southern California on the other side of the continent, where he had family, work, a life. Even if she'd been on his mind last night, would she stay on his mind once he got back into his routines?

But she didn't want to get into her romantic whirlwind over the past week. "One never knows," she said simply.

Lila eyed her suspiciously. "Whatever makes you happy, Kylie. You're the type who can juggle a variety of interests and priorities, get inspired by the fun and the chaos of a family. Singular focus on work can be productive for a while, but it can't last. We need to live life." She shrugged, downing more of her champagne. "Otherwise, what's the point?"

"Are you talking to me or to yourself?"

"Both of us. I'm en route to Vermont. I'm seeing a

guy who wants to take me fly-fishing. Don't laugh. I stopped here to give myself a chance to come to my senses, but it could be a fun couple of days. I have a car, so I'm not trapped in case I hate it."

"You're always good with contingency plans."

"You do beautiful work. I'm proud to be your kid sister. I can now tell my friends that my father inspired Dr. Badger."

"Your friends won't care."

"No, they'll care. I gave them *The Badgers of Middle Branch* for Christmas. Vet humor."

"Christmas? But how—"

"I stumbled on your badger books in a vet waiting room, for kids while they're waiting for their puppies and such. I looked at it and knew it had to be your work. I started reading, and that was that. Case closed. I didn't say anything, since it was obviously your secret. Always a matter of time before it got out, wasn't it? Some good has come from when you used to study flies on the ceiling in algebra class. I remember you sketched a fly squad that would swoop in and save children." Lila grinned, then held up her glass. "What are you working on now?"

"I have some ideas for *Beauty and the Beast*."

"Ah. Do you have a beast in mind?"

Kylie smiled. "He has to be his own self. Enjoy your fishing."

"It's not the kind of fishing where you end up with something to throw on the grill. You toss your fish back into the water. People probably fly-fish around here. Anyway, Kylie, you do live in an interesting little town."

Lila left Kylie with most of the opened bottle of

champagne. Kylie followed her back downstairs. Lila pointed out that she'd only had a few sips of champagne and was good to drive up to Vermont. She got in her car, shaking her head about the prospect of her fly-fishing.

When Kylie returned to her apartment, she noticed she had a text message from Russ. Your cover is blown out here, too. Marty is handing out copies of your badger books to his friends.

She laughed, typing a quick response. Tell him thank you.

He says to tell you he paid full price.

Double thank you. Are you with him now?

Yes, and Daphne. Says to tell you she adores Sherlock's style.

Kylie laughed, told him to thank Daphne and went out to her balcony. The few drops of rain had increased to a deluge, a gray wall of water pelting onto the river. She put out her hand, catching a rush of raindrops. Nothing had changed with her announcement about Morwenna, except she could be less reclusive, less secretive and protective of her identity. She didn't have to worry anymore about people making the connection. They knew, and what they did with it was up to them.

She finished her glass of champagne and went inside, corking the remainder and tucking it in her refrigerator. She wasn't drinking most of a bottle of champagne by herself.

She sat at her worktable. Sherlock Badger stared at

her from his perch on her task lamp. "I know, Sherlock. It's quiet here. I miss Russ, too."

The rain continued through the night and into the morning, nixing a bike ride. Instead Kylie drove out to Carriage Hill for coffee and muffins with Olivia McCaffrey. Kylie showed Olivia her sketches for the grandmother's house in her version of *Little Red Riding Hood*. A graphic designer, Olivia could see how her house had served as inspiration but also was Kylie's own thing. They talked graphic design and illustration, which somehow turned to furniture painting.

"Maggie and I have a new find," Olivia said. "It's a wardrobe Maggie discovered in the attic of her fixer-upper house in the village."

A "gingerbread" house off the common, Kylie knew. Given her pregnancy, Olivia could only do so much to refurbish the wardrobe. Kylie volunteered to help. Sanding and painting furniture would get her out of her apartment, and it was past time to go from acquaintance to friends with people in her adopted town.

"Knights Bridge is your home," Olivia said, as she walked out through the kitchen door with Kylie. "it's not a place that cares about celebrity. Dylan and Noah feel the same way, but at the same time, we can't pretend we don't have to see to security."

Could Russ fit in here, make a place for himself?

Kylie shook off the thought.

Dylan came around from the back of the house and greeted her. "I'm heading to LA tomorrow with Noah. He and Phoebe just flew in. She's staying with her mother for a few days to discuss wedding plans. Noah and I are flying back to LA together to take care of a few things. I hear you're due to head that way. Care to join us on our flight?"

"I have meetings in LA I've been putting off. I probably could arrange a few on short notice. If you're sure—"

"We're sure. Noah's jet is an experience," Dylan added with a wink.

"I'll attest to that," Olivia said.

Kylie did well with her badgers, but private jets were out of her league. But who'd told Dylan she was due to go to LA?

Russ.

She smiled as she got into her car. As she pulled out onto the rain-soaked road, the sun bursting through the last of the clouds, she glanced back and saw Dylan put his arm around Olivia. Olivia leaned into him.

Two people deeply in love, Kylie thought.

They waved to her, and she waved back.

Word was out about Morwenna, and she was more than okay with it.

Twenty-Five

Marty set a beer in front of Russ at his Hollywood bar. "I don't think this guy Daphne's been talking about is real," Marty said, standing back. "The producer, director, whatever he is. I think she's making him up, so we don't worry about her. We're her surrogate sons, like Noah and Dylan with Loretta. They were surrogate sons to her even before they had bazillions."

Daphne snorted, two stools down the bar from Russ. She moved to the stool next to him. "I love when you two bastards talk about me as if I'm not there."

"Might as well," Marty said. "You only hear what you want to hear, anyway."

She fastened her green eyes on Russ. "You do remind me of my second husband."

"I thought I reminded you of Liam Neeson."

"My second husband was nowhere near as cute as Neeson. I'd still be married if he were. I'm that shallow. Kidding. We were young. My first husband was a footnote in my life. I think we were married all of ten minutes. It was a clear mistake for both of us. But my second guy. He could always find a reason to say no to going for it. Sometimes you need to find a reason to say yes."

"You're mad because I'm not staying on at Sawyer & Sawyer full-time," Russ said.

"You can keep them as a client when you go out on your own. You're worried Marty has no life, but you can turn into a grind, too. Kylie Shaw doesn't need you to say no. She needs you to say yes."

Russ drank some of his beer. "Daphne, what are you talking about?"

Marty set a fresh martini in front of her. "She's saying Kylie needs you to get as obsessed with her as the prince who hunted for Cinderella. All he had was her glass slipper. Kylie enjoys her fairy tales. The heroine gets what she wants in the end, right? And she had grand adventures."

"Exactly." Daphne tapped the stack of Badger books Marty had on the bar. "Our Badgers of little Middle Branch are always saying yes to adventure. That's part of their appeal."

Russ shook his head. "I swear I have no idea what you two are talking about."

Daphne tried her martini. "Whoa, strong. Marty, did you go heavy with the vodka?"

"No, ma'am."

"Ugh. Ma'am. I prefer to think I speak with the wisdom of a woman who's lived a full, rich life."

"And you do," Marty said. "Right, Russ?"

"Sure. Right."

She snorted. "That's a strong note of skepticism in

your voice. Do you see why I like your big brother better than you?"

Marty laughed. "You're so full of it, Daphne."

Russ eyed her. "Daphne, are you going to be fit to drive yourself home?"

"I hope not. One of you boys can call me a cab."

"Marty can," Russ said. "I'm clearing out before one of you two hands me a glass slipper."

"I have one at home, you know," Daphne said.

He sighed. "Of course you do."

"It was for a production of *Cinderella* about twenty years ago. I saved it. I save everything."

"This I want to see," Marty said. "Russ Colton, PI, taking a glass slipper through airport security."

By the time Russ finished his beer and left, Daphne was starting her second martini, still talking with Marty about glass slippers and how they related to adventure, romance and a certain illustrator in Knights Bridge, Massachusetts.

Two days later, Russ had coffee on the deck with Julius and Loretta, up from La Jolla for a few days. "Daphne's master class, a stalker, a secret children's book author and illustrator," Loretta said. "My, my. Quite a few days, Russ."

"No argument from me." He picked up his mug. "Are you here because Dylan McCaffrey and Noah Kendrick are on their way?"

"Dylan is a client," Loretta reminded him.

Julius was tackling one of his plants. "Noah and Dylan can't fool themselves anymore that they don't need proper security in Knights Bridge with the adventure travel and the entrepreneurial boot camp."

Loretta nodded. "They know that now. Letting you help them with security will allow them to stay focused on what they do best."

"You'd need to spend some time in Knights Bridge, but you won't have to relocate there," Julius said. "Unless you want to. You can still do work with Sawyer & Sawyer. You'd get to do interesting work and have more freedom and independence. I don't see a downside for you."

"This is perfect for you, Russ," Loretta added.

"We'll see," he said, noncommittal. "Are either of you joining the meeting?"

Julius shook his head. "This is your deal. If you want to talk about your options, I'm available, but I don't need to be in the meeting."

"Same here," Loretta said.

Julius and Loretta stayed long enough to greet Dylan and Noah when they arrived. Then they were off for a walk, with plans to return in time for them all to have lunch together.

Russ had never met Noah Kendrick, but he knew about him from Loretta and Julius's descriptions.

The two friends listened to Russ explain what he could do for them and then asked questions.

It was a business meeting, but the three of them had San Diego in common, and if Noah and Dylan were in love with Knights Bridge women, Russ was halfway there with one.

Maybe more than halfway there.

Daphne awoke at noon. *Noon*, she thought with a self-satisfied snort. She'd worked until 2:00 a.m. She hadn't done that in years. She'd been obsessed with a design, as eager and happy about her work as she'd been at twenty-five.

She scrambled a few eggs with salsa and took her plate out to the patio and sat by the pool. She hadn't been this content in weeks. Months. She could feel herself letting go of the drama. She'd been damaged by her childhood but had found herself in her attic room in Knights Bridge and saying yes to getting on that first bus west.

This place was her home, she thought. She'd emailed a girlfriend last night to start making plans for a long weekend in Hawaii.

She had a good life.

She wasn't ready to retire. Not even close, something that had emerged during her day talking with, teaching, people as passionate about costume design as she was. The emotions stirred up by returning to Knights Bridge had settled. She appreciated seeing friends she'd forgotten she had, making new friends, but that didn't mean she had to make radical changes in her life here, at home in Hollywood Hills. She was where she belonged, where she could be herself.

Everyone had a story. She would tell her friends her story over lunch one day soon.

Where did you get your start, Daphne?

In a secret room in a New England library attic.

She could hear her words, and she knew her friends would understand—and then they would all switch to another topic and order dessert and more wine.

Her doorbell rang, rousing Daphne from her thoughts. She wasn't expecting company.

It was Kylie Shaw at the door. "I seized the moment," she said, explaining that she was in town for long-put-off meetings.

"You're in Morwenna mode," Daphne said.

"It's a big change but I'm excited. I stopped here first because…well, because I haven't told Russ I'm here."

"Oh, how fun."

Daphne saw now that sending Russ to Knights Bridge hadn't been a waste of his time. Her whirlwind trip had helped her get her head screwed on straight, but his stay had also helped him.

She had a strong suspicion he'd be going back.

"Come on," she said to the younger woman. "I'll grab my keys and take you out for a drink. You can meet Russ's brother."

Marty Colton was a lot like Russ and yet not like him.

That was Kylie's first take, at least, when she sat on a stool at the bar. Daphne sat next to her and regaled her with the perfection of Marty's version of a French martini. "It's so much better than the mess I served you in Knights Bridge," Daphne said.

Kylie appreciated the opportunity but ordered champagne.

"Celebrating your first trip to LA?" Marty asked as he poured the champagne. "Or does Morwenna Mills drink champagne and Kylie Shaw drink wine?"

She laughed. "I get to indulge both their tastes and sensibilities."

"Perfect world."

He had a friendly, easygoing manner. Daphne had

warned her about the unprepossessing bar, but Kylie liked it. She had checked into a five-star Beverly Hills hotel. She'd already had two meetings at its restaurant. It was a gorgeous place, a treat, but Marty's Bar was a nice change, a chance to see another side of the area.

"How long are you in town?" Marty asked her.

"A few days at most."

"She hitched a ride with Noah Kendrick and Dylan McCaffrey in Noah's private jet," Daphne said.

Marty gave a low whistle.

Kylie smiled. "I'll be flying coach home." She raised her glass. "To new friends," she said, then took a sip. It was good champagne, if not as expensive as the one she'd bought the day she'd first heard Russ Colton's name. Could it be not even two weeks ago?

As soon as she thought his name, he eased onto the stool to her right, with Daphne on her left. "I didn't know this place had champagne," he said in a low voice.

"And it's good champagne," Kylie said.

"Never underestimate a bar I work at," Marty said with a grin. "What are you drinking, brother?"

"Beer. You choose." Russ turned to Kylie. "The fish tacos here are decent, but I don't know if they go with champagne." He glanced past her to Daphne. "How are you, Daphne?"

"Distracted. I'm in the middle of a project. I drove Kylie over here, so I asked Marty to go light on the alcohol in my drink. Kylie, you can indulge. Can you find your own way back to your hotel?"

"Of course," she said.

Daphne jumped down from the stool. "Marty, seriously—can you get your bosses to at least buy new cushions? It's time. The duct tape holding them together scratches, and it caught on a pricey little scarf I wore before I flew east…" She stopped abruptly. "I'll see you all soon. Kylie, enjoy your stay. Make Russ take you out to an expensive lunch in Beverly Hills. I can recommend restaurants."

Russ touched Kylie's hand. "We can move to a booth and have fish tacos. I won't make you talk."

"I'm talked out after my meetings, I admit."

"Kylie enjoys people," Daphne said, "but she needs recovery time."

Kylie smiled. "That sums it up."

Daphne blew them a kiss. "I'm off. Have a good night."

Marty pointed Russ to a booth and put in the order for tacos. Kylie started to grab her champagne, but Marty picked it up. "My job," he said with a quick smile.

He delivered the glass to the table and went back behind the bar. "Your brother's a happy sort," Kylie said as she sat across from Russ. "He likes Hollywood, doesn't he? He seems content here."

"He loves it. He's convinced his ship will come in, but if it doesn't, he's still happy."

"Because he loves the work itself, and he loves being here, doing his thing."

"He'll like that you get that," Russ said. "It's taken me a while."

"What about you?"

"Are you implying I don't fit in around here?"

"Let's say you don't look as content as Marty does."

"Did I look content in Knights Bridge?"

"I thought so."

"Helped having a pretty, mysterious blonde across the hall."

"Mysterious." Kylie smiled. "I like that. I don't think anyone's ever called me mysterious."

"And pretty?"

"My mother and father." She drank some of her champagne. "I could be projecting about your contentment here. I liked having a studly private investigator across the hall."

"Studly? Is that even a word?"

"I don't know. I like it. It suits you."

"I thought I was a distraction when I was across the hall."

His eyes held hers in such a way she knew he was thinking about their near-lovemaking on the balcony. She felt heat rise in her face, but Marty arrived with the tacos. "Give a shout if you need anything else," he said, heading back to the bar.

Kylie tried one of the tacos. "These are amazing. Definitely won't find fish tacos on the menu at Smith's."

"Don't go near the turkey club here, though," Russ said.

She pointed her taco at him. "And you were a distraction, but an energizing one."

"The studly, energizing PI. I'll go with that."

They talked over dinner, covering everything from baseball to their schedules for the next day.

"Julius Hartley and Loretta Wrentham want to meet you," Russ said. "They're in town. They're having dinner with Noah and Dylan. If you're not too tired, I can take you to Julius's house for a visit."

"I'd like that."

"I've been bunking in Julius's guest room."

"You don't have a place of your own here?"

"Not yet. Right now I don't have my own place any-where. I thought I'd stay in San Diego, but I moved up here after I started doing some work for Sawyer & Saw-yer. I wanted to be closer to Marty, at least for a while."

"You were worried about him?"

"Yeah." Russ smiled. "The guy doesn't drink to ex-cess or do drugs, and he's happy and pays his own bills. But I was worried."

"Because of the past," Kylie said.

"Does your little sister worry about you?"

"Lila. Yes. All the time. It's annoying as hell." She grinned at him. "But it's also not without cause. I move to this small, out-of-the-way town where I don't know a soul and basically hide out for ten months. I don't tell her about Morwenna, so at first she doesn't know how I'm making ends meet since I'm apparently not doing much under my own name. Then she discovers *The Badgers of Middle Branch*, figures out I'm Morwenna, doesn't say anything and frets some more, for some of the same as well as new reasons."

"That's great. I think I'd like Lila."

Kylie laughed, and she noticed Russ did, too, the corners of his eyes crinkling with amusement. But as he shifted his gaze to his brother, a seriousness came over Russ that told her his concern for Marty was gen-uine and not without reason. She reached across the table and touched Russ's hand. "Marty went through hell, didn't he?"

"He still has days he's in hell again." But Russ didn't go further, instead throwing a few bills on the table and getting to his feet. "Careful. Daphne wasn't exaggerating about the duct tape."

When they reached Julius Hartley's Hollywood Hills home, Kylie could feel herself dragging, but she enjoyed seeing Dylan and Noah and meeting Julius and Loretta. As Kylie enjoyed a glass of wine, it occurred to her that what they all had in common was her little New England town.

Julius and Loretta invited her to stay in a guest room. "If we'd known you were coming..." Loretta left it at that.

Kylie thanked them. "I have a breakfast meeting at my hotel. It's convenient. I have meetings through lunch. Then I get to go play and see the sights."

"Are you showing Kylie around?" Dylan asked Russ casually.

"That would be great if you have time," Kylie said.

"I have time."

When he dropped her off at her hotel, he kissed her softly. "See you tomorrow."

"Imagine the Badgers in Beverly Hills," Russ said the following afternoon, as he walked with Kylie down Rodeo Drive, past shops with window displays of clothes, jewelry and merchandise he could appreciate but had little to no interest in owning—regardless of what he could afford. "They could have some serious Badger adventures here."

"Imagine."

"Sherlock Badger could crack a case. One of the Badger kids could get lost. They could learn about greed, envy and ambition. Could be fun."

"You're a man who's comfortable in his own skin, aren't you?" Kylie asked as they passed another shop with a gorgeous window display.

"Sometimes."

The day was very warm and dry, with a cloudless blue sky. Kylie seemed to notice every detail of the sun-washed buildings on Rodeo Drive and tourists like herself, taking in the high-end surroundings. Russ was far more aware of Kylie than he was of anyone or anything else on the posh street.

They found a small Mediterranean restaurant for dinner and sat at a quiet table, with lit candles. A real date, Russ thought.

"Are you going to leave Knights Bridge and find another place to hole up?" he asked her as she sat across from him.

"I love it there, but I don't have any firm plans. Dylan and Noah fit right in. They don't care about celebrity or money. No one's going to behave differently toward me because of who I am." She opened her menu, stared at it a moment, then looked at Russ, the candlelight catching the pale, pretty blue of her eyes. "I want a fuller life than the one I've been leading. It's had its rewards, but it's time for a new approach."

"How do you like my corner of California?"

"It's beautiful and exciting—and sunny."

He laughed. "I thought you said all that sun would get on your nerves after a while."

"I think it makes me bold."

"That could be a plus or a minus. You'd miss George Sanderson staring down at you from above the library mantel if you moved out here. And your spring on Moss

Hill. Did you close your eyes last night and pretend you were there?"

"As a matter of fact, I did."

After dinner, he walked with her back to her hotel. They had a drink at the fancy bar and people-watched. She was a talented woman who had learned to trust her creative process to lead her to what project to tackle next.

Now, Russ thought, Kylie Shaw/Morwenna Mills had to trust herself to know when she was falling in love.

Twenty-Six

Kylie left LA the following day, taking the same red-eye flight he had taken twice last week. He drove her to the airport and kissed her goodbye, but he could see her mind was spinning.

But so was his.

He dove into his non-Daphne work with Sawyer & Sawyer, on a real investigation involving witnesses, evidence, trial prep—different but not radically so from what he would do with Noah and Dylan and their lives and fledgling companies in Knights Bridge.

On Friday evening, Russ huddled with Julius in a booth at Marty's Bar, reviewing and brainstorming options and obstacles. running through what his proposed new venture would be like, the risks, the opportunities.

"Kylie Shaw is both a risk and an opportunity, isn't she?" Julius asked quietly.

Russ wasn't as taken aback by the question as he might have been a week ago. He knew the answer. He nodded at his friend. "You could say that, yes."

Moving to an office and an apartment in Knights

Bridge—at Moss Hill—would put him in the middle of her life. He'd be a distraction for her, whether or not things worked out between them. She was shaking off her months of nonstop work and isolation, wanted more balance in her life.

"Don't overthink it," Julius said. "Do what's right for you."

"Thanks, Julius."

But Russ knew he wasn't overthinking so much as stuck because he needed to figure out his own personal situation.

Marty. Their mother.

The past. His regrets, his worries, his hopes.

The helicopter crash ten years ago had a grip on him as much as Daphne's attic sewing room and her life as Debbie Sanderson had had a grip on her.

The next morning, Russ flew to Phoenix, rented a car and drove to his mother's house in Scottsdale. He'd be back in Hollywood Hills by nightfall.

He hadn't seen his mother in months.

Janet Colton greeted him with a cool smile, as if he were delivering a package. "Please, come in, Russ."

She'd had his tawny hair, but it was elegantly gray now, which suited her cool manner. She led him to her covered patio. A ceiling fan whirred, stirring the warm, almost hot, air. She had a pitcher of water and stack of glasses on a table, her stash for the morning, she explained. She was big on hydration.

She poured Russ a glass of water and handed it to him. "You're looking well. LA agrees with you?"

"It's fine. I spent most of last week on a job back east."

She shuddered. "I don't like cold weather."

"I might be working out there this next year. You can visit when it's warm."

But they both knew she would never visit. "You're always welcome here," she said. "The pool house doubles as a guest cottage."

"It's a nice place. I'm glad you're happy."

"I'm content. I keep happiness at arm's length. Life is easier that way." She smiled, but her eyes remained distant, if not emotionless. "You look more and more like your father as you've gotten older. Marty takes after my father. How is he? He calls every week, but he never tells me anything."

"He's doing great."

It was what she wanted to hear because it was easiest for her.

Russ drank his water, and she let her three miniature white poodles out of the house. She laughed, letting them jump in her lap. He'd never seen her so warm and animated with his father, his brother or himself. As traumatized as she'd been by the helicopter crash, the woman she was now was the woman she'd always been. Bouncing around the country with the army hadn't made a career and family easy, but playing the dutiful wife and mother had also given her an excuse to focus on herself. His father hadn't minded, or if he had, he hadn't needed more in a relationship. She freed him up so he could devote himself to his career without distraction and play with his toys without guilt. They'd worked, in their own way.

But it wasn't what Russ wanted, and it wasn't who

he was. He wasn't his mother, and he wasn't his father. Neither was Marty.

Marty didn't need saving.

Neither did their mother.

Russ chatted with her about her dogs and her hobbies—desert landscaping, yoga, attending lectures at a local college—and she asked a few surface questions about his life. He didn't get into Knights Bridge, Kylie, his plans with Noah Kendrick and Dylan McCaffrey.

She didn't ask about Marty. It wasn't deliberate, Russ realized. Her older son simply hadn't crossed her mind.

"Marty says hi," Russ said as he started out.

"Wonderful. Tell him hi back."

Russ promised he would and left.

She had her poodles and her hobbies and her nice house. They were enough.

He went back to LA, straight to Marty's Bar.

"We aren't the Badgers of Middle Branch," Marty said, joining Russ at his booth with two beers and two plates of fish tacos.

"Nope."

"Probably the Shaws aren't, either."

"Kylie's dad is a vet," Russ said.

"Oh. So maybe they are like the Badgers. That could be good. We're different."

Russ grinned. "Always the bright side with you, Marty."

"I got cozy with the dark side my first months in rehab. Mom was there every day through my dark spell. She might have hated it and resented it, but she was there, Russ. Don't be too hard on her. She's earned her poodles and her pool."

"She's into desert plants, too."

"And animals. She's into all those desert critters. Kylie would like that."

"I'm glad Mom's made a life for herself." Russ didn't tell his brother that duty more than love and empathy had driven their mother to be there for him during his long hospitalization and rehab. Maybe he was short-changing her, but he didn't think so.

"Time for you to make a life for yourself."

Russ leveled his gaze on his brother. "I'm sorry I wasn't there for you after the crash."

"You were. You were serving your country, and that helped me on the dark days. If you'd given up everything for me—I don't think I'd have made it, Russ. I meant it when I said I didn't want you there. It was important to me that you weren't."

"Thanks for that, Marty."

"Now, if you'd been able to take my place in that beat-up, piece-of-crap helicopter…" Marty leaned back, looking at ease with himself. "What a miserable day that was."

"Yeah," Russ said.

"Pop went quick. He did all he could to pull us out of the crash, but it wasn't possible. It was his time. He knew it. I think he focused at the end on making sure Mom and I survived."

"He would."

Marty nodded. "Mom knows that, too. I don't judge her, Russ. If the biggest thing in her day is cleaning up poodle poop and pricking her finger on a cactus, then good for her. Damn good thing I got banged up, though, because otherwise you'd have married that woman—talk about driven. What is she, an admiral now?"

"We haven't stayed in touch." Things had been a blur then, in the weeks after the helicopter crash, and Russ couldn't say for sure he'd contemplated marriage.

Marty was grinning at him. Russ sighed. "What?"

"You can't remember her name."

"I could if you said it."

"I was on morphine. How am I going to remember?"

"Did you meet her? Did I bring her by the rehab facility?

"I met her. She was the only woman I saw for weeks besides nurses, therapists and our sweet mother. She was driven."

"I remember now. JAG. I think she is an admiral, married, a couple of kids. The fog clears. She dumped me."

"Too much baggage because of the crash? Real nice. Bitch. I hate her."

Russ shook his head. "Because we weren't right together."

"Kylie Shaw has her head together. She's driven, but she's about the journey and not just the destination."

"I have no idea what you just said."

"Fight for her. Make the effort for her. She came out here. Now you get off your ass and go back there."

"As it happens, I have a flight east tonight."

Marty glared at him. "Just let me go on?"

"You were mesmerizing."

"You are such a jerk, you know that?" Marty grinned, leaning over the table. "It's great having you in town, but you can't live out of a beat-up duffel bag forever, and you can't put your life on hold because of me."

Russ didn't have a glass slipper, and his kiss wouldn't awaken a poisoned princess. He fit in better with the determined Badgers of Middle Branch.

"I can't get this wrong, Marty."

"You won't. This lady isn't a project with a set of tasks attached to it. She's the love of your life. You're good together."

Noah and Dylan needed an answer.

Russ had one. *Yes.*

Twenty-Seven

After her quick trip to Los Angeles, Kylie took the train to New York for a day of meetings with her agent and publisher. When she arrived back at her apartment that same evening, everything was exactly as she'd left it, but she felt different.

She couldn't un-ring the bell and go back to having Morwenna as her secret.

And she couldn't un-fall for Russ.

She sighed at Sherlock Badger. "Well, you're the same. I should have taken you with me to LA and New York. You're my rock, Sherlock."

She swore he shook his head, swore he said, *No, I'm not. Russ Colton is your rock.*

But, fortunately, Ruby O'Dunn had come home from Boston and was finally ready to talk. Kylie was downstairs, scraping dried mud off her bike, when Ruby stopped at Moss Hill, got out of her mother's car and fell apart.

Kylie grabbed Jess Flanagan, who was working late and called Maggie, Phoebe, Olivia and Samantha. Jess had the key to the apartment Russ had used while he was in town, and they all slipped inside because there were more places to sit than at Kylie's apartment.

Maggie collected a few things she had in the back of her van. A couple of bottles of Kendrick Winery merlot, cheese, olives, artichokes and chocolates, and Ruby poured out her heart. Clearing Christopher Sloan out of her system wasn't easy, but it was right for her, and for him.

"This great guy, and I'm giving him up..." She sniffled. "I pounced on the idea of a children's theater here for the wrong reasons. Daphne saw that before I did. She's put me in touch with people she knows. I have a summer internship in Hollywood. I leave in mid-May. How can I be heartbroken and excited at the same time?"

"Chris could have looked less relieved when he told Brandon and me you two were through with each other," Maggie said. "Seriously. He's a fantastic guy, but he forgot there for a second that you're my little sister."

Ruby laughed, sniffling back more tears.

"Mark's rented this place," Jess said eventually. "The new tenant's moving in next weekend."

"Who?" Kylie asked, startled.

"I didn't get around to asking."

"Tell us about Beverly Hills, Kylie," Ruby said. "I heard Russ Colton took you to dinner on Rodeo Drive."

"Daphne told you?"

"You bet."

"It must be fun now to integrate Kylie and Morwenna," Olivia said.

"Did you buy something wonderful for yourself on

Rodeo Drive?" Jess asked. "I bought an Hermes scarf when Mark and I went to Paris last year. It's so expensive I'm almost afraid to wear it."

"I window-shopped," Kylie said.

"With Russ?" Ruby asked. "Seriously?"

Kylie pictured Russ as they'd lingered at a jewelry display, his arm around her as she'd raised her eyebrows at over-the-top rings and necklaces worthy of Daphne Stewart. Then she'd realized his gaze had zeroed in on engagement rings. Even now, she could feel the leap her heart had taken, the sense that anything was possible when they were together.

"Do people see themselves in your badgers?" Maggie asked.

"My father says the badger vet is better-looking than he is," Kylie said. "I'll be working on a new Badger installment soon. Right now I'm tackling *Beauty and the Beast*. I'm adjusting to integrating Morwenna into my public, day-to-day life. It hasn't been as challenging as I thought it might be."

Olivia nibbled on a piece of cheese. "What are your plans now? Do you think you'll stay in Knights Bridge?"

"I love it here, but..." Kylie smiled. "We'll see."

The women all seemed to guess a man was involved in her decision-making process, and probably who that man was.

But they didn't ask.

They all pitched in to clean up, and Ruby promised she would be there for any of them if they needed a good cry. "Which I hope you never will," she added.

"Especially not over a Sloan," Maggie said with a long-suffering shake of her head and a spark in her eyes.

Samantha concurred. "I love that hardheaded Justin, I have to say."

"Can't wait for that wedding," Maggie said. "Brandon's home plotting a camping trip with our boys and Clare Morgan's son. I have declined to join them. I hate sleeping in a tent."

"You and Chris will both be fine," Phoebe, the quietest of the women, said. "You *are* fine, Ruby."

After everyone left, Kylie returned to her apartment. She had a new request for an appearance as Morwenna, this one at a reading festival in southwest Florida next spring. Her agent was thrilled when Kylie had told her she would be doing more public events to meet young readers, parents, guardians, librarians and teachers. She just needed to budget the time.

But her work was here, in Knights Bridge, she thought, looking out at the river.

This was where she would create more Badger stories, and whatever came next.

She'd only had a few sips of wine across the hall and took her glass onto her balcony. Wine alone didn't hold the charm it once had. She observed this fact with an aching loneliness and a stubborn sense of hope that wasn't as odd a mix as she might have thought when she'd moved into Moss Hill.

She missed Russ, but he wouldn't leave her dangling— and she wouldn't let him. He was honorable in his own way, and she was tenacious in hers. Half her success as an illustrator she attributed to pure doggedness, a refusal to give up even when the work was hard-to-impossible, the financial rewards were meager and uncertain and any appreciation was damn near nonexistent.

Loving the work helped, just as now loving Russ helped.

The warming spring weather only made her miss Russ more. Did he ride a bike? Kylie realized she didn't know. Probably. He could do anything physical.

And right there went her powers of concentration.

She left her wineglass on the balcony—she'd only taken a few sips of a nice pinot noir, purchased at the country store but not on sale—and went back inside. She grabbed a dark green crayon. She smiled. She had her beast now.

In the morning, she rode her bike to the house past the covered bridge, with its sprawling maple tree in the front yard fully leafed out, with wild columbine and chives blossoming along the stone wall and a rooster weathervane pointing west with the steady breeze.

She could see a dog asleep in the shade, and she could hear children laughing—and she could smell the first strawberries of the season, tart-sweet and ready for whipped cream and shortcake.

All in her imagination, she knew. A scene for the *Badgers of Middle Branch*, perhaps.

The youngest Badger adored strawberries.

Kylie eased off her bike and sat on the stone wall, looking across the quiet road to the river. She could do California. Really, she could. If Russ was there, if he wanted her in his life—to build a life together— she could do Beverly Hills, San Diego, a houseboat in a Dutch canal, a loft in Paris, a condo in Chicago… anywhere. Her career was portable. She could fly to visit her parents and sister. With her parents retiring and Lila graduating soon, who knew where they'd end up, anyway?

Everything and anything seemed possible, not because of money or determination but because of love. Crazy as it might be, she felt it was true, and she believed it.

Falling in love not only could happen to her, it had happened.

She'd opened herself up to it, invited it into her life, said yes to it—to all the risks, the uncertainties and the possibilities that came with it. But it wasn't just about how she felt. It was what she wanted to do. She was restless, twitchy, frustrated with inaction. What kind of doing would loving Russ involve?

She smiled at the thoughts that popped into her head. Kissing, stroking, hugging.

Making love.

Talking over glasses of wine, making dinner, picking apples in the fall, taking off for a drive in the country without a map or GPS...

She could think of a thousand ways to love Russ Colton.

She jumped up from the stone wall and looked back at the house, but this time she realized the For Sale sign wasn't up anymore.

Her heart sank. Someone had made an offer on the house? Already?

She fought the tightness in her throat, forcing herself to swallow and take a deep breath. Hadn't she just been picturing herself on a houseboat in Amsterdam?

But it felt like an omen, and she ran across the yard, through a small field and into the woods, leaving her bike behind at the house that never would be hers. She ducked between two white pines onto a trail. Whether it was the wind or tears, her eyes were watery and her cheeks wet when she arrived at her spring on Moss Hill.

Twenty-Eight

Russ wasn't surprised when he found Kylie at her spring. The undergrowth had come to life even more since his last visit. He crouched on a flat rock next to greenery poking up along the small spring pool and the stream. "That's skunk cabbage," she said. "I don't know if you have that in California."

"I don't, either. Not up on my things-that-grow-by-a-stream plants."

"Any plants?"

"Julius took me through his plants on his deck. I learned enough to know which ones to water when. Good-looking plants, but I have a ways to go before I'm a gardener." He sat down on the rock. "But I'm game. I can see myself growing vegetables."

"I could live in California," she said.

"You wouldn't have your spring or your renovated hat factory."

"I'd find something else. I'm not set in my ways."

"But Knights Bridge is home for you."

"Yes, it is, at least in a certain way. I'm not Christopher Sloan. His job and his family are here, and he grew up here. I've created a few fantasies about living here, but that's all they are." She stared at the spring water. "I can live somewhere else, if I have a reason."

"I'd be happy wherever you are," he said simply.

She smiled. "And I'd be happy wherever you are. That's what's happened since I spotted you that Sunday morning at Moss Hill. I want to be with you."

"Why don't you show me the way to the house you rented upriver?"

"I was just there. I left my bike, so I have to go back, anyway. The For Sale sign is down…" She licked her lips, obviously struggling to control her emotions. "One of those paths not taken."

"I'd hoped I'd get to you before you went out there. Kylie, I've been in touch with the art professor who owns the house. I got her to take down the For Sale sign. I think I should tour the place before we make an offer, in case it's too cute for a studly guy like me."

She gasped. "Russ…"

"Kylie, Kylie." He paused, brushing stray hairs off her face, noticing they were damp with tears. "Show me the way."

"You worked out something with Noah and Dylan," she said as she led Russ through the woods.

"Tentatively. They know I won't do this work if it upsets your life. There are other clients, other jobs."

"What about Sawyer & Sawyer?"

"I just have to keep the paperwork up to date, and they can remain a client."

"That will make Daphne happy."

"She's in Hawaii with friends. When she gets back,

Ruby O'Dunn will be there for her internship. I only know this through Marty. Daphne's been unusually quiet."

"The class is behind her, she's off the hook with the theater—she's calm now."

"Either that or she's biding her time until she presents Julius and me with her next drama."

They followed a gently sloping trail into the last of the woods, then crossed a green field with pops of little yellow flowers—Russ had no idea what they were—and finally came to the house.

Russ slipped his hand into Kylie's. She squinted up at him. "It's not far from Boston, and the college towns of Amherst and Northampton are a short drive."

"Convenient." He reached into his pocket. "I have a key."

"Also convenient."

They went inside and through the rooms on the first floor. She showed him the spot in the bay window where she'd worked, living here alone, from July to March. Had she ever imagined a man here with her? *Him?* An ex-navy investigator, a guy who knew more about California spiders than he did New England wildflowers?

They mounted the stairs to the second floor. The house was charming and surprisingly modern, with room to expand, but as much as he fell in love with it, seeing Kylie there made it perfect.

"I'm guessing this was your room when you lived here," he said, entering a small bedroom at the front of the house. It had wide-board floors, white-painted walls and double windows, sparkling in the midday sun.

Kylie followed him into the room. "What gives it away?"

"It looks out on the river." He stood at the window. "I can see you here, in this spot, on a cold winter night. But that's in the past. Right now I see a tire swing, snowball fights, raking leaves..." He turned to her. "A life here with you."

"I can see you painting walls and woodwork whatever colors I want. And just so you know, I tend to escort spiders to safety instead of stomping on them or getting out the spider spray."

"There are exceptions?"

"When one is running up my leg while I'm working."

"Ah."

"I love my work. I love to create stories and illustrations about my badgers, for young readers. You come to life helping people and keeping them safe, figuring out what went wrong when things don't work out. You don't dwell on the past, but you don't deny its influence on you. And you love your brother, Marty, more than anyone in the world—" She stopped herself. "What would Marty say right now?"

"That you're crazy if you think I love him the way I love you."

She laughed, those translucent cheeks of hers turning a pretty shade of pink, telling him what she was thinking. "Well, that."

"He'd say it's good," Russ said, pulling her to him. "All good."

"I think you planned this," Kylie said.

"I think I did."

He swept her off her feet and carried her to the bed,

made with linens she'd left behind. She draped her arms over his shoulders, and he could smell her hair, feel the mud on her pants from her jaunt to her spring. He lowered her to the bed, kissing her, wanting to take his time with her, but the taste of her, the feel of her under him, ignited him. She responded in kind, tackling his shirt, his pants, with hands shaking with desire. His hands weren't any steadier as he dispatched with her clothes, casting them to the floor. He coursed his palms up her hips, over her breasts, and paused, his eyes locking with hers in the sunshine. Her skin was smooth and hot, and he felt her shift her position under him, so that he was almost inside her.

But not yet, he thought. Not yet.

His mouth descended to her breasts, and he heard her sharp intake of air and knew she was lost to the same sensations pouring through him. He ached for her, wanted her. As he tasted her, drew more sharp breaths from her, and moans of pleasure, the reality of this moment, making love to this woman, exceeded any fantasies he'd had since she'd bolted from him at Moss Hill.

When he entered her, she was wet, ready, clawing at him for more, to thrust deeper, harder. He took his time, until he felt her rising to him, matching his rhythm, quaking under him. Her fingers dug into his back, and he plunged into her with such force he was afraid he'd hurt her…but that was his last thought.

She held him inside her, whispered, "Don't stop," and he quickened his pace, finally exploding, crying out for her as he let go, loving her. There was nowhere he'd rather be than where he was, making love to Kylie on a warm spring day.

* * *

They left Kylie's bike at the house and walked back to Moss Hill together. She was spent and yet energized—the result, she knew, of being with Russ. He showed her a text that had come in from Marty. How's it going? Did you give Kylie the glass slipper?

Russ grinned. "Marty and the metaphors."

"What are you going to tell him?"

"Yes. Leave it at that."

When they arrived at Moss Hill, they walked out to the dam, flowing steadily onto the rocks below. She saw ducklings now with the pair of ducks. Russ grinned, and she knew he saw them, too. But he turned to her, took her in his arms. "I love you, Kylie, and I want to make a home and a life with you here in Knights Bridge."

"Russ…" She tried to hold back tears. "I love you. I think I started loving you when I first heard your name at the Swift River Country Store. I swear Sherlock knew before I did."

"No doubt in my mind." Russ laughed, kissing the top of her head. "You've seen my life, Kylie. I'm no prince. I don't have a castle, servants or a crown. What I have—what I can promise to you now and forever—is my love."

"That's all that matters." She smiled, draping her arms over his shoulders. "I can draw the rest."

* * * * *

Author's Note

One of my favorite walks growing up was to a wood-land spring much like the one Kylie discovers. I hadn't been there in ages until researching *The Spring at Moss Hill*. I love to spend time at our family homestead on the western edge of the Quabbin reservoir and protected wilderness. I had no trouble imagining Kylie taking a creative retreat in that beautiful area.

As always, I have many people to thank, starting with my editor, Nicole Brebner, and my team at MIRA Books, and my agent, Jodi Reamer at Writers House. My son, Zack Jewell, a designer, was a huge help in understanding Kylie's visual mind, as well as the technical aspects of her work.

Most of all, I want to thank my mother, who fell and broke her hip while I was writing *The Spring at Moss Hill*. Her courage and resilience are an inspiration. She taught clothing and quilting and can do anything with a needle and thread and a bit of fabric.

I don't have a stuffed badger on my desk lamp, but I have an Irish painting of poppies that helps me keep perspective and makes me smile.

If you're new to my Swift River Valley world, the series starts with *Secrets of the Lost Summer*, Olivia and Dylan's story, and Grace Webster's story. You can find a short video on my website, with photos of the four lost Quabbin towns and the reservoir as it is today. While you're on my website, you can sign up for my monthly e-newsletter! I'm also on Facebook and Twitter. I love to hear from readers.

Thank you, and happy reading!

Carla
www.carlaneggers.com